Baby SEALs Part 1

Beginnings

J. W. Bloomfield

Joe Whitfill

WESTBOW
PRESS
A DIVISION OF THOMAS NELSON
& ZONDERVAN

Scripture taken from the King James Version of the Bible.

This is a work of fiction. All of the characters, names, incidents, organizations, and dialogue in this novel are either the products of the author's imagination or are used fictitiously.

WestBow Press books may be ordered through booksellers or by contacting:

WestBow Press
A Division of Thomas Nelson & Zondervan
1663 Liberty Drive
Bloomington, IN 47403
www.westbowpress.com
1 (866) 928-1240

ISBN: 978-1-5127-6567-0 (sc)
ISBN: 978-1-5127-6568-7 (e)

Print information available on the last page.

WestBow Press rev. date: 12/12/2016

Contents

Dedication

This book is dedicated with love to my wife, Christy, who has always supported me.

Acknowledgements

Many thanks to all my friends and relatives who provided information during my research. I asked a lot of questions, and you always came through. Special thanks to my sister, Jane, for her editing skills, and for giving me the excellent advice, "Just write. We'll clean it up later."

The Beginning

Chapter 1

They met in May when they were six. Danielle LeBeau was walking down the quiet Texas street early in the morning. The neighborhood was mainly middle class with older homes built in the 70's. Nearby was a city park and strip shopping centers containing a variety of food stores and individually owned retail stores such as tattoo parlors and nail salons. It seemed like an ordinary day without a hint of what would come from the choices made today. Spring was well underway, the lawns were green (some with grass, some with weeds), leaves were on the trees, and what flowers there were added color to the scene. Robins, mockingbirds, and blue jays were flitting about as squirrels and the occasional rabbit searched for food. The scent of freshly mown grass filled the air along with the sound of a few lawn mowers. Danielle was trying to think of ways that a six year old girl could make some money. She didn't want a lot, but her Mom and stepdad gave her none, and she would need a new sketchpad soon. As she walked, she spotted a boy crawling around on the ground under a pecan tree and moved closer to investigate. He appeared to be about her age and about her size which was a little larger than average. He had short brown hair the same color as hers that looked as though he cut it himself, jagged and uneven. The jeans he was wearing were worn, with holes in the knees; not distressed, just old and worn out. The t-shirt he was wearing was from a local radio station. Not that anyone would point to her as the model from a clothing catalog, but her jeans didn't have holes, and her shirt was new, if it was from a thrift store. As he crawled, he kept flipping a square made out of wood. He appeared to be picking things up and putting them in a bucket. She drew nearer, pulling the sketchpad from her fake leather messenger bag and starting to draw what she could see. As she drew, she asked in a soft Louisiana accent, "What are y'all doing?"

Jeff looked up in surprise. There wasn't usually anyone on the street this time of day even though it was a nice spring day just right for walking around. Usually the only people he saw were joggers. He found himself looking into the light green eyes of a girl about his age, dressed like him in jeans and a t-shirt, her long, brown hair pulled back in a ponytail. Several answers went through his head, some snarky, some long, some short. He chose a short reply, "Picking up pecans."

Danielle rolled her eyes to herself. Obvious answers were not her favorite, but she calmly asked, "Why?" Jeff looked up at her again with bright blue eyes. She thought at first he might not answer or would answer with a snarky comment, but instead he gave her a decent, complete explanation.

"The man who lives here mows his own lawn. The pecans on the grass make it bumpy to push the lawn mower, and they aren't much fun to walk on. He offered me $20 to pick them all up." He didn't mention his work to put the idea in the man's head or the negotiation over the price or even figuring out what he could do for the man in the first place. He was pretty proud of all three. He might not have been quite as proud had he known that the man, Steve Jacobs, knew what Jeff was doing when Jeff brought up the pecans to him. Steve was a salesman at a local car dealership. At six feet and 165 pounds he was built like a linebacker, and at age 30 he wasn't showing any fat yet. His blue eyes were a lighter shade than Jeff's and twinkled as Jeff negotiated his deal. The conversation

4

went something like: Jeff, "Hi, mister. You have a lot of pecans in your yard." Steve: "Yes, I do. I seem to have a bumper crop every other year." Jeff: "Do you eat them all?" Steve: "No. They pretty much go to the squirrels." Jeff: "I bet they don't pick them all up." Steve: "No, they only get part of them." Jeff: "It must be a pain to mow with them there, getting in the way." Steve: "Yep. They are a pain." Jeff: "I could pick them all up for you." Steve: "Hmmm. How much would you want to be paid for doing that?" Jeff: "$20." In Jeff's experience, everything was $20. ATM's gave out $20 bills. People put $20 worth of gas in their cars. A trip to the grocery store cost $20. $20 was a good number. Steve: "That seems like a lot for picking up pecans. And what would you do with the pecans?" Jeff: "That's a lot of pecans, and your yard is pretty big. I'd give the pecans to you. You could sell them or eat them. I might could shell them for you. That would be a different job, though." Steve laughed and said, "Okay. $20 it is. Let me know when you're finished, and we'll check it out."

Later that day Steve told his wife Amy about the conversation. Amy was the same height as Steve although somewhat lighter with an athletic build. Her strawberry blond hair was curly which suited her just fine. She had no intentions of ever getting an iron near it. Where Steve tanned easily, she freckled just as easily which both of them found hilarious. They had been high school sweethearts, gone to college together, married right after finishing college, and planned their family for the not too distant future. Then they had found out two years ago that Amy couldn't have children, and they hadn't yet decided what, if anything, to do about it. Perhaps adopt, perhaps be foster parents, perhaps plan nothing and just see what God had in store for them. In the meantime Steve coached a local little league team, and they both taught Sunday School for the high school young men and women at their church, 2nd Street Bible Church.

When Steve had finished telling her about his deal with Jeff she asked, "Why are you paying a child $20 to pick up pecans out of our yard?" Steve explained, "Well, he looked like he could use the money. I don't know who his parents are, but it looks like they could use a little extra. We can take the money from our charity fund. Besides, I just have a feeling about this kid, like we should help him and be involved in his life if we can. We can add him to our prayer list. And it would be nice to get the pecans out of the yard." Amy smiled indulgently at him and rested her forehead against his. "You are just a big kid at heart, aren't you?" Steve smiled happily back at her. "Yes. Yes I am."

But that was later. Meanwhile Danielle asked her next question, "Why the square?"

"To give me a place to work in and show where I've been." Jeff was rather proud of this idea.

Danielle thought to herself, "Huh," and asked "What's your name?"

The boy looked up again and replied, "Jeff Mitchell."

"I'm Danielle LeBeau. Do you want some help?"

Did he want some help. On the one hand he had found, more like created, the job. He could use the money. Danielle didn't look like she needed the money with her no holes jeans and new looking shirt. Still, for some reason, he said, "Sure, why not." And maybe she wouldn't want any of the money.

"What do you do with the pecans?"

"Mostly put them in a bag for the man. Some I put on the fence to make it easier for the squirrels."

"Can I get some of the money?" That was chancy, Danielle thought. Did she want to crawl on the grass picking up pecans for nothing if he said no? Would he want to split the money since he came up with the job in the first place?

Jeff thought to himself that there went the idea of no money for her. "How much of the money?"

"Enough to buy a new sketch pad."

Jeff heard his traitorous mouth say, "I just started. If you do half you can have half."

Wow, Danielle thought. That was generous. She said, "Okay," put her sketchpad back in the messenger bag, and sat down to help.

Jeff watched her put the sketchpad away and asked, "Are you an artist?" Meanwhile he ran his hand through the grass, searching for pecans and watching for fire ants. There was nothing like a bunch of fire ant stings to ruin your day.

"I like to draw what I see." She paused a moment and then asked, "Where do you live?"

He replied, "Over on 4th Street. In the Viewpoint Apartments near the park. How about you?"

"Wow! You live right across the street from me. I live on 3rd Street just behind you, the second house from the corner. Who do you live with?"

"It's just me and my Mom. She's a waitress at Sal's. She could do more. She's really smart. But she likes drugs." He paused a moment and added, "And guys who bring them to her".

Danielle frowned. "Bummer. I live with my Mom and stepdad. Where's your Dad?"

Jeff shrugged. "I never met him. I don't think my Mom knows who he is. My birth certificate says Unknown."

Excitement began permeating Danielle as an idea started to form. "Mine, too! We could be brother and sister! Different Moms but same Dad. When's your birthday?"

"February 1st. And why do I need a sister?"

Now Danielle could barely contain herself. "Mine, too! We could be twins! What time were you born? And everyone needs a sister."

Jeff was starting to feel like he was getting in way over his head and wishing he had picked a different day to start working on the yard. And that he'd never seen his birth certificate. Or that he couldn't read, which he could since he was four and his mother, tired of reading to him, taught him phonics and told him, "Read to yourself." At any rate he said hesitantly, "6:47AM."

And now Danielle's idea was complete. "I was born at 6:46AM. We're twins. And I'm the oldest. This is perfect! And how do you know what's on your birth certificate?"

"It's in the box where my Mom keeps her pot and papers. I'm lucky she hasn't burned it up. I read it. I read everything. What about you?"

"I found it in the desk drawer, and my mom told me what it was and what it said. (Unlike Jeff, Danielle's mother had seen no need to teach Danielle to read before she started school.) "I was curious who my real Dad was. Now I know. Unknown." She paused then casually asked, "So do you smoke pot?"

He looked at her scornfully and replied, "Like I need more drugs in my life."

"Pretty bad, huh?" Danielle asked with sympathy.

"I find a lot of reasons to be out of the apartment."

"Me, too. Out of the house, I mean. My stepfather gives me the creeps. Sometimes he looks at me like, I don't know. But I don't like it."

Jeff announced, "We have to take a picture," and pulled out a digital camera.

Danielle exclaimed in amazement, "You have a digital camera?"

Jeff explained, thinking to himself, "I do a lot of explaining around her. Having a sister can be a pain." But to her he said, "I have a friend who bought a mobile phone with a camera in it. He said he didn't need this anymore and gave it to me. I have another friend who lets me store the pictures on her computer." He set the camera on a fencepost, started the timer, and ran back to stand next to Danielle. And the first picture of their time together was taken. Several more were taken as the mood struck them.

The day progressed as they worked their way back and forth

across the yard, talking about the pecan man and the other people they knew, where they lived (Jeff's apartment complex had a swimming pool which Jeff said Danielle could use), what they did all day, what their parents did, and on and on. By the time they had covered the entire yard they knew quite a bit about each other.

They also learned about each other just by hanging out together. Danielle learned that Jeff was fast, but she was faster. If they reached for a pecan at the same time Danielle always got to it first, even if they were the same distance from it and started on a count of three. Excellent eyesight was a common factor as both could read street signs that were far down the street and tell the eye color of the few people they saw when they were a few houses away. Jeff liked to plan but didn't mind when his plans didn't work out. Danielle was happiest when flying by the seat of her pants but could plan if she had to. Jeff was amazed at Danielle's ability with animals. Before they had been working two hours, the squirrels were coming to Danielle to take the pecans out of her hands. At the end of the day, they still avoided Jeff. He thought this was ungrateful since he was putting nuts on the fence for them. They both spoke Spanish as a second language since they were around it so much everywhere they went.

Danielle didn't think Jeff was smarter than her, but he knew more since he could already read and perform addition, subtraction, multiplication, and division. She thought this was wrong since she was, after all, the oldest, and she demanded that he teach her everything he knew. With raised eyebrow, he asked, "Today?" Danielle frowned and said, "Well, maybe not everything today. But we could start." So Jeff began teaching her, using her sketch pad, and by the time the pecans were all picked up she knew the alphabet and the numbers from one to one hundred.

Jeff told her about his mom. "She's really pretty. Her hair is the same color as mine but long. Her eyes are the same color as mine. She had me when she was sixteen, and her mom kicked her out of the house. She moved here with a friend from Colorado, and we've been here ever since. She said she would have gone to college if it wasn't for me, but I don't know. She's really smart, and she can think really fast, and she knows all the answers to the shows on television. She can be really good with people. I think she could have about any job she wants, but she doesn't really want one. She'd rather just sit and do drugs with the guys who are always coming around."

Danielle told him about her mom and stepdad. Her mom was young, too, in her early 20's with hair the same color as Danielle's and the same green eyes. She was tall and graceful and wanted to be a dancer but wasn't quite good enough, or truth be told, dedicated enough. Danielle explained how sometimes she had a strange light in her eyes when she looked at Danielle which was another reason Danielle spent as little time at home as possible. Her mom worked at a nearby food store as a manager, ordering stock, creating schedules for the other employees, and basically keeping the store on its feet while the owner, as she said, "Sat on his butt and made all the money." Her husband of one year was wiry and strong with hard eyes, shorter than her mom, bald, worked as an exterminator, and always smelled like chemicals. Neither seemed to care too much for Danielle. Danielle and Jeff were two of a kind, not in the most loving or even sanest homes in the city.

By the time Steve arrived home from work and parked in front of the house, they were finished. The bag for the man was full (even though Jeff and Danielle had eaten some of the pecans as they went for their lunch), and the squirrels were busy moving nuts from the fence to the tree across the alley. Danielle was waiting down the block when the man pulled up out front, looked over the yard, laughed at the squirrels, and paid Jeff with two tens, which was convenient. The man also offered him another job, which Jeff accepted. He raced down the sidewalk with a squeegee in his hand, gave Danielle her ten, and asked, "Now where are you going?"

"Home, I guess. You? And why did he give you that?"

"Home. He gave me another job cleaning his car windows in the morning. One dollar a week. He said he can probably get some more cars, too. Do you want to help? We'd have to do them before 7. Can I see what you've drawn?"

Danielle said okay to the job and showed him some of her drawings. There were drawings of people and animals and trees, scenes from storefronts and inside stores, some that were probably her room. Those were pretty bleak. Still, they were really good, he thought. Maybe not good enough to sell or be in a magazine, but they looked good to him.

They walked together down 4th street toward their homes. The apartment complex where Jeff lived consisted of several two-story apartment buildings with a pool and laundry room in the center. Stretching between 3rd and 4th streets the property was old, built in the late 60's, and occupied by a mixture of young and old, working and retired, a few college students, and a variety of ethnic groups and languages. It was a virtual United Nations, a friendly melting pot. Jeff and his mother had lived there as long as he could remember, and he knew and was friends with many of the people residing there. As they walked past the swimming pool on the way from 4th street to 3rd street, they met Angela Potts as she picked up her things in preparation for a quick run by her apartment before going out for the evening.

Angela was a single, retired lady in her early sixties with prematurely white hair which she made no attempt to color and a swimmer's athletic body. She led a very busy life with her friends, a life consisting of plays, museums, sporting events, restaurants, and anything else that came to the mind of one of the active group. Their hobbies included an investment club where they decided how to best place their pensions, other retirement funds, and even their salaries for the ones still working, to get a decent return on their money. So far, they were doing well.

However, the skill that meant the most to Jeff to this point was Angela's former work as a lifeguard and swimming instructor. She had invested quite a bit of time the previous summer teaching Jeff to swim in the apartment pool, patiently working with him to improve his form until he was quite a good swimmer and at little risk of drowning, even if stuck in deep water for a long period. Jeff introduced her to Danielle, and after a quick aside to Danielle to learn if she could swim (she could not), asked Angela if she would mind teaching Danielle to swim. Not being able to resist the imploring look on Jeff's face and the identical look on Danielle's face, and not least because she enjoyed teaching people to swim, she agreed. A time was set for the following day, and Jeff and Danielle continued on their way.

They passed through the gate at the rear of the apartment complex and crossed 3rd street to the house where Danielle lived. As they crossed the street, Jeff pointed to his bedroom window, almost directly across the street from Danielle's house, and, as it happened, across from Danielle's bedroom window, which she pointed out. This house, like all the others in the neighborhood, had been built in the 60's, about the same time as the apartment complex. It was a one story, three bedroom, two-bath home with a combination living room and dining room. The master bedroom and bath were at the rear of the house by the garage. This room belonged to Danielle's mother and stepdad. Danielle's room was at the very front of the house near the living room. The third room held mainly junk which could be cleared enough to put down an air mattress if needed, which never happened. All of the floors were hardwood except for the kitchen and bathrooms; these floors were linoleum. There was a two-car garage at the rear of the house off the alley. An identical row of houses sat on the other side of the alley. There were no trees associated with the house, and the front and back yards, such as they were, consisted of weeds and crabgrass, which when mowed, gave a semblance of "cared for". The only other greenery was a hedge along the front of the house, which at one time had a brick border. Many of the bricks were broken now into halves or thirds or quarters.

With a "Meet you in front of your house at 6:30" Jeff left Danielle and went back through the gate towards his apartment while Danielle made a quiet entrance through the front door, stepping into the living room. Her stepfather was leaning forward in an old lounge chair, eating from a TV tray as he watched some show on the television. He was still in his blue work clothes with the Ajax Exterminators logo on the left front of the shirt and his name, Carl, stitched on the right front. Danielle could smell the chemicals from where she stood at the door, and wrinkled her nose. Carl looked at her just in time to see the nose wrinkle, and his face flushed with anger. "My job is as good as any other, and it puts the food on your plate and the roof over your head!" he snapped. Danielle just nodded and scurried around the corner into the kitchen before he could say more, and he returned his attention to the show on the screen. Her mom gave her a glare as she handed her a plate with a KFC chicken leg, green beans, and an apple.

Danielle carried the plate to her bedroom, set it on the bed, and ran water from the bathroom sink into an old McDonald's cup. Closing her door she put plate and cup on the floor and sat down to eat while she reviewed the alphabet lessons Jeff had added to her sketch pad, pausing now and then to glance around the room. The furniture in the room consisted of a twin bed and an old, scarred dresser. Peeking from under the edge of the bed was the corner of an Ibanez ½-size guitar that had been a parting gift when she had left New Orleans two years ago. A few shirts and a couple more pairs of jeans hung in the closet. Another, older pair of sneakers lay jumbled on the closet floor with a pair of flip-flops. The closet shelves, the upper clothes rod, and most of the lower clothes rod were full of her mom's stuff with a bit of common items such as Christmas decorations thrown in.

Room scans were necessary. She had once found a teddy bear with a video camera hidden in it. The joy at the new toy was short lived after she found the camera, and she managed always to have the bear facing sideways or behind something else after her discovery. Eventually the bear disappeared, but she was always watching for something new or different in her room.

When she was finished eating she threw the apple core in the kitchen trash, rinsed her plate in the sink by standing on a stepstool (she couldn't wait until she was tall enough not to need it anymore) and placed it carefully in the dishwasher. Silently she slid out the kitchen door and into the back yard. The yard was surrounded by a four-foot chain link fence that shared a side with Alice Springley next door.

Alice was a large, older woman in her 70's with light black skin offset with short, curly white hair. She lived alone, her husband having died before Danielle moved in next door. Every Sunday morning she drove to her sister's house to go with her to church. Danielle loved her smile and thought her the kindest woman she knew. Unlike the mess of weeds Danielle was standing in, Alice's back yard was a garden just like in a magazine, full of native Texas plants, with gravel in between. Alice once told her it had taken ten years to get everything the way she wanted it, and she was still not completely satisfied.

Crossing to the gate on the alley side of the yard, Danielle quietly raised the locking bar and stepped into the alley, letting the gate latch silently behind her. She moved down the alley until she stood near Alice where she was carefully tending to a patch of Velvetleaf Senna. Before Danielle could greet her Alice said,

"Hello, child. How was your day?" As though she had totally lost control of her tongue, Danielle told her about meeting Jeff, how he was her brother, the day spent picking up pecans in a yard and the squirrels taking the pecans from her hand but not Jeff's, Jeff teaching her to read and write, and that he lived right across the street and could see her house from his bedroom window. Alice listened to all of this with the occasional nod and "uh-huh" and "well how about that". Then she asked if Danielle wanted to help her plant a few Purple Prairie Verbenas that she had picked up that day. Danielle made her way through the alley gate, down the gravel path, and knelt beside Alice to help dig holes for the new plants. When they were all safely planted, she filled up the watering can from the back faucet and carefully watered the new plants, smiling happily at the beauty around her. Alice sat watching her with pleasure of her own and some displeasure at Danielle's parents, thinking that she certainly treated her children much better than Danielle's parents treated her. The girl was smart as a whip, and an artist to boot. She had a couple of Danielle's drawings on her wall, one of her working in the garden, and one of the garden the winter before with most everything dead but full of hope. Her sister even had one of the drawings on her wall, and she was a most particular woman.

She sighed and said, "It's getting dark, child. Time you were getting on home." Danielle smiled at her, told her goodnight, and slowly moved down the path, through both gates, and in through the kitchen door. Both adults were in the living room watching television. She returned to her room and sat cross-legged on the bed to finish her drawing of Jeff and start one of Angela. As always, her hope was that she could get ready for bed and fall asleep with no further interaction with her mom or stepdad.

As Jeff stepped through the gate towards his apartment building, he wondered how bad Danielle's life at home was. Better than his? Worse than his? The same as his? After walking around the side of the building, he unlocked the door and slipped into the apparently empty apartment. Tossing the squeegee onto his bed, he chose a frozen entrée from the freezer, placed it in the microwave, and set the time. He wondered idly how anyone had managed before microwaves. There were directions on the package for cooking one in the oven, but who wanted to wait that long? Once the dinner was heated, he ate it while sitting at the bar on one of the two mismatched barstools he and his mom had picked up at a yard sale. The two stools were a fair representation of their furniture. The scratched dining room table with its two chairs was a cheap buy because of its condition and because there were only two matching chairs. It looked okay with a cheap tablecloth, and the two of them didn't usually need more than two chairs. The sofa had been thrown out on the street with its one broken leg and worn upholstery. A couple of bricks took care of the broken leg, and a decorated blanket from the thrift store covered the rest. It actually was a very comfortable sofa if you didn't look at it. Jeff's bedroom consisted of a twin mattress on the floor and a cardboard filing cabinet for a dresser. His closet was mostly empty. His mom's bedroom looked much the same. If they ever had to move, it would probably take more time to pack and move the kitchen than the entire rest of the apartment. While Jeff ate, he read *The Lord of the Rings*. It was slow going, taking a dictionary because there were so many words he didn't know, but the book was interesting anyway. Jeff had a plan in mind for some time in the future to create an entire elvish language, written and spoken. He was already creating an elvish/English dictionary as he went, adding words as he came across them in the novel with their elvish symbol beside them when there was one.

After he finished eating, he rinsed the plastic tray at the sink by standing on the stepstool that usually stayed under the sink (he couldn't wait until he was tall enough not to need it anymore) and tossed the tray and its package into the recycle sack hanging in the small cupboard. His mom was adamant about recycling. Next, he climbed the stairs to the second floor to visit Grand-mere Claudette. This spry, dark-haired woman was the epitome of an aristocrat and had a look that could freeze ice. Even Jeff's mom, with all her powers to make people's lives miserable, could not make a dent in this older woman who lived with her son and daughter-in-law in the apartment directly above Jeff. The young couple worked the 4PM to midnight shift at a semi-conductor company, and Claudette was alone in the evenings. She was recently arrived from Paris, and had been living there since her husband died earlier in the year. With the use of a French-English dictionary and much patience, Jeff was learning French while Grand-mere Claudette was learning English; she was a much more reluctant student than Jeff since French was the only civilized language in the world, and everyone should already speak it.

After half an hour or so, he said goodbye to Grand-mere and ran to the end of the hall where Ayame Fujioka stood with a plastic trash bag in one hand, her youngest daughter Cho in one arm, and her eldest daughter Hatsu clinging to one leg like a chubby barnacle. Ayame was a tiny woman, hardly taller than Jeff it seemed to him. She had dark black hair and dark eyes that gleamed mischievously whenever she spoke to Jeff. Sliding to a stop in front of the woman Jeff bowed slightly as was proper, said Kon'nichiwa, and asked if he could be of assistance. Perhaps he could take the trash to the dumpster for her? Ayame smiled at him and said, "It would be of the greatest assistance to me if you could do that for me. And dare I ask for a very great favor?" Jeff answered agreeably, "Of course." Ayame said, "Could you possibly run to the food mart for a quart of milk? I have run out, and Harudo has not made it home yet." Jeff smiled as he thought of the logistics involved in herding the two active girls from the apartment to the store and back, even if it was less than two blocks. He said, "I would be glad to do that for you." She gave him money, he picked up the trash, and trotted down the nearby stairs.

After a quick stop to toss the trash bag in the side opening of the dumpster which had fortunately been left open (since it was hard work to force the stubborn thing open on his own), he trotted out the back gate. He glanced over at Danielle's house as he hurried down the block to the Food Mart, wondering how she was spending her evening. At the Food Mart, he quickly found the quart of milk and brought it to Mr. Amir at the counter, who asked him how his day had gone. Jeff had known Mr. Amir all of his life and often performed small tasks for him such as picking up trash in the parking lot, bringing in the stack of daily newspapers that were dropped off, or just arranging products on the shelves. In exchange, Mr. Amir gave Jeff free run of his soft drink machine and the occasional hot dog, privileges Jeff was careful not to abuse. Or, by unspoken agreement with Mr. Amir, let his mother know about. They both knew she would exploit this generosity mercilessly. Jeff paid for the milk, thanked the kind man, and was knocking on Ayame's door soon after leaving it. Ayame thanked him profusely and offered him the change as reward for his kindness, which Jeff politely refused before telling her sayonara and moving towards his next and favorite stop, Lacey Peterson.

Chapter 2

Lacey Peterson smiled as Jeff finished playing the piano piece. She could best be described as average: average height, average weight, neither slim nor stout, eyes average brown, hair average color, clothing average. Her picture would have been in the dictionary under the definition of average. If you passed her on the street, you would not have noticed her. She would have made a great spy. Until music came up. Then her presence filled a room with love and passion. Just now, she was watching Jeff. He had arrived at her door earlier in the evening, right on time, and after politely asking how she was, sat down at one of her two Yamaha keyboards. Her living room had no furniture but chairs and was filled with musical instruments: the two keyboards, two electric guitars, two acoustic guitars, two violins, two harmonicas, and an accordion. As a semi-retired music teacher she taught just enough to pay for the occasional splurge and because she loved seeing her students sharing their gift with other people. It was important to her that her students use their gift somehow, playing at church or nursing homes or at parties; anything besides letting it sit unused in their heads.

She reflected on how much Jeff had grown, in size and ability, since she had first met him when he was four. She had passed him playing in front of his apartment as she was carrying two armfuls of groceries to her apartment. He was humming a catchy tune that she didn't recognize but knew would get caught in her head all day. Coming to an abrupt halt she shifted the bags in her arms and asked him, "What song are you humming?" Jeff glanced up at her and shrugged. "Just a song." "Where did you hear it?" Another shrug. "I made it up." Lacey eyed him suspiciously. "You made it up? You didn't hear it on the radio or something?" Back to his game. "Nope." Excitement started to raise its head. Could she possibly after all her years of teaching music have found someone who had a talent for writing their own music? "Does it have any words?" "Sure." In a clear, childish voice he sang her a song about something he had seen outside his window: a blue jay and a mockingbird fighting over a pecan that a squirrel eventually ran away with. She almost dropped the groceries she was laughing so hard, and as she walked on to her apartment and put the various items away, she decided she was right: the tune did stick in her head.

After that she looked for Jeff, and when she saw him she asked him if he had any new songs. Apparently, he had several, which he hummed or sang for her depending on whether or not he had words for them. Finally, she asked him if he would like to learn to play the keyboard and write his songs down. He excitedly agreed and so began the past three years of teaching Jeff to play the keyboard and the various facets of music theory.

When Jeff was six, Lacey introduced him to Terry who took ten of Jeff's songs and, with Terry's band, created arrangements for the pieces, which he burned to CD; he also took the music on the road so to speak, playing the songs in clubs around the city. The band and the songs were popular enough that Terry uploaded the album to iTunes where it proved to be fairly popular. Terry and the band were scrupulously honest about paying Jeff royalties for the songs, which led to so many unforeseen consequences that it made Lacey's head spin. The cause of it all was Jeff's mother.

Lacey met Jeff's mother about the time she started giving him keyboard lessons. She knocked on Lacey's apartment door one day in the middle of a lesson. Lacey answered the door and found a woman standing there who she had seen around the apartment complex. She was about Lacey's height, 5'6", with long brown hair, slim and pretty in a pale and wasted kind of way with sharp blue eyes that were somewhat bloodshot. "I'm Marilyn. Is my son here?" "I'm Lacey. Are you Jeff's mother?" When Marilyn said yes, Lacey invited her in. She turned to Jeff and found that the funny, talented young man was gone and in his place was a bland faced child with a look of polite disinterest on his face. Lacey thought to herself "Wow, that's....odd." Marilyn asked, "Why is my son here? Jeff, why are you here?" Lacey explained, "He has some talent, so I was giving him keyboard lessons." Marilyn lifted one eyebrow. "My son has talent? Musical talent? Talent that is worth your time? You are calling the noise he is always making that sticks in your head and makes you want to bang it against a wall to get it out music? You must not be much of a teacher."

Lacey refrained from rolling her eyes. Or smacking the woman. She had dealt with parents before: those who thought their kids were the next Mozart, those who wanted a baby sitter for an hour while they shopped and were willing to pay for music lessons to get that hour and be able to say their child was at their music lesson instead of saying, "I went shopping," those who wanted their kids to be well rounded. However, she very seldom ran into one whose child had talent and put them down because of it. So she said, "I like to teach. He likes to learn. He's welcome to the lessons."

Marilyn had no problem rolling her eyes. "Fine. If he breaks something, I don't want to hear about it. And if you could find a way to keep the music here and out of our place that would be great." She turned around and walked away.

Lacey thought the breaking things comment was also interesting. For a four-year-old boy Jeff was one of the most graceful boys she had ever seen. He moved like a gymnast. Or a cat. His mother obviously had many blind spots.

Over the next three years, she ran into Marilyn around the apartment complex. Several things became apparent. Marilyn was very smart. She was also very empathic and could tell almost immediately what your weaknesses were, which she was happy to exploit in a way that would cause you the most pain. She also used drugs, which would explain her low paying jobs and the various men she had in her apartment.

This knowledge led to the deal with Terry. Terry paid Jeff in cash for his songs, and Jeff left the money with Lacey, knowing if he took it home it would be spent on drugs. He didn't spend the money on anything he could take home so he didn't have to explain how he bought it. Mostly it just accumulated to the point where Lacey was afraid to leave it in her apartment in case the place was burglarized and the money was stolen. Which led to the next unintended consequence. A friend of hers, Angela, helped Jeff set up an online trading account (no one asked how Jeff acquired his mom's signature on the forms), and Terry sent most of the money there instead. The possibility of letters from the online trading account and the IRS led to a PO Box at a post office store, which led to a friendship with Bob, the man who ran the post office store. Suffice it to say Jeff had many and varied types of friends by the time he was six and acquired a sister.

After finishing the piano piece, Jeff and Lacey played duets together, some classics, some modern as Lacey accompanied him with the other keyboard, one of the guitars, one of the violins, even a harmonica, and on one song the accordion. Then they spent some time on music theory as Jeff worked to complete a new song that Terry was very interested in. Finally, at 9 o'clock, he left Lacey at her door and made his way to his own door, slipping back inside the silent apartment. He stayed awake until 11 reading *The Lord of the Rings* and adding to his elvish dictionary, checking occasionally to see if Danielle's light was still on. When her room went dark, he turned out his light and went to bed to dream of music and elves and squirrels and sisters.

The next morning Jeff was awake in time to be standing in front of Danielle's house by 6:30, munching on a pop tart in one hand while holding a second one in a paper towel for Danielle. The squeegee was hanging from a piece of cord he had tied to a belt loop, and he had a rag stuck in one pocket. She popped out of her front door, closing it quietly behind her, and ran down the sidewalk. Together they quickly made their way to Steve's house, eating the pastries as they went and describing what each had been up to since they parted the day before. She was very excited to hear about Lacey, the instruments in her living room, and the lessons she was giving Jeff, and asked if he thought Lacey might give her guitar lessons adding, "I couldn't pay her, and my mom and stepdad wouldn't." Jeff replied, "I'll introduce you today, and we'll ask her. Maybe you can pay her with the money we make on these jobs." Danielle felt her day was already off to a terrific start. Having a brother was working out well for her so far.

Arriving at Steve's house Jeff extended the squeegee as far as it would go and wiped the dew off all four side windows, using the rag to wipe the moisture off the tool between each stroke just as he had seen the men cleaning the windows of the various stores in his neighborhood. Then he lifted Danielle on his shoulders so she could clean the windshield and rear window. Danielle took the time to clean the headlights and taillights as well, and used the rag to wipe the dew off the door handle. Steve strolled out the front door just as they finished, he and Amy having watched the activity through slits in the front blinds as the children worked. Amy commented, "You're right. He's adorable. Who's the girl with him?" to which Steve replied, "I don't know. I'll go find out."

As Steve walked down the front walk, Jeff and Danielle stood on the sidewalk side by side to greet him. Steve made a show of examining the windows and was surprised and pleased to see how well the job had been done, exclaiming "Well done!" before turning to Danielle and asking, "And who are you?". Before Jeff could speak Danielle said, "I'm Danielle. I'm Jeff's sister." Steve examined the two of them and said, "Well you look alike. Are you twins?" Again, before Jeff could speak, Danielle said, "Yes. I'm the oldest by one minute." Jeff rolled his eyes, and Steve laughed, reaching for his wallet and pulling out two ones. Jeff rushed to say before Danielle could cut him off again, "Pay us in a week, and it's one dollar. Thanks, though." Steve nodded agreement and put the money back in his wallet and the wallet back in his pocket. He pulled a sheet of paper out of his shirt pocket with a flourish and said, "I spoke with a couple more guys who would like the same service. And one lady who would like you to clean the leaves out from behind her hedge. And one man who would like his hoses moved around. Here are the names, addresses, and car descriptions. You can go ahead and clean the car windows, but you'll need to talk to the other two to see exactly what they want done." Then he eyed the piece of paper questioningly and asked if they could read. Jeff said "Yes", and Danielle said, "Jeff is teaching me." Steve smiled indulgently and said, "That's great! What are you reading? *War and Peace? To Kill a Mockingbird?*" to which Jeff replied, "I've never heard of those. I'm reading *The Lord of the Rings.*" Steve's smiled vanished, and he said, "Really? Isn't that a hard book to read?" Jeff shrugged and said, "Yes. It takes a dictionary. But I'm getting better." Steve said, "Okay, then. Well I have to finish getting ready for work. Thanks for the great job on the windows. It was nice meeting you, Danielle. I'll see you both in a week if not before."

The two children waved goodbye as a flabbergasted Steve backed his way to his front door. Jeff checked the sheet of paper for the next car on the list, and they ran down the street. Back in the house, Steve explained to a wide-eyed Amy all he had learned and everything that had been said. She asked where he had come up with the other names of people who wanted things done, and Steve told her that two were in his men's Bible study, and the other two were next door neighbors of those men who were actually interested in getting small (and even strange in the case of moving hoses around) chores done. And so a plan continued to develop in the two children's lives and moved on to its next step.

Jeff and Danielle cleaned the windows of the two cars on the list and knocked on the door of the man who wanted hoses moved. A short, fat man with short, black hair, black glasses, and a friendly face opened the door. Introducing himself as Frank, he explained what he wanted. Every Saturday morning he mowed his lawn. Sometime before Monday morning he wanted the hoses and sprinklers put back into position so all he had to do on Monday morning to water the lawn was turn on the faucet. He showed them where the sprinklers should be placed and how their hoses should be arranged and admonished them to be careful hooking everything back up so as not to damage the faucet or any of the couplers and to make sure it worked before they left. Jeff and Danielle agreed, thanked him, and ran to the house with the hedge to be cleaned behind. As they ran Danielle asked, "Why are people paying us to do these things? Cleaning off their car windows and moving the hoses around?" Jeff thought for a moment and replied, "People have things they don't like. My mom won't eat at a place again if she's ever gotten sick after eating there. And she won't eat a food if she's ever gotten sick after eating it. So maybe these people don't like cleaning their windows or moving their sprinklers around." Laughing he added, "Maybe they're always late for work, and they can't drive with all the windows foggy, but they don't know they're foggy until they go to get in the car, and cleaning them makes them even later to work. Besides, it's only a dollar a week. That's probably what a candy bar costs at the vending machine where they work. So they give up a candy bar and get something done they don't like or have time to do. Whatever. It works for me."

The next door they knocked on was answered by a very tall, pale, redheaded woman who asked brusquely, "Are you Jeff?" When Jeff confirmed that he was and introduced Danielle, the woman continued, "I need everything cleaned out from behind my front hedge that doesn't belong there: leaves, trash, whatever. Put it in this bag." Handing Jeff a paper lawn bag and a dollar, she added, "I'll pay you now. I trust it will be done properly. Just leave the bag by the front door, and I'll put it away." Then she went inside and closed the door. Jeff raised an eyebrow at Danielle and commented, "Alrighty then." The two children tramped to the end of the hedge, and while Danielle held the bag open, Jeff scooped up handfuls of leaves and thrust them in the bag. In half an hour the job was finished, and there wasn't a single dead leaf or anything else behind the hedge. Jeff and Danielle declared themselves satisfied with the job and stood in front of the house deciding what to do next. Danielle wanted to introduce Jeff to Alice Springley, and Jeff suggested they see if Angela was at the pool yet and would teach Danielle to swim. And they needed to meet Lacey and check on music lessons. Speaking of lessons, Danielle needed to continue with her reading lessons, and she wanted to start on arithmetic.

Plans made, they ran back to Jeff's apartment complex and in the front gate to the pool. Angela was not at her usual spot so they continued out the back gate to Danielle's front door. Using the key from the chain around her neck, Danielle opened the door and checked to make sure her mom and stepdad had left for work. Finding the house empty, she waved Jeff inside and gave him a tour of the living room, kitchen, and her room, scanning her room for anything new or out of place before letting him in. Showing Jeff her room took about a second, but then she brought out the guitar and showed him what she had learned to do so far, rippling through chords and playing the melodies of some popular songs. Jeff was duly impressed and said so. She slid the guitar back under the bed and took Jeff out the kitchen door to see if Alice was out in her garden.

They found her tending the daisies, and Danielle introduced her to Jeff, her brother by another mother. Alice laughed heartily at this and shook his hand, admitting that they did look somewhat like twins, and suggesting that maybe it was best if Danielle did not introduce him to her mom or stepdad in that manner. Together the three spent another hour moving from plant bed to plant bed as Danielle and Jeff told her about their day, their various jobs, Danielle learning to swim, and all the rest while they watered here and pulled out a weed there until Alice declared that the garden suited her for the time being and invited them inside for a glass of lemonade. They politely declined, explaining that it was time for swimming lessons for Danielle. Alice declared that was a fine thing, and they left her puttering around her kitchen while Danielle changed into a swimsuit as Jeff waited by the rear gate to the complex.

When Danielle ran back across the street (there is a lot of running involved with six year olds) they crossed to the pool to find Angela there, reading a book, earbuds in her ears, sunglasses perched on her nose. The two plopped at her feet, and when she looked up, Jeff told her they were ready for Danielle's swimming lesson. Danielle threw her cover-up and towel onto the nearest lounge chair and jumped into the pool. While Jeff went to change into his own swimsuit, Angela began the lessons. Jeff returned and dove in, swimming nearby where he could offer encouragements such as "Don't sink" and "Don't breathe the water," which he thought was the brotherly thing to do.

After Angela threatened to drown him herself, he started swimming laps, stopping occasionally to watch the progress. If

Angela's comments and what he could see were any indication the lessons were progressing very rapidly. Danielle was already swimming properly with her head tucked back to take a breath every other stroke. It had taken him a week to get that down so he could take a breath without sucking in water and choking. It wasn't even 11:30 yet. Angela declared herself satisfied with the morning and left them there as she went in for lunch and an afternoon of bridge and finance with her friends, thanking Jeff as she passed for bringing Danielle to her. Jeff beamed with pleasure at the compliment and at how well his sister had done. Ayame arrived then with Hatsu and Cho in tow, and Jeff introduced everyone. They spent half an hour talking with Ayame and playing with the children before they all left to eat lunch.

Jeff took Danielle to his apartment, and after a quick tour made them peanut butter and jelly sandwiches. As they ate, Jeff tutored her on her letters, had her practice all the numbers, and started her on the phonics. They decided to stop by the used bookstore in the afternoon to find an easy book for Danielle to start with. Jeff planned to have her well on her way, if not to his level, before they started school in the fall, not considering what they would do if they were well ahead of the class on the first day. He also showed her his elvish/English dictionary, which she found really exciting. Their own language which no one else (hardly) would know! She was more interested in that than learning to read, but Jeff pointed out she would need to learn to read first so she could help with the creation. Sighing, she agreed, but she perked up when he said they would visit Lacey next and see about guitar lessons.

Lacey was home and available and pleased to meet Jeff's sister. She also nodded knowingly when Jeff commented that she might not want to mention the sister part around his mother. It was easy to see how she and Jeff could be related, even if that was somewhat unlikely. Even twins as they insisted. Except for the eye color, they looked very similar: same hair color, same general face shape, same lean swimmer's build.

Finding that Danielle was interested in guitar lessons she left the room and returned with a half sized guitar which she handed to Danielle, asking her to play something. Danielle tuned the guitar and then started in on a tune currently popular on the radio, singing as she played. Jeff joined in on one of the Yamaha keyboards. Lacey smiled at the result thinking, "Another one." Danielle played the guitar very well for someone obviously untrained. Better than Jeff played the keyboard, in fact. Small as her fingers were they flew like magic over the frets. Her notes and chords were all clean, and her voice was amazing. At six years old it was obvious she had a pleasing and powerful voice.

After some negotiating in which Jeff participated, she agreed to give Danielle guitar lessons for $10 a week, the same as Jeff, which in itself was something of a fiction. Jeff gave her $10 a week from his odd jobs or from his music royalties from Terry which Lacey then gave to Terry to put in Jeff's account. For Danielle, she'd have to see. It was early days yet. She was pleased to find that Danielle had her own guitar and could practice on her own, and that afternoon she gave her the first lesson while Jeff waited patiently. When a student arrived half an hour later Danielle handed Lacey the guitar along with the ten dollars earned the day before, and she and Jeff took their leave.

Danielle was bubbling with excitement. What an amazing week! A brother, a twin even. Earning ten dollars in one day. Learning to swim. A guitar lesson. And it was only early afternoon on the second day! She was so excited that she grabbed Jeff and hugged him, making his eyes pop, his face turn red, and startling a "Eww!" out of him. She backed away laughing, hands held out in a calming gesture and said, "What next?"

Next was running to the used bookstore to look for books. In the education section, they found what Jeff was looking for:

a *McGuffey's 1ˢᵗ Eclectic Reader*. Walking up and down the aisles Danielle now saw promise where before she had no particular interest. Jeff showed her a copy of *The Lord of the Rings* that he was currently reading, pointing out that it was really three books with a fourth, *The Hobbit*, as a prelude which he had already read. "I'm going to get an eBook reader soon so I can keep all my books on one small tablet. Then I can take all of them with me anywhere I go. We should get you one, too." Danielle snorted, "That will probably take a lot of car windows cleaned and hoses moved and hedges cleaned behind. I don't even have the money to pay for this one since I paid for my guitar lesson." Jeff just said, "We'll see. And I'll pay for this one. You'll owe me. At a zillion percent interest a minute." Danielle laughed. Eventually making their way to the checkout register Jeff paid for the book, and they left, running to Danielle's house to drop off the book in her room.

Walking for a change, they headed for the nearby park to see the swans, discussing as they went the grammar rules for elvish. Danielle was wondering how to show past, present, and future without making it too complicated. "For example, when we were on the way to the bookstore we were going to the bookstore. Now we have gone to the bookstore. Tomorrow we might go to the bookstore again. How do we know if it was yesterday, now, or tomorrow? Jeff suggested the symbol would be today. If it had already happened, they could add a small mark at the upper left of the symbol. If it was tomorrow, they could add the small mark at the lower right of the symbol. Saying the word would be the same. If it was today, then no accent. If it was past, then they would accent the beginning of the word. For tomorrow they would accent the end of the word. He showed her, and she laughed. "That sounds like whale sounds!" Jeff laughed and agreed. "I'm exaggerating, but you see what I mean. We'll have to practice." On the discussion went.

At the edge of the park, they ran into Elena and Tisha, two

girls who lived in the apartment complex, arguing over something with lots of unhappy gestures on Elena's part. The two girls were in the 8th grade at the nearby middle school. Elena was brown with dark hair and brown eyes, a usually cheerful face, and a tall body that loved playing sports. All sports. She was on the school softball team, basketball team, volleyball team, and she had taught Jeff how to throw a spiral with a football and a slowball with a baseball. Tisha was the opposite, mostly. She was tall as well, but pale: pale skin, pale blond hair, pale blue eyes, and was way too intense for sports which caused an allergic reaction in her mind. Jeff wasn't sure exactly why they were friends.

"What's up?" Jeff called when they were close enough. Elena continued the rant she was having with Tisha. "We have to memorize a stupid poem in English, *My Last Duchess*. It was written by who knows who (Tisha chimed in: Robert Browning) in who knows when (Tisha: 1842), it's a million words long (Tisha: it's pretty short, actually), and who cares (Tisha: it's worth a pretty big percentage of our grade)." Elena glared at Tisha, "Of course you don't care. You already have it memorized. You were probably born with it memorized." Tisha replied, "No, I memorized it in class." Elena's glare did not diminish. "That is so much better. Thank you very much."

Jeff tried not to laugh and said, "Maybe I can write a song with the poem for lyrics, and it would be easier to learn." Danielle added, "Maybe we could come up with dance steps, too!" The frown had disappeared from Elena's face, and she was starting to look interested. Tisha commented, "I'm glad I already have it memorized." Elena gave her a push and said, "Come on you wimp." So, Jeff and Danielle turned around, leaving the swans for another day, and walked with the two girls back to the apartment Elena shared with her older sister and brother-in-law.

Along the way Danielle was introduced and she showed Tisha her new book (which impressed her very much), while Jeff and

Elena carried on a conversation in Spanish regarding the soon to be song. At the apartment, Jeff sat at the dining room table with the poem open in front of him and Tisha sitting across from him to explain any words he didn't know. He drew music bars on a sheet of notebook paper from Elena's notebook and began adding notes while Elena listened to Danielle telling her about learning to swim that morning, oohing and aahing and proclaiming they would have to race. In half an hour, he was finished and went over the results with the girls. Elena said, "We need more people," pulled out her phone, and started texting. In another half hour, there were two more girls and four boys in the apartment as everyone started putting together a dance routine to go with the music. They were still going strong when Danielle and Jeff both said they had to get home and left. Elena showed them out the door, hugged Danielle and told her they would have to race soon, and kissed Jeff on the cheek, much to his disgust. To him that didn't seem like much thanks for doing something good. He walked with Danielle to the back gate and let her through, telling her he would see her in the morning.

When Jeff walked in the door, Marilyn was home and had cartons of Chinese food spread out on the table. One of her male friends, Tony, who worked in a headshop, was sitting in one of the two chairs. Tony was one of her nicer friends, and Jeff liked him okay. He had long hair tied into a ponytail with a strip of leather and a full beard. His western shirt had the sleeves ripped off, the cutoff jeans were faded and frayed, and he was wearing sandals. He was several years older than Jeff's mom and used the word Dude a lot.

"Dude! How they hanging?" which Jeff understood to mean hello. "I'm fine, thanks. Is that cashew chicken?" His mom answered, "Among other things," as she handed him a plate. "What have you been doing all day?" Jeff scooped rice and chicken onto his plate, added an egg roll, grabbed packets of sweet and sour and soy sauce, and climbed onto one of the bar stools. "I made a new friend, Danielle. We went swimming and to the bookstore. Oh, and I wrote a song to help Elena and Tisha learn a poem." Just a little information was best, and no lies. His mom said, "That's nice," and started talking to Tony about things happening on the street. Jeff finished quickly, rinsed his plate, placed it in the dishwasher, took his book and dictionary, and went to sit by the pool. The other two didn't seem to notice his absence, which was fine by him. The pool area was empty, and he sat at one of the tables, reading until it grew dark outside and the lights came on, and then watched the bats as they caught insects around the lights.

Danielle's night was a repeat of the one before with different food. And this time she didn't wrinkle her nose when she came in the door. She ate, put away her dishes, helped Alice with her garden, and worked on her pictures, adding Ayame and her two children, and Elena, and Tisha. She had to get another sketchbook tomorrow! She would have liked to practice on her guitar but knew the sound would be heard over the television, and there would be yelling. Instead, she looked through the reader, anxious to get on with the lessons, learn to read, and learn elvish.

Again, Jeff watched out his bedroom window as Danielle's light went out. His mom and Tony were still in the living room, the apartment heavy with the smell of burning leaves. He tied a wet bandana over his nose and mouth to block the smell, went to sleep and didn't remember dreaming in the morning.

Chapter 3

The next morning dawned a beautiful Friday. On the way to meet Danielle, Jeff passed the dumpster and saw a squeegee lying on the ground next to it. Picking it up and examining it he found that the sponge part was ragged and torn, but the scrapper part looked fine. With a smile he added it to his collection of pop tarts and the first squeegee stuck through the loop at his waist. When Danielle slipped out her front door, he handed her a still warm pastry and the squeegee, explaining where he had found it. She smiled as well and said, "Cool!" as they headed down the street at a brisk walk to the first of the cars on the list, finishing the last bite as they drew even with it. With two squeegees, they finished in half the time and were off at a run for Steve's car, which was next. With a few more quick scrapes they were about to run off again when Steve stepped out the door, this time with his wife behind him. Jeff and Danielle stopped mid-stride and waited as the two walked down the sidewalk towards them. As he came even with them Steve said, "This is my wife Amy. She wanted to meet the two of you." Amy smiled and said, "Hi, Danielle. Hi, Jeff." They both said hi in return, and Steve continued, "I have a few more jobs for you," as he handed Jeff a piece of paper. "Two more people want their car windows cleaned in the mornings, two want you to clean behind their hedges, and one wants you to finish watering his lawn for him on Friday mornings. They're all on the list there: names, addresses, and what they need done." Jeff studied the addresses, found they were all nearby, and said, "Thanks, Mr. Jacobs". Amy asked, "Do you two go to the elementary school?" to which Jeff replied, "Not yet. We'll start in the fall." Amy tried not to show her surprise that they were not old enough to be in elementary school. Jeff and Danielle said goodbye and ran off to clean the two new car windows. As Steve and Amy sat at the table eating breakfast Amy commented, "They're even younger than I thought. Do you think their parents know where they are? Should they be out doing this on their own this young?" Steve replied, "I suspect their parents don't care where they are, but I'll see what I can find out. And you know that everyone asking them to do things will be keeping an eye on them." They had to be satisfied with that for the moment and added the two children to their morning prayers.

By mutual agreement Jeff and Danielle cleaned all of the car windows first, moved the hoses out of the way for mowing for Frank, and knocked on the door of the house next door where watering had been requested. Sprinklers were already running, and they looked at each other questioningly. The man who answered the door was pretty normal looking to Jeff although Danielle thought his beard would be interesting to draw. Introducing himself as Tom, he explained that Frank next door had told him about the deal he had made about moving his hoses around for him and wanted to know if the two of them would be interested in finishing the watering out front for him. Tom went on to explain that he liked to get his yard watered on Friday morning so it was nice for weekend use, but to get it all done he had to start very early in the morning on Friday to be finished before he left for work. So, he would get it started at a more reasonable hour, and if they would finish it up for him he would pay them five dollars a week. They would need to move the sprinklers three times, leave them running for half an hour, and hand water along the street for about 10 minutes. Jeff and Danielle exchanged a glance to confirm agreement, and Jeff accepted the deal. Tom pulled out his wallet and handed Jeff a five dollar bill adding, "Here's for this week." Jeff pocketed the bill, and he and Danielle set to work moving the sprinklers to the next spot as Tom watched, nodding approval. I'll leave you to it, and I'll see you next Friday," before stepping back through the front door, closing it behind him.

Jeff pulled a watch out of his pocket, one of the many discards for which he had found a use. The case was broken so a strap could no longer be attached, but it kept time just fine, and Jeff had rescued it from the man who was throwing it away. "We'll come back in half an hour after we check on the hedges." And off they ran. Apparently, all the people they were doing jobs for were speaking with their neighbors because the two new jobs were next door to Marge, their first hedge-cleaning job. They met the two new homeowners, received their yard bags and their two dollars, and started to work, pausing between hedges to run back to move the sprinklers. They cleaned behind the second hedge, and when the sprinklers were finished they watered along the street as instructed, put the hoses away, and ran back to Danielle's house where she put on her swimsuit while Jeff waited at the apartment gate.

By 9:00 they were once again sitting at Angela's feet where she sunned herself by the swimming pool. Laughing as she saw them sitting there (as though she hadn't been hoping the two would show up again) she said to Danielle, "Okay, let's review what you learned yesterday and start on learning new strokes." As they jumped in the water, Jeff left to put on his own swimsuit. Returning shortly he dove in the deep end and swam to the side causing Danielle to comment to Angela, "I want to dive like that." Angela beamed proudly and exclaimed, "Excellent.

We'll add that on at the end," and continued demonstrating the breaststroke she was currently teaching Danielle.

By 10AM Danielle knew the breaststroke, backstroke, and sidestroke, and could dive from the side of the pool, if not as well as Jeff. After thanking Angela profusely for her kindness the two spent the next hour racing each other (sometimes Danielle's grace won, sometimes Jeff's power), splashing and diving. Finally, exhausted they walked to Jeff's apartment to rest, find something to eat, and work on Danielle's studies. With sandwiches, water, apples, oranges, and bananas in hand, Jeff taught Danielle phonics, and she was soon recognizing the words she used every day and learning new ones, complaining, just like school children have since the first English word was ever written down, about the words that didn't follow the rules. Time flew by, and when Jeff glanced up to the clock on the wall and saw that it was 3PM he suggested they practice music. He walked Danielle to the gate so she could fetch her guitar, thinking he needed to find some way to get her a key, and returned with her to the apartment. Reaching in the back of his closet, he pulled out an electronic keyboard. It was faded and cracked as though it had been sitting in the sun after being dropped from a tree, but the keys and electronics all worked, which was all he cared about. He had given it the pawn test by taking it by the local pawnshop to see if they would buy it. When they laughed at him and offered to throw it in the trash he was satisfied that it was probably safe from his mom. They practiced on the song Jeff had written yesterday for Elena and Tisha, and just as they had reached the point where they were satisfied with the way it sounded, there was a pounding on the door. Jeff looked up in some alarm, pulled a chair over to the door so he could see out the peephole, and saw Elena and Tisha standing there. Well, Tisha was standing there. Elena was hopping up and down in excitement. Jeff climbed down, moved the chair to the side, and opened the door. Elena rushed in, Tisha following calmly behind her. Elena picked him up, hugged him, and kissed him on the cheek. Danielle started backing away but not quickly enough before Elena did the same to her. Elena ignored Jeff wiping his face off on his shirt and started dancing around the living room shouting, "It was awesome! Best Day Ever! We nailed it! The poem wasn't due until next week, but all of us said it today. Everyone that was at my apartment yesterday. Everyone learned the song, even Tisha. You should have seen the look on Mr. Lucas' face. It was priceless. It's not like any of us except Tisha are his best students, but we were the only ones ready to say it. He asked us how we learned it so quickly, and I asked him if he really wanted to know. He said yes. I asked if he really, really wanted to know, and he said yes, but you could tell he was getting a little peeved. So the eight of us did the dance for him. The class loved it! Even Mr. Lucas was impressed. And Mr. Ford, the principal, walked by while we were doing it, and he wants us to perform it for the school using costumes. Everyone is excited to the max!"

Elena continued to dance around the room, but then stopped, sat on the couch and asked, "Would you guys mind if we made copies of the music and sold it and taught other kids the song? We'd pay you, too." Jeff glanced at Danielle who gave a quick nod and then said to Elena, "Okay. How about if you give us ten cents for every song you sell?" Elena jumped up and rushed to hug him again, but Jeff was able to dodge this time, so she hugged Danielle again instead. "Thank you, thank you, thank you! Best Day Ever!" Then she grabbed Tisha by the hand and dragged her from the apartment.

It was 4:30, so Danielle picked up her guitar and headed for the door. As Jeff walked her to the gate she asked, "Do things like this happen often?" Jeff laughed and said, "Things like this never happened until I met you!" Danielle laughed, too, and replied, "See. Isn't it great to have an older sister?" Jeff rolled his eyes but said, "Why don't you come over after dinner and I'll introduce you to Grand-mere. She lives above us." As Danielle ran across the street, her "Okay" trailed behind her.

At 5:30 his mom had still not appeared, and Jeff nuked another frozen entrée in the microwave, munching on carrots while it cooked. When the dinner was hot, he moved it to the bar along with his book and dictionary and read while he ate. After he had rinsed the plastic tray and tossed it and its package in the recycle bag, he grabbed a bunch of grapes from the counter and took them and the books to his bedroom where he sat on his bed and continued to read as he munched on the grapes. At 6:30 there was a quiet knock at the apartment door, which signified the arrival of Danielle. After doing the chair and peephole routine, he opened the door, stepped through, closing the door firmly behind him, and led her up the stairs where he knocked politely on the door. Grand-mere opened the door and smiled pleasantly at Jeff, less so at Danielle, and said in French, "And who is this?" Danielle answered in French, albeit Cajun French, "My name is Danielle LeBeau. I am Jeff's sister by another mother." Grand-mere's face returned to the pleasant expression it had when she saw Jeff, and she responded with "Come in. Come in. You speak French well, child, but your accent is atrocious. Where did you learn your French?" Danielle replied that she had lived in New Orleans until she was four and had learned her French there. Jeff followed about half of this but caught the gist of the exchange and burst in with, "I didn't know you spoke French!" Danielle said enigmatically in French, "There are many things you don't know about me. That is why I am the eldest." At this Grand-mere burst out laughing, and had she been younger and American she might have said, "You go, girl!" They spent a pleasant half hour with the older woman, Grand-mere correcting Danielle's French until Danielle was exhausted and Jeff getting little bits in here in there and feeling a bit relieved that it wasn't just his French getting corrected.

At 7:30 they said their goodbyes and crossed the street to help Alice finish up in her garden and tell her about the day. When the sky grew dark Jeff left for home, and another day drew to a close.

The weekend passed by quickly with a lot of time spent in the busy swimming pool with Ayame and her family, Elena and Tisha and their friends, Angela, and others. They also fed the swans in the park and went window-shopping at the many stores in the area, and as always seems to happen, Monday came quickly.

Their various jobs continued and grew: scraping the dew off more and more windows in the mornings, cleaning out behind more hedges, moving peoples' newspapers up to their porches, digging up dandelions and other weeds, and anything else two six year olds could do. There was no end to what people would pay a dollar a week or more to have done, and they were doing various things for various people in a very large area.

One afternoon Jeff took Danielle to meet his IT friend at The Web Factory, a company that created and maintained web pages for small companies. The white brick building was a couple of blocks north on 6th Street. They walked through the front door into the small but cozy reception area. Jeff greeted Debbie, the receptionist, and introduced her to his sister. Debbie, a pretty, heavyset, young, black-haired girl waved hi to Danielle as she deftly handled numerous incoming calls, pausing briefly to tell someone that Jeff was there to see her before returning to the phone. Presently a tall woman in her late 20's with bright, knowledgeable grey eyes and short blond hair opened a door to the right of the reception area and waved Jeff towards her. When the door had closed behind her, she began a rapid tirade, "Hi! Who's this? Did you bring more pictures?" Jeff laughed and introduced her to Danielle. "This is Tina. She stores all the pictures for me." Tina shook Danielle's hand vigorously, pointed them towards her office at the end of the hall and said, "It has been crazy around here lately! We have new clients, and everyone wants to change everything! We need more space, more servers, more everything! Where's the camera?" Jeff took the camera out of his backpack and handed it to her. "This is the first chance I've had to come by. The camera is pretty full." As she looked around the office, taking in the various pictures and framed Master of Computer Science degree, Danielle asked, "How did you two meet?" Tina explained, "Jeff helped me find my contact lens in the parking lot. I was stumbling around looking and trying not to step on it, and this little kid walked up, got down on his hands and knees in the parking lot, and found the thing for me. We've been friends ever since. It's been a couple of years now. When he got the camera, I started storing his pictures on one of our servers. I didn't know you had a sister." Jeff explained how they had just met, different mothers, etc. Tina exclaimed, "Wow, that's really cool!" She started scrolling the pictures across her computer screen. Jeff had to explain why they were behind a hedge, why they were cleaning car windows and moving hoses and sprinklers, and all the other jobs. He described Danielle learning to swim, and Tina was impressed. After all the pictures were moved from the camera to the server Tina gave the camera back to Jeff and said, "I have to get back to work. Come by when you have more pictures." Then she led them back down the hall, opened the door to the reception area, waved goodbye, and disappeared. Jeff and Danielle waved to Debbie and left the building. Danielle said, "Wow! That was wicked! And cool! She was nice. I can't believe you have all these grownup friends." Jeff said, "They're your friends, too. Especially all the new ones we've met since we picked up the pecans in Steve's yard." Danielle glowed inside as they headed back to the apartment complex. "Can you see the pictures online?" Jeff snarked, "Well, duh! It wouldn't do me much good if I couldn't see the pictures without going to see Tina!" Danielle punched him in the arm, he feigned massive damage, and they walked back to the apartment complex.

Danielle had started a project of her own. She wanted her yard to not look like a weed patch. With no hope of anything like Alice's, she had come up with an idea as a result of one of their jobs. A woman had asked them to dig up the grass that was growing along the street. When they looked at her questioningly she agreed that yes, it was nice enough grass, it covered everything smoothly and not in clumps like crab grass, yes it didn't need watering, but it put up slender seed stalks overnight that were two feet tall and looked as though it always needed mowing. It had shallow roots and was easy to pull up, so she didn't think they would have any trouble, and they agreed to try. Sure enough, it was easy to pull up, and as Danielle looked at the first bunch in her hand she said to Jeff, "We should plant this in my yard and see if it will grow. It looks better than what we have now, and my mom and stepdad probably won't notice. Or care if they do notice." Jeff agreed, and when they were finished pulling all of the grass from the woman's yard they carried the paper lawn bag, looking a bit like a body stuffed in a carpet just like in the movies and requiring a few stops to rest along the way, to Danielle's house. They then proceeded to dig up clumps of crabgrass and replace it with patches of the new grass, working as carefully as possible to conceal any obvious signs of their work, hoping no one would notice the change in color or type of grass for a while.

After checking with Alice, Danielle borrowed the watering can from Alice's front porch and gave each of the new patches of grass a bit of water. Knowing how her stepfather ranted over the water bill every month when he saw it, saying the two women in the house used more water than everyone at his job combined, she didn't want to use too much, but she didn't think he would notice the few gallons she was using on the new grass. And hopefully it would rain soon. Jeff commented, "If you don't want them to notice we'll have to keep the seed stalks cut off. If it survives until next spring maybe they'll think they grew on their own." And the yard transformation was begun, Danielle style.

In August, Steve and Amy invited them to church and Sunday School. The church was only a couple of blocks away, and they had passed it more than once as they went on their way around the neighborhood. On the second Sunday in August, they met Steve and Amy in front of the church. It was a medium sized church. The sanctuary would hold perhaps 500 people. It had a raised platform at the front for the pulpit, with room for a praise band as well as the occasional youth choir when they sang. A choir loft located behind the platform held 40 people. An organ sat to the right of the platform and a piano to the left. There were video screens above the piano and organ. Sunday School classes were held in temporary structures outside the sanctuary. There were enough rooms to have a men's class, women's class, couples' class, and elementary, middle school, high school, and college classes as well as nursery and pre-school. There were about 80 families with as many children college age and younger in the church as adults 25 and older. Most of the members were under 50. The church was only two years old, the building having previously been a small warehouse. Under the leadership of the pastor, John Patton, and his wife, Sarah, and members like Steve and Amy the church had grown from an original 20 members meeting in various homes to its current size. Much of the remodeling had been done by the members themselves, most of who lived within two miles of the church.

Steve and Amy took Jeff and Danielle straight to the elementary school room where they were introduced to Mary Johnson who was in charge of the elementary class. Mary was a small, older woman with brown hair worn in a bun and a cheerful smile. She reminded Danielle of a sparrow. Mary introduced them to her helpers who were middle school, high school, and college age volunteers. The volunteers introduced them to the 30 or so other class members as they appeared. The room was broken into five tables, one for each grade level. Graduation had taken place the week before as each class advanced a grade level, so the five others sitting with Jeff and Danielle at their table would be starting school in the fall, just as they would.

That is where the similarities ended. Under Jeff's tutelage, Danielle was reading at a 3rd grade level, while Jeff had advanced to a 5th grade level. They were both performing 5th grade math problems, and had spent the summer learning such fun things as every state and its capital and drawing a map of the US starting from a blank piece of paper. Danielle's map was always more accurate than Jeff's, but his was pretty accurate as well. One of their games was to play on the map of the US painted on the elementary school playground, taking turns racing from state to state in alphabetical order, shouting out the name of the state and its capital. If either got one out of order, they had to perform some exercise such as a lap around the schoolyard or a trip back and forth across the monkey bars without stopping. Now they were learning the world map. The American continents were already committed to memory, and they were working their way across Europe.

Not to mention that they had spent the summer working for and with adults, so on the one hand they felt like they were adults sitting at the children's table. On the other hand this was all new to them. They had never read the Bible or heard a Bible story, so there were new things to learn.

Class began with music. While one of the helpers played on a keyboard in the corner, the entire room sang songs Jeff and Danielle had never heard before. There was no sheet music. Everyone seemed to know the songs, even the younger children at their table. After a few songs, Mary said a prayer, another first for Jeff and Danielle, and activities began at the various tables. This morning their student helper, Denise, told them the story from Matthew 19:13 about people bringing their little children to Jesus to bless. There was a page to color of a man with a beard dressed in a robe with children around him.

For Jeff and Danielle this was wrong on so many levels. First of all, the story made no sense. Who was Jesus? Why were parents bringing their children to him? What would blessing them do for them? What were disciples, and why were they trying to stop the parents? And the picture. Who colored a picture that someone else had drawn? What kind of artwork was that? Jeff and Danielle looked at each other, and while Danielle turned her sheet of paper over and began redrawing the picture with charcoal from her messenger bag, Jeff asked questions.

At Jeff's first question, "Who is Jesus?" the other children at the table laughed. They had learned about Jesus all their lives, and even if they couldn't read, they had heard the stories for years now. Jeff ignored the laughter and watched Denise, waiting for her answer. Denise, a somewhat overweight young lady of 13 with black hair, black glasses, and intelligent brown eyes answered, "The Son of God who takes away the sins of the world." Jeff came back with, "Who is God, how is Jesus his son, and what are the sins of the world?" The room had grown quiet during this exchange, which had not taken place at a whisper, and Mary watched with interest to see how Denise would hold up under these questions. Denise responded, "God created the heavens and the earth, the sea and everything in them. Jesus was conceived by the Holy Spirit, born to the virgin Mary, suffered under Pontius Pilate, was crucified, died, and was buried. On the 3rd day he rose from the dead and ascended into heaven where he sits at God's right hand. From there he will come to judge the living and the dead." Jeff didn't even know where to go from here.

Mary spoke up, "Thank you Denise. You have done a wonderful job of explaining, but I think we will have to back up a little further for our two new visitors, and our time is almost up."

Denise told Jeff, "I will explain better later," as she went around the table, admiring all the coloring. When she came to Danielle's, the boy sitting next to her said, "She didn't color hers." Denise stared at the drawing Danielle had made. With charcoal she had redrawn the scene with Jesus replaced by Tony from the head shop with this long hair tied back, his sleeveless western shirt, cutoffs and sandals. The parents had been replaced by Mary, Steve, and Amy. The children were Denise and the children at the table. Jeff and Danielle were missing from the picture. The drawing was quickly done without a lot of detail, but every person in the picture was easily recognizable.

Denise asked if she could show the picture to the rest of the room, and Danielle handed it to her. Denise held the picture up and said, "Look everyone. Danielle redrew the picture with Mrs. Johnson, Mr. and Mrs. Jacobs, me, and the others at this table. She taped it to the whiteboard, and everyone crowded around to see it. As they did, Mary came over to Jeff and Danielle and said, "Danielle, your picture is marvelous. Steve and Amy said you can both read. You're starting a bit behind everyone else in the room because they have been hearing these stories all their lives. How about if I give you each a Bible and some things to read in it. Then next week you can bring your new questions. Or you can ask any of your friends from the church. Steve and Amy say you already know several people. And I'll introduce you to Pastor John and his wife Sarah. They can answer your questions as well."

Jeff and Danielle had been wondering if they even wanted to come back, but with a look between them they agreed to at least give it one more week, and they agreed to see Mary again the following week.

The room emptied as everyone left for the sanctuary, the children from the room finding their parents and dragging them to see the picture that had been left on the whiteboard. Dodging everyone, Jeff and Danielle made their way to the side entrance where they found Steve and Amy waiting for them. Waving the pair inside, they took them to the front of the church where Pastor John was greeting people, and introduced them. Pastor John smiled and shook their hands saying, "I'm pleased to meet the two of you. I've been hearing all summer about two children who have been helping out all over the neighborhood. I can't tell you how thrilled Toni Patterson is to have you watching her two year olds so she can work around the house a couple of times a week."

Jeff and Danielle thanked him and went with Steve and Amy to sit in a row near the front. If they noticed various people around the sanctuary pointing at them, they didn't show it. The organ began playing another song they didn't know, and just before the song ended and Pastor John stepped up to the pulpit to greet the congregation, a young couple with a five year old girl made their way down the row, and the little girl plopped in the seat next to Danielle. She smiled at Danielle and then opened a coloring book and began coloring.

Pastor John welcomed everyone and asked them to greet each other, especially the visitors. Jeff and Danielle were greeted by everyone around them, and they waved to the people they knew from the jobs they had done for them. Then the singing began. Guitars and a drum set joined the piano, and Jeff and Danielle looked on with interest. A band. At least this part they could understand. The words to the songs were shown on the two screens, but not the music, and none of the songs were ones Jeff and Danielle had heard before. After hearing the first verse, they could join in on the second. Following the music there was reading from the Bible. Steve showed Jeff how to find the book, chapter, and verse in the Bible Mary had given him, Jeff showed Danielle, and they followed along. This reading was from James 3 verses 1-12 and spoke about controlling what you say. Jeff listened to the Pastor read, re-read it himself, and thought, huh.

Following the Bible reading, an offering was taken while

more music was played. As the offering plate was passed down their aisle, Jeff and Danielle both placed a dollar in it. Steve and Amy looked at each other, knowing it represented one of their jobs. After this song ended, Pastor John stood behind the pulpit again to speak. He told a local story that everyone knew, a lie that led to great harm for several people, and tied it in to the verses. As he spoke, Jeff listened with interest and took some notes on the back of the church program.

Meanwhile the little girl sitting next to Danielle was growing restless and looking for something to do to occupy herself. Her mother tried valiantly to keep her occupied and listen at the same time, but it was a losing battle. Danielle, seeing all this, pulled her sketchpad out of her ever present messenger bag and began drawing a picture, or pieces of a picture. She could see the whole picture in her head but only drew parts of it on the paper, putting dots with numbers by them at strategic points, creating a connect the dots picture. The little girl watched her work, and when she was finished, Danielle gave the sheet of paper to her. With her mother's help and a crayon the little girl connected the dots and ended up with a cute puppy with a bone in its mouth just as the sermon ended. Pastor John offered a final prayer, and the service was over. The young mother introduced herself as Carolyn Brandt, her daughter as Allison, and her husband as Roger, and thanked Danielle for the picture and for helping with Allison. They knew Steve and Amy and said hello. Walking towards the front door everyone greeted those they knew and were introduced to those they hadn't met yet. Jeff and Danielle were swamped with the parents of the kids in their Sunday School room who had seen the picture and by those who had heard about the jobs they were doing in the neighborhood or had had jobs done by the two. When they were asked about their parents and bringing them to church, they were very non-committal, and at that point Steve and Amy hurried them out of the church. On the sidewalk in front of the church, they invited Jeff and Danielle to lunch with them, and, knowing no one would miss them, they accepted.

As they ate, Amy remarked on their excellent table manners. Jeff replied that last Christmas his mom had given him *Miss Manners Basic Training: Eating* which she had picked up at the used bookstore, not saying that his mom had added when she gave it to him, "Learn this so you aren't disgusting to eat with." Danielle chimed in, "He's been teaching me so I can eat right, too." Amy looked at Steve and thought, "If we had kids I'd want them to be like these."

Jeff and Danielle spent an enjoyable two hours with Steve and Amy, asking many questions, the answers to which led to more questions. Steve and Amy did their best with answers, but many times just wrote them down to research and answer later. Steve did give them his copy of the *New England Primer* pointing out that the book was written to teach children the Christian faith. "If you memorize this book you will have the answers to a lot of your questions. You may not realize it when you do the memorizing, but later you will ask a question or be asked a question, and you will realize you already know the answer." Amy told them that the entire Bible pointed to Jesus and gave them a list of verses to read from Genesis to The Revelation, which she said would tell about Him from the beginning of time to the end. "You won't know everything today. Or tomorrow. All you need to know today is that God loves you." At 2:30, they left Steve and Amy to enjoy the rest of their Sunday afternoon together, promising to return for church that evening at 6:00.

Jeff left Danielle at her front sidewalk, promising to meet her in front of her house at 5:30, and walked through the gate to his apartment. He found his mother sitting on the sofa reading the newspaper, when he unlocked the door and slipped quietly inside. Looking over the top of the paper she asked, "Where have you been?" Jeff answered, "At church." Marilyn laughed a smirky sort of laugh and said, "Really? And what is that in your hand?" to which Jeff replied, "They gave me a Bible." With a mean glint in her eye, Marilyn said, "Seriously? Let me see it!" Jeff handed her the Bible, and she went through it, ripping out pages at random, wadding them into balls, and throwing them across the living room accompanied by comments such as, "This is bunk! I never liked this section! You don't need this one!" Jeff watched in blank faced silence until she handed the book back to him with, "Now it's more accurate!" He took the Bible, picked up the papers from the floor, and went to his room followed by his mom's jeering, "Don't cry over it, okay?" Jeff had expected something like this when she found out and already had a backup plan, which involved buying a used eBook reader and downloading the Bible onto it. He spent the rest of the afternoon looking up what verses he could from what was left of the Bible, but not really making much headway. The words Amy had said stuck in his head, though, "All you need to know today is that God loves you."

He might have understood his mom's attitude better had he known more of her background. Marilyn had grown up in a religious home and had been to church her entire life. She knew quite a bit of the Bible by memory, having had to memorize verses every week and recite them to her parents. To her, religion was about rules, mainly what not to do, and avoiding anything that resembled fun. Her parents were very strict and seldom smiled. When the chance came to run wild, she grabbed hold with both hands, and in her mind, one of the best things that happened was her parents kicking her out of the house. When she left her parents behind, she left the church as well and anything associated with it. Jeff's birth was indeed a miracle, and his survival may well have depended more on Marilyn's desire to get even with her parents than any love she had for him.

During the afternoon, Marilyn exited the apartment, and

at 5:30, Jeff left to meet Danielle. Her afternoon had not gone any better than his had. When she walked in the front door, her mom and stepdad were sitting on the sofa, her mom reading the newspaper while her stepdad watched a ballgame. He asked brusquely, "Where have you been?" When she explained that she had been at church her mom looked up and said, "Great! That's what you needed: adding a holier than thou attitude to everything else! Is that a Bible?" Danielle confirmed that it was indeed her new Bible, and her mom stood up, grabbed it from her, and threw it in the kitchen trash, making sure it landed on the greasy paper towels from their morning bacon. Danielle walked quietly on to her room, and as she closed her door, she heard the two in the living room discussing her. With no Bible to study she pulled out the *New England Primer*, thankful her mom hadn't seen this book, and began reading through it, following Amy's advice and simply memorizing things without trying to understand them. Even new as she was to it all, parts of *A Lesson For Children* were pretty clear: tell no lies, do not swear, do not steal, cheat not in your play, etc. Use no ill words was not so clear, however. What was an ill word? At 5:30 she grabbed an apple from the kitchen and walked out the front door. The two adults, engrossed in a television program, paid no attention.

Meeting Jeff at the sidewalk, she continued with him to the church, both relaying their afternoon experience to the other. After hearing about the fate of her Bible, Jeff told her about his backup plan. "We'll find an eBook reader for you, too." Danielle agreed that it would at least be worth a try.

They reached the church and found Steve and Amy inside. Amy jokingly asked if they had forgotten their new Bibles already, and Jeff explained what had happened to them. He also explained the backup plan to which Steve exclaimed, "Well I can help with that plan. I have my old eBook reader that I was about to donate to Goodwill, and Frank has one as well. I'll check with him and let you know. You can get mine tomorrow, and I'll let you know what I find out from Frank. Does one of you have an online account? If not I'll help you set one up."

Sunday evening went pretty much as Sunday morning had, without the Sunday School part and without a little girl who needed entertaining. For the evening sermon, Pastor John spoke about love from 1 Corinthians Chapter 13. At the end of the sermon Jeff and Danielle both began asking Steve and Amy questions. "Are we supposed to love everybody? Even people who don't love us? What about people who are really bad to us? Or hurt us?" Steve and Amy did their best to explain that love is not a feeling but a choice, and 1 Corinthians Chapter 13 shows what that choice looks like. And that sometimes someone has hurt us so badly that we can't do it on our own, and God has to step in to help us.

With Jeff and Danielle still skeptical, they let it drop for the time being and introduced them to Adam Nichols, the music minister, who was happy to hear that both Jeff and Danielle played instruments and excited to hear that Jeff wrote music, asking to hear a sample of his music. Jeff stepped to the piano and played one of the songs Terry had recorded. Adam said, "I've heard that song. You wrote it?" Jeff explained that he had written it, and his friend Terry and his band had recorded it along with nine others for an album. Adam asked if, first, they would be interested in playing with the Praise Band and, second, if Jeff would be interested in writing songs for the band to play at the church services. Jeff and Danielle said they'd see to both questions, still not sure if coming to church all the time was something they wanted to do, much less join the church. Becoming Christians was not even on their radar. They returned to their homes that evening to more comments from the parents and stepparents, making the love sermon seem like some unattainable goal.

Chapter 4

On Monday they were back at their usual routine, although this was the last week of summer. Next week was the start of school. They stopped by Steve and Amy's at 5:30, just in time to meet Steve as he pulled up to the curb. True to his word, he had two eBook readers sitting on the kitchen table. As Amy prepared dinner, he created an online account for them using his credit card and home address. Then he loaded the account with the $50 online gift card Jeff and Danielle had purchased earlier in the day. After he removed his credit card from the account, he helped them set up the eBook readers to the new account and purchase a Bible that then downloaded to both readers. "You're all set," he commented as Danielle placed both readers in her messenger bag. Do you need any help learning to use them? When the two sets of eyes rolled his way, he laughed and added, "Okay! Okay! I know! Kids today can do all things electronic."

From eBooks, the conversation shifted to school starting, and what they would be doing with all their jobs then. Jeff told him they had already spoken with everyone they were doing things for weekly. "Some things we may still be able to do. We'll have to see what kind of time we have. Everyone said they understood, although some of them seemed really unhappy, especially Frank. He really likes not having to move his own hoses. And some of the people think they'll be late for work every day if we don't clean their windows for them." Steve laughed. "Me included." Amy asked if they wanted to stay for dinner, but both said they needed to get home, and they left. The rest of the week passed quickly for them.

Public school lasted almost a week. Four and a half days to be exact before they were expelled. It started well. In spite of not wanting to be bothered, Jeff's and Danielle's respective moms had enrolled them and supplied all the necessary documentation. Both of them had all their vaccinations. All of the required school supplies were in their backpacks. On the first day, they were both in the right room at the right time, Mrs. O'Malley's first grade class.

It was perhaps a sign that there was trouble on the first day. Mrs. O'Malley gave them the assignment of practicing their alphabet by writing capital A across the first line of their paper one finger width apart with capital B on the second line, and so on. Danielle rolled her eyes, wrote on the paper, turned it over, and started drawing a picture on the back. Jeff didn't roll his eyes, but wrote on the paper and then turned it over and began drawing an organizational plan he and Danielle had in mind for Steve's workbench. Mrs. O'Malley walked around the room checking on each student's progress. When she reached Danielle's desk, she paused like an oil tanker slowing to a stop in mid ocean. She was a very large woman with a heart to match, and she asked kindly, "Are you having trouble with your letters, dear?" Danielle turned her paper over on which she had written all of the letters, capital and small, on one line. Under that, she had printed "I know how to print." And under that she had written in a very nice script, "I also know how to write." Mrs. O'Malley read all three lines, said, "I see. Continue with what you were doing for now," and moved on down the row. When she came to Jeff, she asked the same question and was not totally surprised when he turned the page over and she saw the same three lines as had been on Danielle's sheet. Jeff's printing was perhaps better, and Danielle's script was neater, but they were both obviously ahead of the rest of the class. The question was by how much. She told Jeff to continue with what he was doing and finished reviewing the rest of the class. At recess, she asked them to remain inside, and after asking a student aid to watch her class during the break, she gave the two a mini quiz to see what she was dealing with. She asked them to read for her. She asked them to do math problems. She asked questions from the science book, the geography book, the civics book. By the time recess was over, she had an idea of where they placed in their education, and for the rest of the day she kept them busy with individual assignments. When the class left for the music room, she strode purposefully to the principal's office to announce her discovery. He called in a counselor. Together they planned a schedule that they thought would challenge the two children. They needn't have bothered.

On Friday at lunch, basically the same thing happened to both Jeff and Danielle at two different restrooms at opposite ends of the building. Three 3rd grade boys and three 3rd grade girls demanded lunch money from them. In Jeff's case he responded by saying, "No." One of the boys shoved him and said, "What do you mean no?" That is when the three boys discovered that what they had thought was a kitten was indeed a bobcat. A short time later, Jeff walked out of the restroom into the arms of a teacher, who was running into the restroom because of boy number three's screaming exit. Meanwhile in the girls' restroom almost the exact same thing had happened. The three 3rd grade girls demanded Danielle's lunch money, and, outraged, she said no. The largest of the three girls shoved her. A short time later Danielle was standing over the first girl as the vice principal ran in the door, alerted by the third girl as she ran screaming from the restroom. All parties told their stories, and although the 3rd graders' tale of being attacked for no reason was not believed, the rules against fighting were clear, and everyone involved was expelled.

Jeff and Danielle took their backpacks with their new, barely used school supplies, and, leaving all school owned materials behind left the school property alone, phone calls to their parents having produced no results. On the way back to their homes, they came across the Shepherd family leaving their home for a field trip to an art museum. The Shepherds lived across the alley from Frank, knew all about his dislike for moving hoses, and had spoken with Jeff and Danielle before. Kathy, a tall, dark haired no-nonsense mom, asked them if their school day was over already. Danielle, still a bit mad over the whole thing, said a bit bitterly, "No, we were expelled." Kathy looked shocked, and as her two children, Sam Jr., 7, and Bailey, 5, looked on with interest, she asked, "Why? How?" Danielle explained what had happened. Sam Jr. said, "You beat up three 3rd graders? Cool!" which earned a stern look from his mother. Kathy asked, "Where are your parents? Didn't they call them?" Jeff replied, "They couldn't get hold of them." Kathy pondered for a moment and asked, "What are you going to do now?" Danielle shrugged and replied, "Don't know." Kathy then said, "I'll have to check with Sam, but why don't you join our homeschool group? You'd need your parents' permission, but I don't think it would be a problem with anyone. I can check this weekend, and maybe you could start on Monday." Jeff and Danielle looked at each other, then back at Kathy, and Jeff said, "That would be really great! Thank you very much!" Kathy finished loading her two kids in the car and said, "Stop by Sunday when you have time, and I'll let you know what I find out." Jeff and Danielle agreed and continued to their homes. It seemed that someone was looking out for them, although they thought looking out for them should include not fighting 3rd graders and getting expelled in the first place. Strangely, they had no real fear about what their parents would say. First, because it was a totally new experience, and second because their parents had no real interest in what they did anyway, so this was just one more thing to not be interested in.

The announcement to their parents went about as expected. Marilyn thought it was hilarious, especially in view of the church attendance. She had a good time ridiculing Jeff for his lack of "church attitude". Homeschooling sounded fine with her as long as it kept her from trouble. Danielle's mom and stepdad were very angry at first, thinking about the effort that might be required from them such as visits with teachers and principals and monitoring Danielle's behavior, but they calmed down when Danielle explained about the chance at homeschooling. With the pressure to help Danielle gone, Carl thought it was pretty funny that Danielle had, as he put it, "kicked three 3rd grader's butts". And so the plan for their lives progressed.

The following Sunday was their third visit to 2nd Street Bible Church. Word had gotten around after the first Sunday about Danielle's artistic ability, their instrument playing, and Jeff's song writing. Danielle had been asked if she would provide a connect the dots picture each week for the younger classes that matched the lesson for the day, and she had agreed. They were also asked to play for the singing time at Sunday School, which they did, with Jeff on the keyboard in the classroom and Danielle on her guitar. Using the verses given them by Amy and their new Bibles on their new eBook readers as well as the *New England Primer,* they were much further along in their knowledge than that first Sunday, although their understanding was still a little sketchy.

News of their expulsion had started to filter through the church family. Sam Shepherd had told Frank who had told a neighbor who attended the church who had told another church member who had told his Sunday School class. By the time Jeff and Danielle met Steve and Amy for church they had also heard about the expulsion. There were a variety of opinions in the church ranging from "Good for them for standing up for themselves," to "They should learn to turn the other cheek," and "If any man will take away thy coat, let him have thy cloak also." Steve and Amy just asked if they were okay and knew what they were going to do. Jeff and Danielle explained about the Shepherds offering to add them to their homeschool group, and Steve and Amy were excited for them. They knew the Shepherds and knew the group they belonged to did an excellent job of teaching all the kids.

After church and lunch with Steve and Amy, they walked over to the Shepherds, who welcomed them into their home. Sam Sr. was the opposite of his wife, short and easy going. After some brief pleasantries, Kathy jumped right to the point. She had spoken to everyone in the homeschool group, and they were all eager for Jeff and Danielle to join. There was paperwork for their parents to sign, and they could bring it with them Monday at 8:00. The first day would be spent determining what their level was in each subject, and then the real teaching would begin. Sam Jr. and Bailey chimed in that they would help them get to know anyone they didn't already know. On that note, Jeff and Danielle left, taking the paperwork with them. Neither one had difficulty getting the paperwork signed since the only effort required was a signature. It seemed to be an easy solution to what could have been a major disruption in their parents' lives.

Monday morning they arrived bright and early at the Shepherd's house. After receiving the paperwork, Kathy ran Jeff and Danielle through basically the same testing they had received from Mrs. O'Malley the previous week, with the same results. Kathy started them on their assignments, part of which was helping the other kids with their reading and math. This set the tone, and they continued their briefly interrupted education, continuing to advance quickly.

The congregation at 2nd Street Bible Church was growing,

and the growth seemed to be because of Jeff and Danielle. There were several reasons. First, the two were fun and interesting to be around. They asked some really intriguing questions that kept the teachers and helpers scrambling for answers. Complacency was not the word of the day. The connect the dot pictures Danielle came up with were fun to do. Even adults were interested in seeing the outcome when their children connected all the dots. Second, Jeff and Danielle were playing in the Praise Band at the services, and their young presence was a novelty. Third, Jeff was now writing songs for the band to play. He would write the song, Adam would help with the arrangement, the band would learn it and by the third week play it for the church, which seemed as a whole really to like the new songs. The kids were telling their friends at school, who would visit, brought by their parents. The adults would tell their friends at work or in the neighborhood who would visit, bringing their families.

This was a time of change for Jeff and Danielle. They were spending a lot of time doing things associated with the church: music, Sunday School (helping and attending), church twice Sunday and once Wednesday night, reading their Bibles, etc. They now had homework not of their own choosing on subjects they hadn't spent time on before such as science, history, and civics. And both of them were trying to make a difference at home. Danielle tried to do things at home such as cleaning or dusting, but after her mom made a comment about Danielle thinking Melanie didn't keep the house clean enough to suit Danielle, she stopped. Everything she tried seemed to make things worse. Even trying to be kinder and practice 1 Corinthians Chapter 13 love seemed to make things worse. It was no better for Jeff. Any acts of patience or kindness were met with sarcasm and "Uh-oh, holier than thou attitude." So they prayed and kept on and perhaps sometimes wished that someone like Steve and Amy were their parents.

Thanksgiving came and went. At Danielle's house, it wasn't much different than any other day, except for all the football games. Jeff's mom spent the day with her friends, leaving Jeff to fend for himself. He and Danielle spent much of the day with Steve, Amy, and the Jacobs' relatives.

Christmas, though, was shaping up to be pretty nice. Danielle put up a little tree in her room, along with decorations on the walls and every surface. Even Marilyn put up a small tree in the living room and helped Jeff put up decorations. In addition to the Sunday morning songs for the church, Jeff wrote songs for the Christmas concert in December and ten new Christmas songs for his friend, Terry. Jeff and Danielle taped flyers for the concert to all of the apartment doors at the apartment complex, except for their friends. Those, they hand delivered. They added a note at the bottom saying that Jeff had written some of the songs, and please come. They did the same for all the people they had helped during the summer. Alice and her sister received special ones Danielle drew just for them. The church concert was well attended by a standing room only audience. Terry did well with the Christmas album both in gigs around the city and on iTunes, and Jeff's online trading account continued to grow. They exchanged small gifts with each other and gave small gifts to their friends. As Danielle said emphatically, "Best Christmas Ever!"

One Sunday towards the end of January in the new year while Jeff and Danielle were eating lunch with the Jacobs, Steve asked, "Have you two considered giving your lives to Christ?" to which Danielle answered, "We did that back in December." Amy asked, "Why didn't you tell us? That was an important decision!" Jeff replied, "We wanted to be baptized on our birthday, and we were waiting to tell you; then, we wanted to ask if you would be with us." Amy felt her heart swell, and tears started running down her face as she said, "We're so happy for both of you, and you know we would love to be with you. But your birthday is coming up soon! Are you going to ask Pastor John to baptize you?" "We've already asked him, and he said yes," was Danielle's reply. "The 1st is on a Saturday. He's going to announce it this Sunday morning. There's going to be another family baptized with us, a Tom and Audrey McAdams."

Tom and Audrey McAdams were two former alcoholics who the church, the neighbors, and the police were delighted to see join the church. Tom and Audrey, tall, dirty blond haired, and sharp featured were not happy drunks, or sad drunks, or loud drunks, or even mean drunks. They were psychotic drunks. When they drank, any inhibitions they had towards evil went away, and they were willing to do anything that came to mind with no thought to the consequences. It was a miracle they hadn't killed anyone yet. Or worse. Tom was a master craftsman and Audrey was a bookkeeper at the Cabinet Shop, a small factory that made custom cabinets for homes. Since they never arrived at work drunk, and Tom was one of the best cabinetmakers the owner, Tod Jenkins, had ever seen, he kept them on, hoping he would never regret it. The day one of the members of 2nd Street Bible Church had caught them at the right time and led them to Christ was an especially happy moment for Tod as it was a load off his mind. Tom and Audrey grabbed hold with a childlike faith that never looked back. They, too, were enchanted with Jeff and Danielle, and were looking forward to being baptized with them.

The baptism took place as planned on their 7th birthday. Many of the church members were present even though it was a Saturday, and all four of them were warmly welcomed into the church family.

As the year continued, Jeff had written enough songs that the church made a CD. Most of the families in the church bought at least one copy, and some bought extras to give to family and friends as gifts. There were enough requests that they decided to add it to iTunes, where the album was well received. It was good enough, in fact, that the church decided to enter the Praise Band as one of the bands at the Main Street fair held every year in June. Hopes and expectations ran high as the entire church prepared for the event, choosing what to wear on stage, how the church would support the event with pamphlets to hand out and prayer teams and witness teams. The Praise Band practiced many long hours so the music would be perfect.

During this time Jeff and Danielle attempted more than once to tell their parents about the changes that were going on in their lives, their love for God, the Sunday School, the church, the band, and the new friends they were making. Marilyn and her various boyfriends met the attempts with laughter and derision, so Jeff returned to blank faced silence when around them. Danielle's attempts were met with stony silence. So, at the end of their prayer time they always added on their parents.

With school, church, and the upcoming event, the days flew by until the Saturday of the street fair arrived. They were scheduled to play at 2 PM, and at 1 they were in place, beginning the setup. At 1:55 the prayer team prayed for them and they stepped up on stage. Jeff looked around for everyone's nod that they were ready, got the nod from Danielle, and played the notes of the opening song on the keyboard, and the earth stood still. Everyone within hearing range stopped what they were doing, stopped what they were saying, and stopped moving to listen. Part of it was seeing the two seven year olds on the stage. Part of it was the quality of the music itself. The biggest part was a God thing. As the music continued with song after song, the crowd around the stage grew as people moving up and down the street stopped when they could hear the music and then moved closer. Danielle sang the last song herself, and when the final chord was played at exactly 3 PM, the crowd stretched as far as the sound from the stage could be heard. There was thunderous applause as the Praise Band left the stage, and the table selling CD's of the music was swamped, selling out in less than 20 minutes. They told everyone still trying to buy the CD that it could be found on iTunes, thanks to Adam's foresight in putting it there. The team handing out pamphlets inviting people to visit 2nd Street Bible Church ran out of pamphlets and spoke themselves hoarse. Even that was not the pinnacle.

As the band was leaving the stage a man walked up and introduced himself as the manager from the radio station putting on the big 4th of July concert at the nearby city. He explained that one of the groups had had to drop out due to illness in the family, and if they were interested, the radio station would like for them to take over that slot which was at 2PM, the same as today, although it would be hotter then. Pastor John told him they would tentatively say yes but would let him know in a couple of days after everyone had time to check their schedules, and especially Jeff and Danielle had time to get permission from their parents. Blessings were pouring in on the church, Jeff, and Danielle.

The next day at church Pastor John announced the news to everyone. After church, committees were hastily formed: one for a booth at the concert to sell CD's and hand out pamphlets, one to make the CD's, one to make the pamphlets, one to organize the prayer team, one to organize transportation, one to arrange audio/visuals, etc. Jeff and Danielle had written permission. It had been surprisingly easy to obtain. Marilyn just laughed, said sure, why not, and signed. Carl and Melanie were strangely quiet on the matter. Her mom signed the permission with no comment. Jeff and Danielle made sure everyone they knew, around the apartment complex and among the people they had performed tasks for all summer, who didn't belong to the church, knew about the concert and that they would be playing in it. Several, including Lacey, said they would be there.

The day of the 4th of July concert arrived. Jeff and Danielle, the Praise Band, and several members of the church arrived early to find the crowds had already begun to arrive. More than 100,000 people were expected at the event, which would spotlight several well-known artists as well as lesser known local talent. One of these less well-known groups was the one that had dropped out at the last minute, making room for the 2nd Street Bible Church group. It promised to be a typical hot July day in Texas with only a few scattered clouds that would not interfere with the fireworks late in the evening. Everyone set up their blankets, coolers, and umbrellas as near to the stage as possible and spent the day wandering around, visiting with the many spectators, and checking out the various vendor booths, while the band members tried not to think about playing in front of so many people. It was a huge step up from the street fair, well attended though it had been. Jeff and Danielle felt like they were in heaven. They were surrounded by a huge crowd of people who had the most important thing possible in common and who considered them part of their huge family. The two of them were overjoyed at the thought of sharing their music with these people, and their joy was too contagious for the other band members not to tap into, and their nervousness faded as their excitement and joy grew as well. They were scheduled to play at 2:00, and at 1:00 they moved their instruments to the stage, did sound checks, and made last minute bathroom runs.

At 2:00 on the dot the DJ checked to make sure they were ready and announced them to the huge crowd. Jeff played the opening notes of the first song, and from that point on the music was out of their hands. Just as at the street fair, the huge crowd went silent, cheering, whistling and screaming at the end of each song, continuing the noise for a good while after the last song was played and the band left the stage. As at the street fair, all of the CD's they brought sold out, and many more people were told they could find the songs on iTunes.

Jeff and Danielle and the other band members were exhausted.

Putting out that much energy while standing in that heat took its toll, and they spent a long while at the misting station, cooling down and accepting congratulations from event goers. When everyone was cool, they made their way back to their blankets and the rest of the group and spent the remainder of the day and evening enjoying the music and the fellowship and, finally, the fireworks. It was a tired group of people that headed out for the drive home. Steve and Amy dropped them off at the rear of the apartment complex at 3AM. Jeff and Danielle returned to their respective dark homes and were happily asleep by 4AM with no hint of what was ahead. In her excitement and sleepiness, Danielle forgot to lock the front door behind her when she slipped silently inside.

Chapter 5

Michelle Strong signed in to the pediatric ICU at 7AM to begin her 12-hour shift. She was a trim, loving, but no-nonsense woman with ebony skin and a heart as big as the great outdoors, as her friends liked to say. She really needed the work today. It had been one year since her husband was killed in an auto accident, and everything she saw on the drive to work reminded her of him: the restaurant where they met, the shop where he bought her flowers, the high school their daughter, Elizabeth, might one day attend. Who would have thought that at 31 this is where she would be, struggling to pay the bills and raise their daughter by herself. They were doing okay, but if her mother wasn't taking care of the baby sitting, she wouldn't be making ends meet as well as she was, and she was one major repair away from big trouble. Oh, well, enough of the pity party. She had a lovely, 5 year old daughter to love and a roof over her head today.

She greeted the rest of the staff and checked to see which doctors would be on staff and on call. The night nurse, Elaine, her best friend, greeted her. Elaine was the same age as Michelle but tiny, tan, and blond with a wicked sense of humor. She would sometimes babysit Elizabeth when Michelle's mom needed a break, was great company for the occasional girl's night out, and would visit to watch movies and eat ice cream with Michelle and

Elizabeth. This morning, looking as chipper and cheerful as when she had arrived 12 hours earlier, she handed Michelle the list of current patients. There were only five: two from auto accidents, one who had fallen from a tree, and two cancer patients who had come out of remission. Michelle looked over the list and took a moment to lock her heart in the place she kept it so she could deal with the suffering of the children. Then she said goodbye to Elaine and started to work.

Officer Robert Freedman placed the hoof trimmers in his briefcase along with paperwork and a box of ammunition for his service pistol before loading the briefcase in the trunk of his police cruiser. He planned on a relaxing afternoon working with his horse and replacing a shoe that had pulled off in a patch of mud the previous day. He would have replaced the shoe the day before when it came off if he hadn't forgotten to pick the hoof trimmers up from Chris, his fellow officer whose daughter wanted them for show and tell. At least Robert had his own place, 10 acres a few miles outside the city with a nice sized two-story wood home built in the 20's with a wrap-around porch, shutters that actually functioned, and a real storm cellar. Not to mention the small barn where he kept his horse, Chester. The 10 acres provided hay and a place to ride when it wasn't raining as well as an agricultural exemption on taxes. The steer he let his neighbor graze there provided some free fertilizer, company, and entertainment for Chester. All of it, the land, house, barn, even the storm cellar, was the legacy his parents had left him. They had both died while he was serving with the army in Iraq, she from a stroke, him shortly after from missing her. Robert was definitely better off than Chris whose daughter's horse was kept in a boarding stable. Rob had offered to let him board the horse with Chester, but the stable gave lessons and took the girls to horse shows, so at the moment that wasn't an option for Chris. Robert thought to himself, "Wait until he realizes he's making a house payment for that horse every month. Or his daughter needs braces. Then we'll see." He gave his bulletproof vest a tug to settle it, climbed in the cruiser, and pulled away from the station to begin his patrol.

The ambulance crew from unit 601 finished prepping their Mobile ICU after their latest run to the hospital and headed back to the station down 2nd Street. The ambulance crew from unit 591 picked up their Mobile ICU from the repair center where general maintenance had been performed and headed towards their station, also driving down 2nd Street but from the opposite direction, heading towards the freeway and the station farther north.

Alice Springley added water to the coffee maker to begin her morning ritual. While the coffee was brewing, she would make the bed, check for emails from her children, and cook her breakfast. She would usually be at her sister's house on Sunday morning, but her sister was at a class reunion. The kitchen window was open to the fresh air before the day grew too warm and she had to close up and let the window AC units do their job of keeping the house at a decent temperature.

Many of the members of 2nd Street Bible Church who had attended the music festival the day before were still asleep, exhausted from a long day in the sun, eight hours on a bus, and not much sleep. Jeff was already awake, still excited from the day before. After a quiet breakfast of cereal so he wouldn't wake up his mother and whoever else might be in her room, he would be heading over to meet Danielle before walking on to church.

Danielle was awakened a little before 8AM by her mother, who pulled her out of bed, telling her she and her stepdad had a surprise waiting for her in the living room.

At about 8AM Alice heard the sound of a nail gun coming through her kitchen window from next door. Shortly after that, she heard sounds like a carpet being beaten. She wondered briefly to herself what they were up to so early on a Sunday morning, but after a bit she continued with her morning routine.

Jeff left his apartment around 8:45 for the walk by Danielle's house before they continued on to church together. Shortly after that, Alice stepped out on her front porch to retrieve the Sunday paper. Alice dropped her coffee cup on the porch and grabbed at her chest as the screams tore out of the house next door. With shaking hands, she pulled her cell phone from her pocket and called 911. She told the dispatcher that it sounded like the little girl who lived next door was being murdered. The dispatcher could hear the screams coming over the phone and immediately dispatched a car. Officer Freedman took the call and started for the address with lights and siren. He was close instead of at the other end of his beat due to stopping to give a ticket to someone who ran a red light in front of him. Jeff heard the screams as he stepped through the apartment complex gate and broke into a run. As he raced up the front sidewalk, Alice yelled at him, "Don't go in there, boy! I've called the police." Jeff ignored her, stopping only long enough to pick up two pieces of brick from Danielle's flowerbed before tearing through the unlocked front door. He threw both pieces of brick and tried to pick up a chair.

Officer Freedman screeched to a stop at the curb and jumped out of the car. Over the sounds of Alice yelling at him to hurry he called for backup as he stormed up the walk, drawing his pistol. Soon Alice heard pistol shots from next door.

In a few moments, Robert was calling for ambulances. Rush on the ambulances. Officer Kendra Taylor burst through the door, gun drawn. Officer Freedman waved her to the girl and said, "Do what you can," while he ran to the boy. Then four paramedics burst through the door. A few moments later Alice watched Officer Roberts run to his car and retrieve the hoof trimmers from his briefcase. Two minutes after that, the children were on stretchers, in the two ambulances, and on their way to the hospital.

Soon the crime scene was covered with yellow police tape,

more police, the coroner, detectives, crime scene investigators, and neighbors. Some of those neighbors belonged to 2nd Street Bible Church, the prayer chain was activated, and before 10am, church members were at the hospital, and prayers were going up for Jeff and Danielle.

At 9:30, the two ambulances pulled up at the ER. Jeff and Danielle were rushed into surgery, and two teams of surgeons, plastic surgeons, and other specialists worked for twelve hours to save the lives of the two children. Throughout the surgery, members of 2nd Street Bible Church including Tom and Audrey McAdams came and went, bathing the two children, the operating rooms, and the doctors and nurses in prayer. Danielle's mother was in another part of the hospital with a concussion. Jeff's mother was a no show. At the end of the surgery when both children were stable, they were placed in rooms in the pediatric ICU where Michelle worked. They were unconscious for the rest of Sunday and most of Monday before awakening Monday afternoon. Jeff's mother showed up Monday morning, asked where he was, looked in his room, and left. She stopped at the nurse's station long enough to say, "I hope no one is expecting me to pay for this," before leaving.

At the church service Sunday morning, Pastor John stood in front of the congregation and told them the news. "I thought I would be up here this morning to tell you how well the Praise Band did at the concert yesterday and how well received they were. All of the albums we took were sold." Those in the congregation who had not heard the horrible news applauded. Pastor John continued, "Some of you may have heard by now, but this morning before Sunday School Danielle LeBeau's mother and stepdad tried to kill her. Jeff Mitchell was on his way to meet her to walk to Sunday School. He went inside, and they tried to kill him as well. Both children are in surgery at East Side Memorial in critical condition. My wife and other members of our church are up there. Please keep Jeff and Danielle in your prayers."

Michelle was there when each one awakened. She explained to each one where they were and told them they were safe and that no one else would be hurting them. She was surprised when Danielle looked her in the eyes and told her, "You can't promise that." She was stunned when Jeff looked her in the eyes and told her the same thing. When Robert Freedman stopped by Monday evening to check on them she spoke with him about what the two had said.

"Why would they say that?" she asked as the two stood in the hall? "Do you know what kind of life they have?"

Robert thought about what he'd seen, what he knew, and what the investigation had turned up so far and replied, "Her step father is dead. Her Mother won't be getting her back if she survives jail. Danielle will go into the foster care system, and her chances there are iffy. Some foster homes are incredible, some not so much. Jeff lives with his mother. I'm pretty sure she uses drugs, but she doesn't have a record, and as far as I know she hasn't done anything to bring her to the attention of child protective services. For that matter, Danielle's mom and stepdad didn't have a record either. They were just psychopaths waiting to happen."

Michelle nodded towards the waiting room where a number of people were talking and praying together. "They have a lot of support there." But that wasn't going to go as everyone expected which they found out the next day.

On Tuesday morning, knowing neither child would have a parent visiting them, Michelle allowed Sarah Patton in to visit Danielle. The next thing she knew Danielle's readings were alarming, first heart rate, then blood pressure. As Michelle rushed to the room she heard Danielle screaming, "You lied to me! God hates me, and I hate him!" Michelle grabbed Sarah by the shoulders and pulled her from the room. Then she came to stand by Danielle's bed, looking down at the wild-eyed little girl. She sobbed, "I asked Him to save me. I begged him to forgive me for whatever I had done wrong to deserve what was happening. And it just went on and on and got worse and worse. And Jeff came to save me, and it happened to him, too. How could we have been so bad that God would hate us so much?"

Michelle was at a total loss what to say, so she just said, "Hush, baby. It will be okay," as she administered the allowed sedative. The heart rate and blood pressure dropped back to normal and Michelle stepped back into the hall to find a white-faced Sarah. I'm sorry, ma'am, but I think they shouldn't have any more visitors for a while. Maybe when they move to a regular room. Sarah asked, "What about Jeff? Do you think he feels the same way?" Michelle said she'd check with him and let her know. She wanted to look in on him anyway to see how he had taken all this. His heart rate and pulse had skyrocketed when Danielle's did. Stepping into the room she found Jeff with his face turned towards the door. He asked, "Is Danielle okay? What happened?" Michelle told him that Sarah had gone in to see Danielle. Jeff's eyes turned cold, and his face set in a mask. "They all lied to us. We learned God is love and let the little children come to me. Why did He let that happen to Danielle?" Again Michelle was at a loss for words, so again she said, "Everything will be okay, baby." To which Jeff replied, "Nothing will ever be okay again."

Michelle left the room and told a waiting Sarah, "It would probably be best if you don't see Jeff either. Not right now." Sarah nodded and went down the hall to the waiting room where a stunned group of church members waited. With tears running down her face she told them what had happened. Most sat down and said they would continue to pray for the two children. If only Sarah could have known the many things that happened to get the children safely to the hospital. Such as Alice Springley being home that morning when she was usually at her sister's house.

Or Officer Freedman being so close to the scene instead of at the other end of his beat. Or two ambulances being so close instead of at their respective stations. And the cloud of prayers kept going up for the two children.

As the week in ICU went by Danielle grew angrily bitter. It seemed that every day was worse than the one before with pain and bad news and no friends to help share the load. Seeing Sarah made the betrayal seem real all over again. Every day Danielle looked at her fingers and wondered if she would ever draw again. Or play the guitar. She would feel the pain in her feet and wonder if she would walk again. She wondered if the fire on her back would ever end. And she continued to brood.

Jeff was growing into an icy stoic. He was enraged beyond reason at what had happened to Danielle. Looking at his hands he would think, "I will write music again, but will Danielle be able to draw or play the guitar?" When the pain in his feet caught his attention he would think, "I will walk again, but what about Danielle?" His back was on fire as well, and although they were off the critical list, their condition was still listed as serious.

It didn't help that they couldn't talk to each other or even see each other. Michelle would spend time with each of them, updating them on each other's status, but it wasn't the same. They had been together every day for months, sharing thoughts and dreams and ups and downs, and this sudden isolation was driving them both crazy. Unknown to each other they had both made plans to pull out the IV's, rip off the sensors, and go find the other one. Unfortunately they were both on strict watch because both were refusing adamantly the pain killers prescribed for them and had been stopped just in time from pulling every tube and monitor off preparing to leave the hospital to get away from the pain killers. Jeff was refusing them because of his mom, and Danielle was refusing them because of Jeff. After that, they were allowed to dose themselves as needed even though it broke the hearts of the nurses on duty to watch them suffer through the long hours.

Finally, on Friday, Jeff was allowed out of bed. A male nurse named Ben scooped him from the bed and set him in a wheelchair, then rolled him next door to see Danielle. This began a flurry of elvish starting with, "Sister!" "Brother!" Michelle and the other nurses looked at each wondering, "What in the world?" Ben, a big Lord of the Rings fan, laughed and said, "It's elvish!"

Ben was also the one to give them their nicknames. He walked into the nurses' station after taking the vital signs of both children and said, "They look like a couple of baby seals," and the name stuck. Everyone started using it, even Michelle. To tell the difference between the two they called Danielle Green Seal and Jeff Blue Seal because of their eye color. Even the church and their other friends picked up on it after overhearing the nurses using the names.

Jeff regarded Danielle who was curled in a ball on her side. Her face was pale, and her eyes were sunken with dark rings around them. "How do you feel?" Danielle gave a little shrug and replied, "Pretty bad. I hurt all over, my back feels like it's on fire when I move, and my hands and feet hurt. Better than when I woke up, though." Tears started rolling down her cheeks. "What if I can't draw again?" Jeff smiled and said confidently, "You'll draw again." Danielle snorted, "How do you know," feeling better just hearing him say it. Jeff put on a superior air. "I just know. Just because you're the oldest doesn't mean you know everything." Danielle gave a little laugh. Out at the nurse's station the nurses smiled at each other when they heard that laugh. They were really worried about their young charges, and a laugh was a step in the right direction.

Also on Friday, a harried woman from Child Protective Services stopped by to talk with Danielle and tell her they were arranging foster care for her. There were families at the church who were certified for foster care and other families who were willing to be certified to take care of her including Steve and Amy, but she would have none of it. The woman was annoyed at this since she had children she had trouble placing, and here was one with people begging to take her who refused to let them. She perhaps did not leave with the most charitable thoughts about Danielle.

To cap off the day Jeff's mother stopped by. "How are you feeling?" Jeff was lying on his side facing the door since it still hurt too much to lie on his back for very long. He responded, "I'm okay." Marilyn commented, "You don't look so hot." Jeff just shrugged. "Anyway I wanted to let you know that we're moving. We can't afford to stay at Viewpoint Apartments. I've rented an apartment a few miles to the east. It's not as nice a neighborhood, but whatever. I guess you can ride the bus or walk if you want to keep getting homeschooled by those people. Anyway, I'm moving this weekend. Everything will be moved by the time they let you out of here. Oh, and here are some clothes in case you want to get out of the hospital gown."

With that she left Jeff to think about what he was about to give up such as his friends at the apartments and in the neighborhood, the ones who didn't belong to the church. He would miss the swimming pool. And, always in the back of his mind was where would Danielle be going?

The following Sunday Pastor John stood in front of the congregation again and updated them on what had happened the past week. Again, some knew the news and some did not. "Jeff and Danielle made it through surgery and are out of critical condition. They are doing well and will probably move out of ICU and into a regular room tomorrow." Again, many in the congregation applauded, but many did not, and those that had looked around the room, suddenly expecting the other shoe to drop. "The bad news is they blame the church for misleading them and are very mad at us and God for what happened to them. They haven't wanted to see anyone from the church. Worse than that, when my wife spoke to Danielle her blood pressure and pulse skyrocketed, and she had to be sedated. Jeff is just as angry, but those of you who know them well know that Danielle has always been fire to Jeff's ice. Jeff's anger is much more controlled. Please continue to pray for them, for their physical healing, for their mental and spiritual healing, and that God would show them His love and show us how to reach out to them." At this news, the congregation sat in shocked silence again for the second time in two weeks, many with tears running down their faces, wondering how the church could have gone from such a high to such a low so quickly.

The weekend went by, and the children were recovering well. So much so that by the end of the week they were ready to move to a regular room. They were put in a room together since they claimed to be brother and sister and acted like it, and really, their birth certificates didn't disprove it. Robert stopped by every day to check on them, and, once he found out Michelle was a widow, to check on her as well. A like was growing there, on both sides. The children asked who Officer Freedman was, and Michelle told them, "He's the one who pulled the nails out." After that their love and respect for him grew enormously.

Michelle brought her daughter, Elizabeth, by one day to visit. Elizabeth was two years younger than Jeff and Danielle, as dark as her mother with curious brown eyes. She was not a shy person and walked right into the hospital room, carrying her stuffed rabbit with her and talking a mile a minute, stopping only to breathe. She said, "Mom says you're the baby seals, everyone calls me Lizzie," commented on the size of the room, the view from the window, all the gadgets on the bed, the way the bed could adjust (making sure they knew all the ways the bed would adjust using the remote which also controlled the television and called the nurse), were they walking (it was very important to be up as soon as possible; oh, their feet were hurt, well they should move as much as they could), and on and on. Jeff and Danielle couldn't help but laugh which made Michelle smile. And finally, would they like to have her bunny to keep them company? She had to put on a brave face for this because it was her favorite toy, but she felt they needed him more than she did. Michelle could tell that the children were touched, and she was touched herself. She was so proud of her daughter's big heart since she knew how much that stuffed rabbit meant to her. It was the last present her husband had given Elizabeth before he was killed. A strong bond was growing between this woman and these children, and now her daughter was being added to the bond with them as well.

Once Jeff and Danielle were moved out of ICU they continued to improve physically. A physical therapist came to work with them, and both children sighed with relief when he said he saw no reason why Danielle should not be able to draw and play the guitar again, assuming, he added with raised eyebrow, that you could draw and play before. Giddy with relief Danielle assured him that she could. Although movement was painful, they both performed over and over the exercises to strengthen their hands and restore flexibility. Leaning on each other, they hobbled about the halls, Jeff in shorts and a t-shirt his mom had left, Danielle in shorts and a t-shirt Robert had dropped off from her home. Working until the nurses made them get back in bed, they were determined to get out of the hospital as soon as possible even though they didn't know what they would be leaving it for.

On Wednesday, Robert brought word that Danielle's mom had died in jail, an apparent suicide. Michelle asked him if it was really a suicide, thinking the woman had come to her senses, realized what she had done, and killed herself because of it. Robert said, "It will probably be ruled that, but I imagine she had some help. Everyone in there knew what she did, and people like that don't last long in jail." Danielle didn't know what to think. She didn't believe her mother loved her or cared about her even before "that day", but still it was another change. Jeff was much clearer in his opinion as all he said was, "Good riddance."

On Thursday, the woman from CPS reappeared to tell Danielle that a foster home had been found for her, and she would be taken there as soon as she was released from the hospital. No, she couldn't tell her where it was located except to say it was east of where she lived now. When Michelle and Lizzie came to visit later that day, Jeff and Danielle told her how they would both be moving east of where they used to live. Michelle commented thoughtfully, "You know, Lizzie and I live east of your old homes as well. Wouldn't it be something if you were both moving into my neighborhood?" They asked about her home and the neighborhood. "Well, it's an old neighborhood, and the homes are small. Mine is a two bedroom with a bath and a half. I live across the street from the high school, 9th and 10th grades. It's not the quietest neighborhood, and there's some gangs around because of the high school, but mainly it's just folks like me, going to work to pay their bills."

They were still full of anger and resentment, especially against the members of 2nd Street Bible Church and God. They spoke to Michelle about this as well. She was quiet for a bit, and then she said, "Children, bad things happen to good folks all the time. I don't know why. My Charles died in a car wreck when someone ran a stop light, and I did a lot of asking why. I can tell you that it does no good to get mad at God. He does what He does for His reasons. But it sounds like you had some good friends at the church. Don't you have any friends that don't get along with each other? You like them both, but if you get them together the fur just flies, so you keep them apart?" Jeff and Danielle smiled as they thought of a couple of people in particular at the apartment complex just like that. Michelle continued, "So you just don't see them together, right?" The children nodded. "So maybe you can treat this the same. I don't know. Maybe it's too hard, but maybe you can just see your friends without God, you know? You can see them outside of church, and when you're with them you talk about something else. Didn't you talk about other things before?" They said maybe they could try it, with some of them anyway.

Oddly enough they still prayed. The prayers might be somewhat irreverent and maybe even sarcastic, but they were prayers of a sort. Neither one would ask for anything for themselves believing the personal requests would not be granted. Jeff asked that Danielle be able to draw and play guitar again. He asked that Danielle be sent to a good foster home. He thanked God for Officer Freedman and Michelle. Danielle asked that God heal Jeff's lungs and make him good as new. She also thanked God for Officer Freedman and Michelle. And for Lizzie. And the bunny.

Funerals were held for Danielle's mom and stepdad on Saturday. Danielle and Jeff had both said they would not attend, so the funerals were not delayed until their release from the hospital. There were no known relatives to claim the bodies, and they were cremated. A few of their co-workers attended, but most stayed away, unwilling to be associated with the horrible crimes they had committed. Steve and Amy went so that if the children asked about it in the future they could describe it to them.

On the following Monday they were released, Jeff to his mom, Danielle to her first foster home.

Chapter 6

On Monday morning Michelle and one of their other nurses, Mary Ann, rolled their wheelchairs to the hospital entrance. Ben stopped by as they left the room and told them goodbye in elvish to which they laughingly responded. It helped to lighten their mood a little since they were heading to new homes, and in Danielle's case, new parents. Steve and Amy were there as well. They had been to visit the children a few times after they were moved to a regular hospital room and, acting on Michelle's suggestion, Jeff and Danielle had tried to treat them like friends who had a friend they didn't like. It was awkward, but for Steve and Amy it was at least a beginning. As the wheelchairs were rolling through the hospital Michelle and Mary Ann were chatting with each other and the children, and Michelle made a comment to Mary Ann that stuck in the minds of the kids. Laughingly, she said in response to a comment Mary Ann had made, "I'm just one major expense away from big trouble."

At the entrance, while Marilyn and the CPS lady waited impatiently, Michelle hugged them both goodbye. Danielle handed her Elizabeth's toy rabbit and said, "Please give this back to Lizzie and thank her. It really helped get us through this." Michelle urged her to keep the rabbit, but Danielle and Jeff both told her it was time for the rabbit to go home. Danielle and Jeff hobbled into their respective waiting cars, and the two cars drove away. As they watched the cars turn the corner Mary Ann commented, "It's going to be tough on them not being together. They're obviously very close." Michelle smiled. "I don't think they'll be apart very long."

Indeed, Jeff and Danielle had worked this part out with Steve and Amy. There was a plan and a backup plan. Plan A was that as soon as they had their new address each one would call and give it to the Jacobs who would pass it on. Plan B was to meet at the Shepherds for homeschooling. Sooner or later they would be back together. This was a comforting thought as they drove to the new area of the city. It was obvious this was not as nice a part of town as where they had lived previously. The apartment complexes were smaller and didn't have swimming pools. Homes were smaller and fewer had nice yards. Stores and shops were older and dingier. There seemed to be a mix of older people and young families with children playing in the streets and white haired men and women sitting on front porches in cheap plastic lawn chairs.

As they drove, Jeff asked his mom, "Whose car is this?" to which she replied shortly, "A friend's." Jeff noticed that they were following the car Danielle was riding in and wondered if by any chance they would be living near each other again, but when Danielle's car turned off on Seminole and Marilyn kept driving straight his spirits sank a little. Then, six houses down his mom turned into a driveway and parked across the street from a vinyl siding business. He shouldered his backpack and hobbled after her as she unlocked the door to what must have at one time been a detached garage. Inside, the building had been divided into a living/dining room, a small kitchen, a bathroom, and a bedroom. Marilyn pointed to the cardboard filing box Jeff used as a dresser and said, "You'll be sleeping on the sofa." Jeff set his backpack on top of the filing cabinet and asked, "How will you get to work at Sal's?" From the kitchen he heard, "I don't work at Sal's anymore. I work across the street at the siding place." That was a new one.

"What do you do there?" "Whatever. I keep the books, answer the phone, make sales calls." She added, "I put that piece of junk keyboard by the sofa. I don't know why you keep it." Jeff just said, "Thanks," as he found the keyboard between the filing cabinet and the wall, none the worse for wear as far as he could tell. "Is it okay to look around outside?" Marilyn stuck her head around the corner of the kitchen. "Yeah, just don't go near the house."

Jeff shuffled back out the door, wincing as he turned the doorknob. His hands hurt less than they had a week ago, but between the injuries and the exercises to restore flexibility they were usually sore. Painfully he made his way to the back of the apartment and looked out over what appeared to be a park, or maybe a pasture. In the distance to the right stood an old barn. Across the pasture were the backs of another row of houses. His mom came to stand beside him. "This area is called the reservation. All of the streets have Indian names. We live on Cherokee. The street on the right is Seminole. The one on the left is Sioux. And the one on the other side of those houses is Navaho." Jeff asked if the vacant area in front of them was a park. "No. It used to be a horse pasture. The guy with the barn owned it. He just sold it to a developer and moved. I think they're going to tear down his house and barn, and that will be the entrance into the development. They'll put in a bunch of houses, probably nicer than any of the ones here now. Then it will be the new place to be and will get too expensive to live in anymore." With that cheery thought, she went back inside.

Meanwhile the CPS lady had turned onto another street and pulled up in front of an older but well-kept house. A middle-aged man and woman and a girl about ten walked out onto the front porch. When Danielle painfully exited the car, the man hurried to grab her backpack. He was tall, well over six feet, with dark hair greying at the temples and a stern face not showing many laugh lines. Starting to reach out to shake her hand, he saw the bandages and stuffed his hand in his khaki pockets instead. "I'm Randy Brown. Me and my wife Susan are your new foster parents." Waving the backpack at his wife and the girl he said, "The girl is Cindy Rogers. She's our other foster child." Danielle nodded at all of this and slowly made her way to the house. Susan was a female version of Randy. Putting her hand out in greeting she said, "Hello, Danielle. I'm Susan." Noticing the bandages on Danielle's hands, she started to change the handshake into a hug, but stopped when Danielle backed away in alarm. The CPS woman commented, "Her back was also injured, and hasn't healed yet," by way of explanation. She finished with, "I'll leave you all to get acquainted," handed her card to Danielle with, "Call me if you need anything," nodded to the Browns, jumped in her car, and drove away as though she had a million other things to do.

Randy, who owned an auto repair shop nearby, said, "Well, I have to get to work. I'll see everyone tonight," handed Danielle's backpack to his wife, climbed in his older model Ford, and drove away. Susan led the two girls inside saying, "Cindy, why don't you show Danielle around." Looking questioningly at the backpack she asked, "Danielle, is this all of your things?" to which Danielle replied, "Officer Freedman said he would take me by the house tomorrow to get the rest."

It turned out that Danielle's mom and stepdad had made no provisions for her in case of their death (not much of a surprise since they planned to kill her.) There was no will, which meant the courts would have to figure out what Danielle would get from their estate. They'd only lived in the house a couple of years so there was little equity, and the bank was taking it back. Danielle was going to be able to take the items that were obviously hers such as clothes, but that was about it. As with most foster children, she was going to her foster home with few material possessions of her own.

Cindy waved for Danielle to follow her. She was tall for a ten year old and very thin. Her long black hair hung to her waist, and her face had a slightly oriental look to it. The front door led into an entryway. The kitchen was ahead and to the left and opened into the living room/dining room. Cindy led Danielle down a hallway to the left. The first door on the left held a twin bed, bedside table, and dresser. This would be Danielle's room. The door at the end of the hall opened into another small bedroom furnished just the same. This was Cindy's room. A short hall to the right led to the master bedroom. Just before this bedroom was the bathroom that Cindy and Danielle would share. The little available space was covered with hair dryer, combs, brushes, scrunchies, and everything else a ten year old girl thought she would need to get ready for school. Cindy waved at the clutter and said, "I can make some room if you need it." Danielle just shook her head no. Randy and Susan had their own bathroom off the master bedroom. That was it for the tour, and Cindy tossed Danielle's backpack on her bed.

Danielle noticed that Cindy look a little, well, scared. She stared at her and said, "What?" Cindy moved back a step and said, "You're her!" Danielle was confused. "Her who?" Cindy moved back another step and said, "The one who beat up the three 3rd graders and got expelled and never came back to school." Now Danielle was annoyed. "So? I don't beat up everyone I meet." "Why'd you beat up them?" "They tried to take my lunch money. Which I didn't have, by the way." Cindy looked unconvinced but said, "Okay. Come on, I'll show you the back yard. Danielle trailed slowly behind her as they passed Susan and went out the back door. The yard shared a six-foot wooden privacy fence with the yards on either side, but the backside of the fence was chain link and opened onto a large open space of some kind like a park. There was an old barn off to the left in the distance.

Danielle slowly made her way to the chain link fence with Cindy following her. When she reached the fence she asked,

"What's it like, having foster parents?" Cindy said, "It's not so bad. The Browns are okay. Mr. Brown doesn't really pay any attention at all. He goes to work, comes home and reads the newspaper or watches TV. Mrs. Brown cooks and stuff. I think we are just one more thing to add to her list. She likes it best if you just stay out her way." Danielle asked, "Why do they even bother?" and Cindy replied, "I think they were guilted into it, and I think CPS needs foster parents so bad they don't care as long as they weren't serial killers or something." Danielle just sighed and muttered, "Not being killers would be nice."

The rest of the day and evening went quietly. The stress of leaving the hospital and moving to her foster home tired her out, and she spent much of the day sleeping. Mr. Brown came home from work, and they ate a quiet meal. Danielle borrowed Mrs. Brown's dish washing gloves and cleaned herself off with a wash cloth as best she could. It would be at least another week before all of the bandages were off and she could actually take a shower. One thing she did was get the house address and call Steve and Amy to give it to them. They asked how she was doing, told her they were thinking about her, but told her Jeff hadn't called yet. Amy said, "They just moved, and Jeff may have trouble getting to a phone to call. You know he'll be in touch as soon as he can." Danielle didn't like it, but she agreed. That night Danielle gave another one of her not-prayer prayers saying, "Please watch over Jeff wherever he is, better than you did before," making sure to ask for nothing for herself.

On Tuesday morning, Robert drove to Danielle's foster home. Danielle was waiting on the front porch and slowly made her way to the car. Robert held the door open for her, and she hugged him and said, "Good morning, Officer Freedman." He hugged her gently back with a hearty, "Good morning, Danielle," and she slid into the back seat. As they drove she answered Robert's questions about how she was feeling, how she liked her new home, if she had heard from Jeff yet. The closer they came to her old home the angrier she grew, and by the time they pulled up in front of her old home she was shaking. Robert asked if she wanted to stay in the car, and she answered shortly, "No!" The two of them walked up to the front door, and Robert unlocked the door with the key given him for this purpose. Danielle looked in the living room, then she walked on to her bedroom, Robert beside her. Robert took in the scene, noticing the TV, bookcases full of books, pictures on the walls, and other signs of solid middle class prosperity. As he watched Danielle gather up her few clothes and possessions he was filled with anger over their meagerness. All of the clothes and shoes from the closet and drawers fit in one paper bag. Robert thought to himself as he helped fold the clothes to fit in the bag, "I've lived paycheck to paycheck and still had more than this!" He helped Danielle remove her pictures from the wall and gather up her sketchbooks and art supplies and the guitar in its case under the bed, which also contained her eBook reader. As they left the room Robert asked, "Is there anything in the house you want? Any pictures or whatever?" Danielle replied, "There aren't any pictures of me out here." She moved to the desk drawer and removed her birth certificate, storing it in her messenger bag. She touched the laptop on the desk and asked, "Do you think I can take this?" Robert assured her he saw no problem with her taking the laptop, and she added it to the messenger bag as well. Then she walked back out the front door, shuffled over to Alice's house, and rang the doorbell. When Alice answered the door and saw who was standing there she knelt down in front of Danielle and wrapped her in her arms, squeezing more gently when she felt Danielle wince. "You poor, poor, child. I am so sorry!" she said over and over again. Danielle hugged her back and said, "Thank you for saving my life. Officer Freedman said you called the police." She introduced Robert, who had come up behind her, to Alice. Alice asked, "Where are you living now?" Danielle pointed towards the east. "Over that way. It's not as nice as here. No one has a garden like yours." Alice laughed. "Well you were putting in a lawn of sorts over at your house. Don't think I didn't notice what you were doing." About a quarter of the front yard was thickly covered by the native grass, the tall stems sticking up everywhere. "It was very clever of you. That would have been a nice looking yard by next year." Then, glancing over at Robert she said, "Have you seen Jeff?" Danielle shook her head. "Not yet. I will." Alice assured her that she surely would and told her to come visit when she could, and on that note, Danielle and Robert climbed back in the car and returned to the Brown house. When they exited the car at the Brown's, Robert carried the paper bag of clothes and the guitar case, and Danielle carried her pictures. Susan met them at the front door, introduced herself, and invited Robert inside. When Danielle's things had been safely deposited in her room, they all sat in the living room and chatted for a bit before Robert left, hugging Danielle gently before moving out the door.

Meanwhile, Jeff had taken a bus. There was a bus stop right in front of his house, and he boarded the first westbound bus that came by, planning to ride until he reached a payphone. The bus wasn't crowded, and he sat near the exit. He hadn't ridden far when he saw a gas station ahead with a 7-11 across the street from it. He pulled the bus cord and shuffled his way down the steps when the bus stopped. Making his way to the payphone on the outside wall of the 7-11, he realized his lack of planning: he wasn't tall enough to reach the phone. Sighing he looked around for something to stand on and saw a plastic crate near the dumpster. Carrying it awkwardly in his bandaged hands, he dropped it at the foot of the payphone and scrambled on it. Perfect. He checked for dial tone, slid his coins in the slot, and called the Jacobs house. Amy answered just before the answering machine picked up and greeted him joyously when he said, "Hi. It's Jeff." "Jeff! Where are you?" When he gave her the address he heard her typing on a computer keyboard, and then she laughed. "Jeff, you aren't going to believe this! There's an open field behind your house, right?" When Jeff agreed she continued, "Well Danielle lives almost directly opposite you on the other side of that field. You can see her house from your back door. God is watching out for you!" There was silence on the other end, and Amy added, "Jeff, just be patient. You'll see. I'll let Danielle know where you are when she calls again." Jeff thanked her and hung up. He thought, not for the first time, as he winced his way aboard the eastbound bus that he and Danielle had to get a couple of prepaid phones.

As it happened, Jeff and Danielle didn't need Steve and Amy to find each other. After Robert left, Danielle went out the back door and stood by the back fence, looking across the pasture, thinking about the morning and everything that had changed in the past two weeks. Jeff, stepping down from the bus and not wanting to go into the apartment, walked through the back yard, and stood at the back fence looking across the pasture. He spotted Danielle immediately and flung himself over the short fence, ignoring the pain in his hands, feet, and back, and moving as quickly as he could, crossed the pasture. Danielle had the advantage of a gate in the fence, and she hurried to meet him. Jeff was in less pain, and moving a little faster, he crossed 2/3's of the pasture, saying, "Hello, sister!" as they drew even. Danielle hugged him and exclaimed, "I can't believe we live this close." Jeff told her about his phone conversation with Amy, and that she had said it was God looking out for them. "Nice. Watch out for us in the little things." They brought each other up to date, and Jeff told her about his idea to get them prepaid phones. "I'll find some tomorrow morning. I'll call when I have them set up, we can meet here again, and I'll give you yours." With that, they parted, already feeling better than at the start of the day.

True to his word the next morning Jeff rode the bus to a

store and bought two phones and prepaid cards. Arriving back home he set them up and used one to call the Brown's house to tell Danielle to meet him. Susan answered the phone, and called for Danielle, telling her there was a young man on the phone. When Danielle answered the phone all she said was "Hello" and "Okay". After she hung up Susan asked, "Who was that?" in a disapproving voice. "My brother," Danielle answered in a neutral voice, one that she had used many times in her own home. "He lives across the pasture. I was going to go meet him." "Really?" Susan's voice was friendlier now that she knew she wouldn't have to deal with a seven year old already interested in boys. "How long has he lived there? What a coincidence that you moved so close to him." Danielle explained that his mother had moved there the previous week, but Jeff had arrived the same day as she had arrived at the Brown's. Susan told her to invite him over, and Danielle, with a shrug, called him back and explained. Telling Susan "He's coming," she walked out to the back gate to meet him. When he had made his way across the pasture and into the house accompanied by Danielle, he was greeted by Susan and Cindy, who had come out of her room. As they were walking across the yard to the back door of the house, he gave Danielle her small phone, which she slipped into her pocket, relieved at having a way to stay in contact. Susan reached to shake his hand before noticing the bandages on his hands that were the same as the ones on Danielle's hands, and noticing the careful way he walked realized that he had the same injuries as Danielle. Embarrassed she apologized, "I'm sorry. I didn't realize. I didn't mean for you to walk all the way over here in your condition. I can drive you back home." Jeff shrugged and said, "It's no big deal. I need to be exercising to get back to normal. If I wasn't walking over here I'd need to be walking somewhere." An hour went by quickly as Jeff and Danielle explained how they were twins by different mothers, attended home school in their old neighborhood, and the rest of their brief history including Jeff's song writing, the street fair, and the concert. Susan asked if they would be going back to 2nd Street Bible Church, and both said no. Randy and Susan were not churchgoers, so she had no opinion on this. Through all of the conversation, Cindy sat silent, uncomfortable in the presence of the two 1st graders who had each beaten up three 3rd graders.

After the hour, Jeff and Danielle left to cross the pasture to the apartment, Cindy went back to her room, and Susan returned to clipping coupons. As they slowly crossed the pasture Jeff commented, "We need bicycles. We should keep our eyes open for a garage sale." With a thoughtful expression Danielle added, "We need to find one for Cindy, too." Danielle told him about the trip to her house with Officer Freedman to retrieve her things and seeing Alice. Walking around the apartment Danielle commented, "Wow! This is smaller than what you had! You don't have a room? You sleep on the sofa?" At Jeff's shrug she added, "Oh. Sorry." After saying he didn't expect to be there much anyway, Jeff told her about his mom working across the street and about the bus stopping right out front. "We're only three miles from the old neighborhood, so it shouldn't be a problem going back there. We can ride our bikes when we find them or take the bus if the weather is bad. And I guess maybe this neighborhood won't be too bad." They spent some time calling all their old friends to give them their new phone numbers. Looking at his hands Jeff said, "I don't think I'll be doing any more work this summer. It's already August. We need to get in good enough shape to go back to school. When I gave Mrs. Shepherd our phone numbers she said they were ready for us whenever we can come back." And so the goal for the next few days was set: buy bicycles and get in shape to go back to school. However, as the saying goes, "Man proposes, but God disposes".

Chapter 7

Mike Smith (don't call me Michael), an Iraq war veteran, lived across the street from the Browns. He returned home after his honorable discharge to the job he was in before he joined the service: building homes. He stood over 6 feet tall, weighed 230 pounds, and was heavily muscled. On this Sunday in the middle of August, he was bent over the engine of his Ford F250 when he felt eyes on him, a sense he had developed in the Navy. Looking behind him, he saw two kids, a boy and a girl, watching him over the hood of a car, the girl doing something with a notepad and pencil while the boy just stood there, eyeing him curiously. He'd seen the girl before and understood she was one of the Brown's foster kids.

The boy was new, but he resembled the girl, so maybe they were related. Straightening, he faced them and nodded, saying, "Hey." The boy responded with a wave. The girl stopped writing in the notepad, and the two of them moved around the hood of the car and crossed the street. Mike noticed both of them were wearing what appeared to be weight lifting or biking gloves and that they moved like two cats, smooth and supple. Injured cats, he amended to himself. They were a bit stiff, especially the girl, and you could tell there was an occasional hitch in their movement. He asked, "What are you writing?" to which the boy replied, "She's not writing, she's drawing." The girl turned the notepad around, and Mike saw that it was unlined and contained a pretty nice drawing of him bent over the truck. Not a lot of detail yet, but it was easy to see that the guy in it was him. "Not bad." Nodding at the girl he added, "Can she speak?" The girl said, "Yes. I'm Danielle. He's my brother, Jeff." Mike looked at them and saw the pain, the anger, the determination, and, just like that, decided to take them under his wing. "You look like you're moving a little stiff." Jeff said, "We were injured over the 4th of July. We're still getting well." Mike asked "How were you injured?" "Her parents tried to kill us."

Then Mike knew who they were and what had happened to them, and probably why they were wearing the gloves. He didn't follow the news much, but he had read that story and boiled with anger. "So, what are you doing to get well?" Jeff explained the exercises the physical therapist had given them. Mike watched them a little more and said, "Do you want to do more? Learn more? Be more?" Jeff and Danielle looked at him, looked at each other, seemed to reach a decision, and both said yes. And so it began.

Mike's house was similar in layout to the Brown's house. It had the same three bedrooms, two baths, kitchen, living room/dining room, garage. His use of the rooms was not the same. At all. One bedroom was an office for the construction work, with file cabinets, racks for drawings, desk, laptop, and monitor. Everything was neat and orderly. Nothing was lying around haphazardly as though it didn't belong where it was. There was even a fire extinguisher mounted on the wall by the door. A second bedroom was an armory. The closet had been completely lined with metal with the folding door removed and replaced with a metal door. Racks for rifles and shotguns, as well as drawers for pistols, replaced the lower shelves and clothes rod. Reloading supplies and ammunition for all the weapons was organized neatly on the upper shelf, and various items of hunting gear hung on the upper clothes rod. The bedroom contained a bench along one wall with a Dillon reloader mounted on it, and in the middle of the room sat a large table for cleaning weapons. Cleaning supplies were organized in the drawers under the table. This room also had a fire extinguisher mounted on the wall. Unlike the Brown's garage, which held their car and the usual junk, Mike's garage was a workout room. Along one wall stood a rack containing free weights of various sizes. Three adjustable benches for different types of weight lifting lined another wall. Next to them, mounted floor to ceiling, was a weight bag for punching and kicking. Mats covered the entire floor, and a window AC unit kept the room cool during workouts. Mike had walled off the garage on the inside, leaving enough room so that the outer garage door actually opened to a space big enough to store the lawn mower, edger, tools, a workbench, etc. It wasn't the most convenient when the weather was bad, but the weather wasn't bad that often, and a carport protected everything from rain if he needed a tool on a stormy day.

The first thing Mike did was introduce them to the weight room and proper exercise. Starting with a book on stretching he showed them all the muscle groups and how to stretch them, giving them a list to start with and instructions on how to build on the list, stressing over and over taking it easy to start with. "Work on those for a few days. If you're stiff in the morning, the exercises will work the stiffness out. When you aren't stiff in the mornings, we'll add something new." He gave them the stretch book and kicked them out, telling them he'd see them later, as he went back to working on his truck.

Jeff and Danielle took the book back to Danielle's room telling Susan along the way that they had met Mike and receiving her, "That's nice," in response. Leaving the book on Danielle's bed, they poked their heads in Cindy's room and asked if she wanted to go look for garage sales with them. Bored with her handheld video game she said, "Sure, why not," and followed them out the front door. Making their way slowly around the bend of Caddo, up Pawnee, and down Seminole, they found what they were looking for halfway up Iroquois. A yard sale was in full swing, and sitting on the sidewalk in front of the house were three bicycles: a green girl's bicycle in 7-year-old size, a blue boy's bicycle in the same size, and a red girl's bicycle in 10-year-old size. Although not new they were in good shape, and someone had taken the trouble to clean them up and air up the tires. The three children stood in front of the three bicycles and looked them over, Danielle and Jeff appraisingly to see if they suited what they needed, Cindy wistfully, thinking she couldn't afford one unless it was free. A woman walked over and introduced herself as Kathy. "Those were our kids' bicycles. They are all out of the house now and won't be needing them again. I can let those go for $25 each if you want all three." Jeff and Danielle looked at each other and did the nod thing. Then Danielle asked Cindy if she wanted the red one. Cindy shrugged and said, "Doesn't matter. I can't afford it." Danielle said, "We've got this," and Jeff pulled eight $10 bills from his pocket, all he had left for the time being. Cindy was surprised and ecstatic. Kathy went to get the $5 change, and when she came back, she brought three bicycle chains saying, "If you want to spend $5 more I'll throw in these bicycle chains. Smiling happily Jeff agreed, and the three children rode off on their new bikes. Riding the bicycles turned out to be about the same amount pain on their feet as walking, although they covered more ground for the same amount of pain; however, it was harder on their hands, and Jeff and Danielle went straight back to the Brown house while Cindy went for a ride around the neighborhood.

Jeff and Danielle sat in the back yard with the book on stretching and went over the exercises, trying them one at a time to see which ones hurt. After three weeks, most of the external injuries were healed, although their hands and feet were still tender, and the internal injuries were healing nicely. They were hopeful that when they went back to the hospital for the next checkup they would be healed enough to do anything they wanted. The tender hands and feet were a problem, though, and they took it to Mike.

He had finished working on the truck and was inside, drinking a beer and watching a game on the TV, when they knocked on his door. He opened the door and saw the two of them standing there, and his first thought was, "Have I created a monster for myself?" and his greeting was a gruff, "What?" Jeff and Danielle held out their hands, and Danielle said, "Our hands and feet are tender. What do we do?" Mike raised an eyebrow and asked, "Why are they tender?" Removing their gloves Jeff and Danielle showed him their hands. Seeing the round scars in the middle of each palm Mike felt a spike of rage, but he just said, "Feet, too?" When they nodded, he sighed. "Is there a sandbox in your yard? They shook their heads no, and he walked to the back of his truck where a bag of sand was lying. Lifting it out, he carried it across the street and set it on the ground by the front porch. "Pour this in a bucket or a pan or something or even in a hole in the ground. Move your hands in it like this." He made a motion similar to kneading bread. Making a twisting motion with his foot he added, "Move your feet in it like this. Don't hurt anything or make anything bleed. Just start a little at a time. They'll toughen up." They thanked him, and he returned to his home, his beer, and his ballgame, wishing he could get his hands on her parents and knowing from the news stories that it was too late for any of that. Someone higher up the food chain than him would have to deal with them.

Together they carried the bag of sand to the back yard and went inside to ask Susan for a bucket, pan, or something to put it in. She asked why they needed it, and hearing the reply, "To put sand in," she rolled her eyes and gave them a disposable aluminum foil pan. While they talked, they filled it with some of the sand and began pushing their hands in it as Mike had demonstrated. Jeff commented, "I'm almost out of cash. We need an easier way to get our money. We need bank accounts. You couldn't get one before because of your mom and stepdad, but do you think Mrs. Brown would sign the paperwork?" Danielle thought so but added, "What about your mom?" Jeff replied, "I'll have to put her signature on the paperwork. We can go to the bank tomorrow and talk to someone. We should start with maybe $100 each and then send money there from the online trading account. We need ATM/debit cards, too. The less people see us the better." Having reached this decision, they moved from the sand to the stretching exercises, and being young and determined they overdid it, as they found the next morning. The entire conversation was carried on in elvish with English words thrown in as necessary. Jeff suggested that each day they use a different language, which Danielle thought was an excellent idea. Then she suggested they learn sign language so they could converse with no one listening to them if necessary, and Jeff thought that was a great idea. Danielle said she would check that evening to see if they could learn online. Cindy arrived home for dinner, so all three bicycles were lying in the yard when Randy arrived home. When he heard that the three kids had found them at a nearby garage sale, he congratulated all of them on their initiative. Just before dark, Jeff walked back across the pasture to the apartment. Later that evening Cindy stopped by Danielle's room to thank her for the bicycle and ask where Jeff got the money. When Danielle explained about the various jobs they had done before they were injured Cindy just said, "Huh," and returned to her room. Danielle logged into the internet using the Browns Wi-Fi connection and did a search for sign language, finding what she wanted on YouTube. She studied and practiced until she fell asleep, exhausted after another long day.

The next morning, as expected, Jeff and Danielle could barely move. It seemed as though every muscle was sore. Both of them started painfully going through the stretching exercises again, and in twenty minutes felt almost human again. Danielle texted Jeff, "Sore. You?" to which he replied, "Yes. Stretched. Better now. Leave for bank at 9?" Danielle replied, "Yes. Leave from where?" Jeff, "There. Be over soon." Danielle, "Okay." Danielle dressed and went in to breakfast with Randy and Susan. At the apartment, Jeff poured cereal and milk in a bowl and was sitting by the sofa with his bowl and spoon when his mom came in to make a cup of coffee before leaving for work. Knowing her pre-caffeine condition Jeff ate silently. With her coffee in hand Marilyn opened the door, said, "Stay out of trouble," and left.

At 9, Jeff knocked on the front door. Danielle let him in, and as they passed Susan, laughing on the phone with one of her friends, Danielle whispered, "Jeff and I are going to ride our bikes." After Susan nodded in understanding, the two went out the back door, pushed their bicycles from the back yard to the street, and rode away. Riding up Seminole they turned left on Cherokee, crossed the creek on the bridge, and turned left again onto the bike trail. They rode along it until it ended and then took back streets to reach the bank. Locking their bicycles to a post out front, they pushed through the glass doors and made their way to the information desk where they stood, waiting to be noticed. The tall, dark haired young man sitting on a stool at the counter looked up from the computer where he had been typing, smiled at them, and said, "Hello, there. How can I help you this morning?" Jeff answered, "We need to open an account." Still smiling the man asked, "By yourselves? Is there a grownup with you?" Danielle's turn. "They said it would be a learning experience for us to do it on our own," to which the man said, "Well I'm Eddie. Let me find someone to help you." Making a quick scan of the service representative space he found someone with no one sitting in front of them and said, "Walk with me over here." He then proceeded to lead them to a large desk with a pretty woman sitting on one side and two empty chairs on the other. "Adeela, these two young people would like to open bank accounts." Jeff and Danielle thanked Eddie and sat in the two empty chairs. Adeela smiled at them, asking, "And who might you be?" Jeff replied, "I'm Jeff, and this is my sister Danielle," with Danielle adding, "Older sister." Adeela laughed and said, "Really? And how much older? You look the same age. Are you twins?" to which Danielle replied, "One minute." Adeela exclaimed, "How nice! Well, what can I do for you today?" Jeff explained that they wanted to open one bank account for both of them with ATM cards. Adeela explained that they would need a parent's signature, but she could set it up for them. She prepared the paperwork and marked the spot for the signature. Then Danielle explained that they had different last names and different parents because Jeff lived with his mother and Danielle lived in a foster home. Adeela's eyes softened with sympathy, and she asked, "Are you sure you want one account? You'll both need the signature of a parent or guardian." Jeff said vigorously, "Definitely, one account." Adeela added, "You'll also need a form of ID. I don't suppose you have government ID of any type?" Jeff and Danielle pulled out their official ID's. Surprisingly both of them had one. Their mothers had signed them up for Social Security numbers as soon as possible. Then, when Danielle's mom applied for a Texas driver's license after they moved from New Orleans, the DPS office had a special desk set up to make ID's for children, and Melanie had one made for Danielle. For Jeff, just this past year his mom had to renew her driver's license, and the same desk was set up to make ID's for children. In a rare moment of parental responsibility, she had an ID made for Jeff. Adeela smiled and made the changes to the paperwork. "Danielle, you need to get a new picture on yours. You've grown quite a bit since that one was taken." She continued, "You can open the account with this amount, but to avoid a monthly fee you'll need this amount," highlighting the two figures. Danielle looked at Jeff, and he nodded. Adeela folded the paperwork and put it in an envelope, which Danielle tucked in her backpack. Standing, Adeela ushered them to the bank door and told them, "Just bring back the signed paperwork and the money you want to deposit, and I'll set everything up for you." They thanked her and left. As Adeela passed Eddie on the way back to her desk Eddie asked, "Do you think they'll be back?" She replied, "I'm pretty sure they will. There is something special about them."

Jeff and Danielle unchained their bicycles and stowed the locks in their backpacks. Gazing around the neighborhood Jeff asked, "Where next?" Smiling Danielle replied, "The Shepherds first. Then let's go see Alice."

Shortly after leaving the bank, Jeff and Danielle were knocking on the Shepherd's door. Kathy answered the door and immediately leaned down to hug them both, tears running down her cheeks. "Oh, it's so good to see you up and about. We've been thinking about you, wondering when you would be back. Sam Jr. and Baily are with their Dad on a field trip to the zoo. You just missed them." They sat and chatted with her for a while, discussing the lesson plans for their future and deciding they would start the next week, after all of their bandages were finally off. Jeff and Danielle both felt relief that something would finally be returning to normal.

Alice did not answer the door when they knocked on her front door at 11AM, so they left their bicycles chained to the front porch and walked to the back, finding her in the garden admonishing the weeds trying to grow among her Blackfoot Daisies. When they walked up to her she hugged them saying, "I'm not sure that telling the weeds not to grow helps, but I have to try. Jeff, you're looking almost as good as before, just like my girl here." Jeff assured her he was almost as good as new, a slight exaggeration. They knelt with her and helped as she tended this plant and that, telling her about their new lives. After a bit Alice commented, "Danielle, the bank wants to sell your house. And there's people that want to buy it. My sister is interested. Her house is too big now that her kids are grown, and she's looking for something smaller but still big enough to have company. And a family from your old church is interested in moving into the area. What do you think?"

Danielle didn't know what she thought. Her heart clutched in confusion. It was the home she remembered best, but the memories weren't great, and she wouldn't mind giving them up. Still, it was another piece of her life gone. Although if Alice's sister moved there she could probably visit if she wanted to. "I think it would be great if your sister could move in next to you." With a smile she added, "Jeff and I already got the lawn started for her." Alice laughed at that. "Indeed you did." They ate lunch together, chatted a while more, and then pushed their bikes across the street to see if anyone would let them in the rear gate to the apartment complex. A woman they knew well enough to wave at was leaving as they reached the gate, and she held it open for them. They found Angela at the pool, and she dropped her book to hug them hello. "How are you? Are you going to come back and swim? You can swim with me anytime, you know."

Elena saw them from her apartment and knocked on all the apartment doors she passed on the way to the pool telling everyone that the baby seals were here. In a short while, many of their friends were there to greet them, and they spent an hour telling everyone over and over again that they were getting better, where they were living, about Danielle's foster family, continuing their home schooling, and all the rest. And they spent the time basking in the love of the apartment family. Everyone pretended to ignore their gloves and what they hid although more than one person turned away from time to time to hide tears and sometimes anger.

Finally, Jeff and Danielle said they needed to get home. When everyone heard that they had ridden bicycles to the apartments, there were shouts of "No way! I'll run you home!" from several of the people there, but Jeff and Danielle stood firm, stating that it was only 3 miles, and they would be riding over for home schooling anyway. Eventually they got their way. Before pushing their bicycles out of the pool area, they asked everyone to tell the people they had missed hi and that they would be back to visit soon. Once on the street Danielle said, "That was really nice. I feel happier than I have in weeks. We'll see Lacey tomorrow when we get money to open the bank account." Lacey had been one of the few people missing from the impromptu get together. Jeff agreed all around, and they started riding slowly home, arriving half an hour later in time to help Susan with dinner.

Susan liked to cook and was an excellent cook, which don't always go hand in hand. The Browns seldom ate out as anything anyone else could cook Susan probably could cook as well, and they could eat it in the comfort of their own home. After only a couple of days, she had begun teaching Danielle the basics, and when Jeff appeared, him as well. She was leery about letting the two children use knives but soon discovered that they both, especially Danielle, seemed to have a natural skill for using knives. There didn't seem to be any danger of the knife slipping or being used incorrectly, and after some initial hovering and observation, she left them to cut up vegetables and fruits and meats. At one point after Danielle had brushed away and shrugged off a fly that had snuck into the kitchen, she cut it in half in the air with the paring knife. Susan, observing this with a touch of disbelief, simply said, "You need to wash that knife off dear. Germs, you know." Jeff grinned at her and whispered,

"Nice!" Cindy, who had come to sit at the kitchen bar to play her video game, missed it all.

After the meal and the cleanup, Jeff and Danielle set up the foil pan with sand again and spent some time toughening their hands and feet. Cindy wandered out to ask what they were doing. When they told her she said, "You two are so weird!" and wandered off. Danielle watched her leave and said, "She wants some friends, but she thinks she's too old for us." Jeff laughed. "Too bad. She could be playing in the sand, too!" After working with the sand for a while, Jeff pulled out *The Lord of the Rings* and the dictionary, and they read to each other, Jeff defining the words Danielle didn't know and Danielle looking up the words neither of them knew. Just before dark, Jeff left through the gate, crossed the pasture, climbed the fence, and slipped quietly into the apartment. The bedroom door was closed, and the smell of burning leaves filled the apartment. He sighed, took a shower and brushed his teeth, texted Danielle goodnight and received her goodnight in response, tied the wet bandana over his mouth and nose, and drifted off to sleep.

Their trip to the bank had not gone unnoticed. As they were leaving the bank, Marty from the Jacob's Bible study group was pulling in, and she recognized them. Marty was a short, brown haired, logical, computer programmer who worked at one of the local tech companies. She liked rules. She led her life by rules. Her car came to a complete stop at every stop sign. Coupons were thrown away when they expired, even if stores would still take them. The house where she and her husband, Scott, lived was always in order with everything in its place. Interestingly, she didn't mind dust as long as the dust was in order. Her big flaw was a lack of empathy for people. She had rules for dealing with people as well: don't talk about yourself; don't list more than one problem during Bible study prayer time and not more than once every other week; ask about people's spouses and children; etc. New people rules were always being added. Scott was the opposite. He lived in chaos. He was very much a people person and had great empathy for others. He also disliked dust. Between the two of them, their house was immaculate. Marty kept the house running physically, and Scott kept their relationships running. Marty did not understand what had happened to Jeff and Danielle, and she didn't understand what they were feeling. Scott understood completely how messed up people could be, and his heart ached for the kids. He shared this with the group as Jeff and Danielle were discussed.

Ronnie and Marie told about the problems they were having with their children, trying to explain what had happened, and why Jeff and Danielle didn't come to church anymore. Marie said, "I brought up Job, and that ended badly. My youngest was furious. She said "God used Job to win a bet! Are you saying God used Jeff and Danielle in a bet?" I didn't know what to say." Dan and Marla pointed out that the church had grown by twenty families when Jeff and Danielle started coming, mainly because the kids wanted to be in class with Jeff and Danielle, and the families came with the kids. Since they had stopped coming, growth had slowed way down. Dan also pointed out that that didn't say good things about the rest of them. Jim and Sherrie pointed out all of the growth just within their own Bible study because of the questions the two kids raised. Jim said, "It was fun getting together with everyone once a week, and we learned before, but it was nothing like the research and study we were doing trying to come up with answers." Finally, Steve pointed out that they knew who the enemy was. "Think about it. What a brilliant attack. With one stroke he removed Jeff and Danielle, has our kids questioning God's sovereignty and love, and church growth has slowed. The Praise Band was hit really hard right after playing at the concert. Adam was hit particularly hard since he spent so much time working with Jeff on his music. The whole church has been shaken up. But we have to believe that God has a plan, even if we can't see it. We still talk to the kids. They still believe. They just think God hates them, and they are really, really mad at Him right now. All of you parents have been through that with your kids at one time or another. We just have to pray, do what we can, and wait and see." That evening during prayer time Jeff and Danielle were both lifted up in prayer.

Tuesday morning at 9:00, Lacey heard knocking on her apartment door. When she opened it she found two serious faces looking up at her. Stooping, she hugged them both gently, having heard about the gathering the afternoon before and how tender the children were. Jeff and Danielle brought her up to date and picked up cash to open the new bank account. At 10:00, they presented themselves to Adeela. Before they left the Brown's house Danielle had signed Marilyn's signature to the forms, copying the signature from a document Jeff had brought from the apartment. They handed over the documents and $200 of the cash they had picked up from Lacey. Danielle asked if they could get the fee waived long enough to transfer in a buffer to cover the minimum balance, explaining that they would request it later that day now that they had the account number to transfer the money to, but they didn't know how long the transfer would take. As she created their ATM/Debit cards Adeela told them that wouldn't be a problem. She would watch the account and call them if there were any issues. Jeff and Danielle made sure she had both of their mobile phone numbers, shook hands with her, and left. Eddie waved and wished them a good day as they walked past the information counter, and they had added two more friends to their growing number.

The bicycle ride back to the Brown's house seemed shorter even though they had only "rested" in the bank for a short while. As soon as they arrived home, Danielle logged into the online trading account site on her laptop and transferred $2000 to the bank account. Money still seemed to be coming in regularly in varying amounts, and Jeff assumed this was Terry making royalty deposits. Little money was leaving the account since there wasn't anything Jeff could buy that his mother wouldn't sell, and the Browns would buy the new clothes and such Danielle would need. Jeff took over long enough to add Danielle's name to the online trading account, which earned him a hug. While she was on the laptop, Danielle submitted requests for two new state ID's with their new addresses, reminding Jeff he would need to check the mail before his mom to avoid questions like how he had paid for the new ID.

After transferring the money, the two went out to explore the open field. Houses surrounded the field, most with a fence of some type. Barbed wire fences were common, apparently more to keep animals from the field out of the back yard than to keep anything in. Some of them were tall wooden privacy fences. Many were chain link. In one of the yards with a chain link fence, lay a large, black German Shepherd, tied by a long chain to a doghouse set near the covered patio. When the dog saw the two of them, it rushed towards the fence barking, but stopping just as it reached the end of the chain. Danielle began crooning, "What a smart dog! You knew just how far you could go before you reached the end of the chain, didn't you? And you're such a beautiful dog, too." Listening to her voice the dog stopped barking and then sat with its head cocked to one side. To Jeff's shock Danielle opened the gate and slipped inside the yard. Jeff hissed, "Are you crazy? That is not a squirrel!" Danielle ignored him and walked slowly up to the dog. When she reached him, she held out her hand, which the dog sniffed and then licked. Still talking to it, she began rubbing its head and scratching its ears. "Your collar says your name is King. Is your name King?" The dog responded by licking her face. She laughed and said, "Okay, King it is. Would you like to meet my brother Jeff? He's nice, too." Still petting King, Danielle waved for Jeff to come forward, which he shrugged and did. King eyed him warily as he slowly approached but didn't bark or snarl. When he was close enough, Danielle told him to give King his hand to sniff, and after a thorough sniffing King licked Jeff as well. Jeff joined Danielle in petting King, although King seemed to tolerate him while he appeared to love Danielle. She asked the dog to lie down, which he did, and she and Jeff knelt beside him to continue the petting as they looked around the yard.

It was a scruffy looking yard that appeared to have once been nicer. Grass in need of water covered most of the space, with one big tree in the middle shading the house from afternoon sun. A swing set was erected to one side with the typical scuffmarks under the seats. Bushes covered the fence on both sides so the yards next door were not easily visible. A sliding door opened onto the covered patio, and two windows faced the yard. On a table on the patio sat a familiar looking rabbit. Danielle stood and walked over to take a look at it, King by her side. When she picked up the rabbit to examine it, King bumped her with his head as if to say, "That's not yours." Absently she scratched behind his ears and told him, "I'm not taking it. I'm just looking at it." Presently she called softly to Jeff, "This is Lizzie's rabbit!" "Are you sure?" "Yes! Here's the torn spot on the back that Michelle fixed with yellow thread!" "So we moved across town and ended up next door to Michelle and Lizzie? Wow!" "I know. It makes you wonder." She didn't elaborate on what it made her wonder about.

Eventually they left, making sure King had fresh water and crossing the field to Jeff's apartment, where he helped her over the back fence before swinging over himself. They made themselves a lunch of peanut butter and jelly sandwiches with bananas and crossed back over the fence and field to eat in the Brown's back yard. After lunch, they toughened their hands and feet in the sand, read, and explored the neighborhood, following the bike trail as it meandered through the greenbelt and alongside a creek.

This set the tone for the remainder of the week. They were getting well quickly. Jeff's breathing was normal, and the pain from the injuries was fading away. On Friday, all of the stitches were removed, and if their hands and feet were not totally normal yet, it at least appeared that eventually they would be. Danielle could draw and play the guitar, Jeff could play his keyboard and write music, and the stretching exercises Mike had given them were removing the remaining stiffness. They no longer woke up sore in the mornings and were ready to move on.

Sunday morning they went to see Mike. He was repairing a broken paving stone as they walked up, kneeling in the grass as he pried up the old one, with the new one beside him. Examining them he said, "Well you two are looking better than the last time I saw you. You don't look like death warmed over. Have you been stretching?" They nodded yes. "Still stiff and sore in the mornings?" They shook their heads no. He stared at them some more. "Okay, here's the deal. If you want, I will work with you. It will be hard, harder than anything else you've ever done or probably ever will do again. It's okay if you don't want to. It's okay if you start and quit. But if you quit I won't help you again. Do you understand?" Jeff and Danielle stared at each other for long moments in silent communication, nodded in agreement, turned back to Mike and said at the same time, "Yes." Mike said, "Okay, I'll teach you everything I know." Jeff asked, "What do we call you?", and Mike replied, "Call me Mike." Nodding at a spot on the ground, he added, "Sit there until I finish this." They sat cross-legged on the ground at the spot indicated and watched as he finished prying out the broken paving stone and replaced it with the new one, waiting while he threw the broken pieces in the back of his truck.

Coming back to them, he picked up his tools and said, "Follow me." Leading them to the raised garage door, he placed the tools back in their places and said, "Everything has a place, and it goes in that place. Always. Your place may not be the same as mine, but when you need something, you don't always have time to search for it. So, you put it where it goes every time. Start with your stuff at home. You should have a bag or a backpack or something at home with your important stuff in it. I don't mean stuffed toys. I mean changes of clothes, toothbrush, soap, a bottle of water, some protein bars. Things like that. Stuff that if, say, there was a fire and all you could grab was that bag, you could live out of it for a few days if you had to. Understand?" They nodded. "When you touch my stuff it always goes back in the right spot. If I have to look for something there will be problems."

Leading the way inside he took them to the weight room. "Today we'll start on weights. It will be the same tomorrow morning as it was with the stretching. You'll be sore. Stretch it out." He wrote on a white board on the wall all the exercises they would be doing, then led them through a warmup routine. Giving them each a set of light weights, he ran them through one set of 10 reps of the first exercise, then the next, and on until they had completed the list on the board. "Tomorrow we'll do something different, then next time we'll increase the reps a little. We'll keep increasing the reps, then we'll increase the weights, then we'll increase the number of sets." Next, he took a set of throwing knives from a cabinet and led them to his back yard. Setting up a cork backstop on his wooden fence, he tacked a bullseye target to it and handed a knife to Danielle. "Take it by the blade and try to hit the target. You're aiming for the X in the middle. Try not to throw the knife over the fence. That would disturb me." Danielle took the knife by the blade, stared at the target, and threw. The knife stuck in the center of the X. Mike considered where the knife cut the X and observed, "Lucky first throw. Try another one." Danielle took the second knife, stared at the target and threw. This knife lodged beside the first one on its right. Another knife. Another throw. This one lodged beside the first one on its left. Mike sighed. "You already knew how to throw a knife." Danielle shook her head. I've never thrown one before. It just feels right." She took two more knives and threw them one after another, holding the handles this time. One stuck above the first one, one below it. Shaking his head Mike retrieved the knives and said, "Okay, let's see what Jeff can do." Jeff threw the knives one after the other. He did not do as well as Danielle, but each knife stuck in the target at some spot or another. Mike was impressed. "Not bad at all for beginners. You seem to have a natural ability for this. Keep practicing."

They spent the next hour throwing the knives. Danielle's consistently clustered around the X while Jeff's moved closer and closer to the X. Towards the end of the hour Mike took the cork board and started throwing it while Jeff and Danielle threw the knives at it. Danielle's consistently stuck in the X while Jeff's sometimes hit the target, sometimes didn't.

At the end of the hour, Mike kicked them out and told them to show up the next evening at 6. Jeff and Danielle said, "Thank you, Mike," and left. Mike sat down to think about what he had done. His idea about training the two kids had been a spur of the moment thing. Life had been boring since he left the military. He was building houses and was busy enough, but none of it really mattered that much. He worked, he drank, he slept. This, though, seemed to be something he could sink his teeth into. He liked these kids, he was really angry at what had happened to them, and if nothing else he could teach them to take care of themselves. He knew the Browns, and he couldn't imagine them as good parents. Not crazy parents like the kids had run into before, just a couple of cold fish. He spent the rest of the day planning their training, calling friends, setting up favors.

Jeff and Danielle walked back across the street discussing what to do about the bags Mike had described to them. After going through the pros and cons of paper bags, plastic bags, backpacks, duffel bags, luggage, and so on, they settled on backpacks used for camping. They would use those for everything instead of a dresser or a closet. Everything they owned would go in the backpack. If it wouldn't fit they didn't need it or it could be left behind. This did not work with the Marilyn problem. She would sell a backpack. After chasing the problem up, down, and sideways they decided Jeff's backpack would stay with Danielle. He would keep his things in a couple of paper bags that could be transferred into the backpack if necessary.

Having made such a momentous decision the two went inside to help Susan make dinner. Neither Susan nor Randy made any comments regarding all the meals Jeff ate with them. Susan seemed happy to have someone around to teach cooking, and Randy may not have even noticed Jeff eating with them. Cindy seemed unable to pull her face away from her video game. After dinner Danielle walked with Jeff to the gate, they said goodbye, agreed to meet the next morning at 7, and Jeff crossed the field to the apartment.

Chapter 8

On Monday morning they rode their bicycles to the Shepherd house to resume school. The happy reunion with Sam Jr. and Bailey was marred by only one incident. As they were working on their science lesson with the Shepherd children Jeff and Danielle had removed their gloves. Sam and Bailey were examining and commenting on the scars. Bailey, touching the scars in Danielle's hands asked, "Did it hurt?" just as her mom walked in the room. Kathy saw the scars, thought about what had caused them and the child whose hands they were in, thought about something like that happening to her children, rushed to the nearest bathroom and threw up. Jeff and Danielle looked at each other with raised eyebrows, pulled their gloves back on, and continued with the lesson. Kathy returned with a pale face to begin their civics studies. Other than that, the first day back went fine.

After school, they rode to The Web Factory to see Tina and upload more pictures. The two had really gotten into documenting everything with pictures. Now they were storing them on Danielle's laptop as well, organizing and labeling them, even discussing making a movie of their lives, which Danielle laughingly called Life Behind the Hedge, or Moving the Hoses, or The Yard and Its Pecans. As they entered the reception area Debbie squealed, yanked off her headset, jumped from her seat, and rushed to hug them. "We were so scared! We heard about what happened to you and then we hadn't seen you in weeks, and we didn't know where you were or how you were! How are you? You look good! Ish." Goodish was right. The marks of their ordeal were on their faces. The childish baby fat was gone. So was the cheerful childish attitude. They appeared to be healthy, moving with the usual catlike grace. However, where their eyes before had been happy now they were cool. Their features were sharper. And they were bigger. A little taller, maybe, but stockier with definite muscle tone. "Have you grown since the last time I saw you?" Danielle shrugged. "Maybe a little. We eat a lot." Debbie hugged them again and returned to her desk to call Tina.

Tina appeared at the door in seconds, and they went through it all again before she led them back to her office. As they told her everything that had happened since they saw her last, she connected Jeff's camera to her computer and downloaded the pictures to the server. As they scrolled through the pictures, Jeff and Danielle took turns explaining all of them to her, identifying the different people and events. When she came to the pictures taken in the hospital, tears started rolling down her cheeks, and she said, "Are you sure you two are all right now?" They assured her that they were, but she scrolled to the earliest pictures she had of them and then to the most recent to compare them and shook her head. "You've both changed. A lot." Jeff and Danielle had nothing to say to that and remained silent. They left shortly after, but as Jeff stored the camera in his backpack Danielle shyly handed Tina a picture saying, "I drew this for you." It was a picture of Tina sitting at her desk between two computer monitors and smiling. Tina stared at the picture, then hugged Danielle and said, "Thank you." As she walked them back to the reception area she asked, "Would you like to learn more computer stuff?" to which they both agreed readily. "Can you come over on Saturday morning? About 9:00? They agreed, and she left them at the front door. Waving goodbye to Tina, and to Debbie who had come to the door to see them off, they climbed on their bicycles and rode for the Brown's.

That evening they knocked on Mike's door at 6, and he pointed them to the weight room where they spent time performing completely different exercises than the day before. Next, he sat them at the cleaning table in his gunroom and began his instruction. Over and over he told them the two cardinal rules and made the two repeat them: 1) I will assume every gun is loaded unless I check myself that it is not, and 2) I will not point a gun at anything I do not intend to shoot. Then he put a semi-automatic pistol in front of each of the them and showed them first, the proper way to check that they were not loaded, second to break them down for cleaning, and finally to clean and reassemble them. He demonstrated what a correct amount of oil looked like and how to use a thumbnail to shine light down the barrel to make sure it was clean and oiled. Then he tested them, picking the gun up, turning around, turning back and placing the gun in front of them to make sure the first thing they did was check that it wasn't loaded. As they grew more confident with this step, he had to remind them not to point the gun where they did not intend to shoot. When they had these two points mastered, he told them to go ahead and clean them, and started to work reloading some ammunition at the reloading station.

It didn't show, but Jeff and Danielle's minds were in turmoil. First, they thought about how things might have been different if they had had guns or even knives on that fateful day and were trained in their use. Then they thought how it probably wouldn't have mattered because they had been betrayed, and it is hard to be prepared for betrayal. This led to thoughts about how much it hurt to be betrayed by someone they were supposed to be able to trust. Which led to thoughts about how they felt betrayed by their church friends, and especially by God. And finally came the feeling that they couldn't trust anyone, but that thought quickly fell because they trusted each other, and that one thought produced light that kept total cynicism at bay.

It helped that they were able to focus on disassembling, cleaning, and reassembling the guns instead of their thoughts, especially when Mike had them reassemble the guns blindfolded. First, it was straightforward. Then he mixed each gun's parts up and sometimes even pulled one part out. Eventually he declared himself satisfied and told them it was time to go. Before they left he gave them each a small box. In each box was a stainless steel folding knife. Mike told them, "These are not as balanced as a real throwing knife, but I think you'll be able to throw them just fine, and they're just good knives. Stay out of trouble with them because these take things up a notch if you use them on a person." When they tried to thank him, he told them, "Yeah, yeah, get out. I have to finish reloading."

Back at the Brown house, Jeff and Danielle were using the sand on their hands and feet while discussing their schedules. School took six hours. Mike took three hours. Exercise on their own was another one to two hours including swimming at the apartment complex four times a week. Homework took two to three hours. Sleep was eight hours. That left a couple of hours to get to and from school, eat, bathe, etc. Danielle quipped, "We're wasting a couple of hours here," making Jeff laugh. She continued, "It was nice of Mike to give us the knives, but one is not enough. I'm thinking four." Jeff agreed four was a better number and added, "We need more pockets. We need cargo pants. We also need boots. It's time to go shopping. During all our free time," which set off another round of laughter.

On the Saturday after Danielle gave Tina the picture they met her at The Web Factory, and she began their computer training. She ran them through the basics and gave them a quick course in web design, setting up a web page for them with the header

Baby Seals. After a quick search on the web, she found a picture of a baby seal they liked, changed it into a minimalist drawing in an editing program, and at their request copied it so there were two of them, mirror images of each other. To finish she gave one blue eyes and one green eyes. These went at the top of the page just under the name. Finally, Tina password-protected the site so only the three of them could access it until and unless they wanted to open it up. "If you mess up the password three times it will be five minutes before you can try again, then ten minutes, then twenty minutes, and so on. Don't mess up." Together they came up with a password they could all remember, full of letters and numbers and special characters. This began several weekends of computer training that they all enjoyed, Tina because she had fun watching them learn, and Jeff and Danielle because they loved to learn new things. Really, though, the two of them learned just enough to be dangerous. Tina was the expert, and their go to person for computer issues.

Leaving The Web Factory, they went shopping for clothes and a laptop for Jeff. Beginning at an army navy store, they purchased cargo pants with lots of roomy pockets. They also found the boots they wanted, and they exited the store wearing their new pants and boots. Next stop was an electronics store where they spent an hour examining laptops for Jeff. Based on Tina's recommendations they finally picked one with the software they needed to manage all the pictures and video Jeff was taking plus a memory card with enough memory to max out the camera memory. Explaining to the sales clerk that the laptop had to fit in Jeff's backpack, they convinced her to unpack it after the purchase, and after seeing it safely stored in the backpack she walked them to the entrance where she explained the situation to the security officer who was checking people out of the store as Jeff showed him the receipt. He smiled, checked off the receipt, and waved them out of the store. Jeff and Danielle thanked them both, unlocked their bicycles, and rode to the Brown's house. On the way Jeff said, "I'll need to leave my laptop at your place. It wouldn't last a week at mine." Danielle shook her head and agreed. "No problem. Back everything up to the website every day though, just in case." Sadly, both were aware just how uncertain the future could be.

More evenings were spent with Mike, and they progressed from breaking down, cleaning, and reassembling every pistol Mike owned to the same for his rifles. At first, they had asked when they would be able to shoot something, but after a couple of curt, "When I think you're ready," they had stopped asking. In September, the doctors declared them completely well, and the training intensified. Mike increased the amount of weight and the number of sets in their weight training. The Browns were complaining a bit about the constant need for new clothes as Danielle added weight and outgrew her old clothes, but since all she wore were cargo pants and t shirts the expense wasn't great. As she and Jeff used their bank account to purchase some of her clothes, the Browns really didn't have much room to complain. A more legitimate grievance might have been the amount of food they consumed, but since they ate light for breakfast and took a lunch to the Shepherd's, dinner was the only big meal. Susan liked to cook so much that more people eating a large dinner was more of a blessing to her than a curse, and it all worked out.

In addition to the weight lifting and gun cleaning, Mike added the classroom work for SCUBA diving. Jeff and Danielle were learning everything that would be required to pass the written exam to receive their certification, but Mike wasn't waiting until they were old enough to be officially certified. He planned to have them trained in a swimming pool before winter and ready for open water the following summer when they would be eight. So they sat at the gun cleaning bench and worked out decompression times for dives of varying times and depths, became familiar with Mike's SCUBA gear, and practiced "finding the boat" in the field between their houses. This game, created by Jeff and Danielle, involved starting from a point in the field, then walking to various places around that point, and then picking a compass point to follow back without looking around the field. They became very good at this game in the field, but Mike pointed out it could just be because they were very familiar now with the field, so they began playing the game in different places: the greenbelt near their homes, the high school campus, and city parks. Any open place, really, worked for the game. Mike was impressed by this show of initiative and rewarded them with another knife each. They very much appreciated this as they hadn't yet had time to buy more and still wanted four each.

One evening in September there was an extra car parked in front of Mike's house when they crossed the street. When they knocked on the door, Mike ushered them into the weight room where a tall blond haired man was waiting. Mike introduced the man as Mac and told them to warm up. They responded with "Yes, Mike" and began warming up. Mac and Mike went into the gun room and spoke softly for 45 minutes until Jeff and Danielle appeared in the doorway to say, "We're warmed up, Mike." Mike pointed at Mac and said, "Mac is here to teach you unarmed combat and knife fighting." The two children smiled. It was a feral smile, making Mike wonder for just a moment what he was creating before he dismissed it.

Mac led the way back into the weight room and said, "Mike says you know some things. Show me what you know." They spent 10 minutes remembering and showing Mac the things Harudo Fujioka had shown them, and Mac nodded. "Okay. What I'm going to teach you is all aggressive. There is no gently convincing someone to leave you alone or doing the minimum of harm. I'm going to teach you to take someone down hard and permanent so you don't have to deal with them again in a fight." They spent the next two hours learning blocks and strikes, weak points and strong points, which parts of their bodies to strike with and which ones to avoid if possible.

By 9 they were tired and bruised, but the fire in their eyes was undiminished when Mike sent them back across the street. As he and Mac sat in the living room Mac said, "You're trying to train them to become what? You have those kids learning guns, knives, SCUBA, unarmed combat. Are you going to teach them skydiving? Sniping? Explosives?" Mike took a drink of his beer and said, "Do they look unhappy with it? Do they look ready to quit?" Mac sighed. "No. I've never seen anyone more eager to learn. And they'll be good at it. But what are they going to do if someone their age bullies them? Shoot, what if someone older bullies them? Someone bigger? Will those kids cut their throats in self-defense?" Mike answered savagely, "Better than them ending up in the hospital again like last time. Let it be the other guy for a change. And if you don't like it, why are you helping me?" Mac smiled. "I didn't say I didn't like it. Just making sure you know what you're getting yourself into. And them. Personally, I like those kids. I'll teach them everything I can, but I think it won't take them long before they surpass me. That girl is scary fast. The boy, too. And I think they have complete spatial control. No matter where they are, even thrown through the air, they always know where they are and where everything else is, too. Like time slows down for them or something. I've only seen it one other time. I don't have it." Mike took another drink of beer and said, "Well, we'll see."

It was a Wednesday morning in the next to last week of September, and Michelle was standing at the back door of her house, glaring disgustedly at King, as Elizabeth stood behind her. She needed to leave NOW to drop Lizzie at her mom's house and get to work on time, and the dog stood there as happy as could be after having rolled in something dead and smelling absolutely terrible. There was nothing she could about it before tonight, and what a great thing to look forward to after a twelve hour shift. She glared at him one more time, said "Bad dog!" and closed the door. Elizabeth ran ahead of her to the car, knowing a bad mood when she saw one, and presently Michelle was driving away. When Jeff and Danielle arrived home from school, they ran out into the field and eventually made their way to Michelle's house to say hi to King. He wagged his tail happily as they walked up to him, and Danielle, catching a whiff of him, said, "King, what have you been rolling in?" Jeff spotted the dead squirrel in the middle of the yard, well within reach of King's chain and pointed. Danielle rolled her eyes and said, "We need to give him a bath. Let's go to the store and get some stuff." Running back to their bicycles they rode off to the nearby store and bought dog shampoo, rinse, and a couple of towels. Returning to Michelle's, they hooked up a hose and gave King a bath, washing and drying him thoroughly. Jeff buried the dead squirrel in the field so King no longer had access to it and thoroughly hosed down the area where it had been. Then, with final hugs for King, they returned to the Browns to finish their homework before crossing the street to Mike's for whatever he had planned.

Michelle pulled into her driveway that evening fulling expecting an evening of water and mayhem washing King. Elizabeth ran to the backdoor to say hello to King and called to her mother, "Mom, King is clean!" which didn't make sense to Michelle. "What do you mean clean, baby?" Elizabeth responded, "He's clean, Momma! He even smells good!" Michelle came to inspect King, doubting her daughter's sense of smell but found that Elizabeth was right. King didn't smell bad. At all. He even smelled good. It was as though he had had a bath. She was beginning to doubt her sanity. "He did stink this morning, didn't he, baby? I wasn't imagining that awful smell?" Elizabeth laughed and said, "No, he smelled really bad this morning. And there was a dead squirrel in the yard." Michelle looked at the yard. No dead squirrel. Now she was puzzled. And concerned. Who would have cleaned up the squirrel, washed her dog, and not left a note or something. "There isn't a note or anything is there?" They both looked around the patio and the yard. No note. Stranger and stranger. Coming inside to fix their dinner Michelle thought over the possibilities and came up with nothing.

Jeff and Danielle were now spending time at the swimming pool of a friend of Mike's. First Mike had them prove that they could indeed swim, which didn't take long. Next, he had them prove that they could swim for extended distances and time. After watching them swim for an hour, he had them tread water for another half hour. That was it for the first session. The next time at the pool, they learned to snorkel by swimming and diving with the snorkel and clearing it when surfacing. Mike taught them to retrieve items off the bottom of the pool and clear their ears both going down and coming back up. It was fortunate for the two that both could clear their ears easily. Mike made the retrievals more and more difficult and taking longer and longer underwater. At the end of day two he rewarded them with dive gloves, green for Danielle, blue for Jeff.

For their third session, Mike taught them to mount air tanks in a Buoyancy Compensator, attach regulators to the air tanks, read the pressure and depth gauges, and use the mouth piece and purge valve. They swam laps around the pool along the bottom and practiced swapping between air hose and snorkel at the surface. They practiced clearing the mask and swimming without the mask. They practiced swimming with one using the other's buddy air hose and with both sharing one air hose. Finally he put all the gear on the bottom of the pool and had them swim down, begin by using the air hoses, putting on their masks and clearing them, putting on the BC's and tanks, and returning to him. After this, each session began the same way. They would prepare the equipment, Mike would set it in the deep end, they would swim down and put everything on, and then training would begin. Some training would require a larger and deeper body of water, but they learned the basics of search and recovery and even a little of night diving by swimming in the dark using a flashlight or glow stick to find items. They spent a lot of time performing underwater tasks such as opening locked boxes, arranging bricks into shapes, etc.

They also learned how to fight underwater. This was very different from fighting out of the water. Their speed was not as much of an asset as it had been. Mike taught them to think quickly, act aggressively, and not panic. They practiced attacking him singly and together, with their bare hands, with practice knives, even with simulated bang sticks. Mike found that he had his hands full when they attacked him together. This training went on in the swimming pool until spring when they moved to Texas lakes for real, open water training.

One Saturday after they had been SCUBA training for several weeks, Danielle turned to Jeff as they practiced their navigation skills. "I'm going to cut my hair. It's always getting in my way when we're training, and I don't want to bother with it. Even if it's in a ponytail it's something for someone to grab." Jeff nodded and asked, "How short?" "Short. Military short. I've been doing research online, and there is a site that will take it and make a wig for someone who has lost their hair to cancer. I'm going to cut it off and mail it to them." "When?" She shrugged and said, "Now. Want to come?" "Sure. I'll get mine cut, too." The two of them went back through the Brown's back yard and grabbed their bicycles. By now the Browns were accustomed to seldom knowing where the two were, but Jeff and Danielle had decided to give Susan their phone numbers after stressing that Jeff's mother could not know he had a phone, to which a bemused Susan agreed. The two rode to a salon in their old neighborhood near their bank and walked in. The receptionist at the counter smiled as they walked in. "How can I help you today?" Danielle explained that she would like for them to do everything they could to make her hair nicer since she had spent so many days in a swimming pool without really caring for her hair." The receptionist, whose name was Kay, said, "We can certainly do that. Are you going to something special?" Danielle explained, "No. I'm going to cut it off and mail it to a place that makes wigs for children with cancer." Kay exclaimed, "How nice of you! Did you want to cut it into a bob or one of our other shorter hairstyles? We can make you really cute," to which Danielle replied, "No, I need it cut short like this," and showed them a picture of a new recruit with almost a shaved head. Kay wasn't as excited anymore. "Oh, you don't want to do that!" Danielle just looked at her and said, "That's what I need." Understanding grew in Kay's eyes. "Oh, you're going to have treatment and want to save your hair." Danielle didn't try to correct her, but just kept staring at her. "Michael can help you." Michael came over and Kay explained what Danielle wanted. He nodded and took her back to his chair, and Kay turned to Jeff. "What about you?" Jeff said he wanted the same as his sister except he wasn't saving his hair. Tears came to Kay's eyes, and she said, "Oh, that is so sweet! Michael will take care of you next." Jeff sat in the empty station next to Michael's as he washed, rinsed, and dried Danielle's hair and then carefully cut it off, laying the hair on his counter. When he was finished, he brought a box from the back and carefully placed the hair in the box for her. She looked in the mirror and at Jeff. He nodded. "Just like the picture." She traded places with him, and Michael took a pair of clippers to Jeff's hair. In a very short time, his hair looked just like Danielle's. She nodded, thanked Michael, left a tip on the counter where her hair had lain, and went to the front to pay. The manager was waiting there with Kay and told them there was no charge. They explained that they could pay, but she adamantly refused to take any money. They were puzzled but thanked her and left. Kay turned to the manager after they were gone and asked, "Do you think she has cancer?" The manager replied, "I hope not, on top of everything else. Those are the two that were almost killed by her parents. My friend Tina was telling me about them." The two watched out the door where Jeff and Danielle had left just a short time before.

Jeff and Danielle left their bicycles at the salon, and, carrying the box, they walked down the street to the post office store. Bob greeted them with a "Hey, guys! How's it going? When did you cut your hair?" when they walked in the door. Danielle explained that they had just had it cut, and they needed to mail a box. Pointing towards the back Bob said, "Sure. Get it ready," and turned back to the form he was completing. Danielle set the box on the table, spread out a sheet of bubble wrap, and placed the hair from the box carefully on it. Jeff held the sides in place while Danielle used packing tape to seal all four sides. Then she placed the hair back in the box and filled it with packing peanuts. She sealed the box, wrapped it in brown paper, and attached a shipping label. The she brought the box to Bob who had been watching the procedure as he wrote. He confirmed his thoughts with the address and said, "So that's where your hair is going. That's a really nice thing to do." Danielle just shrugged and asked how much for everything, and Bob said, "This one's on me." Danielle asked, "Are you sure? I have the money," and he said, "Nope. I got it." Danielle hugged him, Jeff bumped fists, and they left. Bob shook his head as they closed the door behind them and said to himself, "Those kids."

Time passed, and fall was in the air. Jeff and Danielle were at the outdoor gun range on a Saturday afternoon the middle of October. Mike had finally decided they were ready to start shooting and loaded the kids, his .22 pistols and rifles and an AR15 into the truck and drove to an outdoor range a couple of hours away. It was a well-placed range pretty much in the middle of nowhere, with miles of brush and open field on the down range side. In addition to the usual short range for pistol shooting and a 100-yard range for sighting in hunting rifles, there were 200-yard, 500-yard, and 1000-yard ranges. Shooters walked to the 200-yard targets, but there was a golf cart available to take people to the 500 and 1000 yard targets.

Jeff and Danielle were ecstatic. For weeks they had been breaking down, cleaning, oiling, and reassembling all of Mike's guns with apparently no hope of ever firing any of them. Mike had even taken the guns to the range himself, and as they cleaned away the residual gunpowder, they knew he had been firing them when they weren't allowed to. Now, finally, their day had arrived.

Tommy, the owner of the range, greeted Mike, Jeff, and Danielle as they walked in the range store with a loud, "Hi, Mike! Haven't seen you in a few weeks. Who do you have there?" Mike introduced Jeff and Danielle to Tommy, and they bumped fists with him. Ever since "the day" they were reluctant to shake hands with strangers. Some they wouldn't even bump fists with, but if Mike would vouch for them they would at least get a fist bump. While Mike and Tommy got into a discussion on the best gunpowder to use to reload a .50 caliber round, Jeff and Danielle wandered around the shop gazing at the various guns. At one counter, a sales clerk was demonstrating breaking down an AR15 for cleaning and was in the process of reassembling it but was obviously having some difficulty. Jeff and Danielle watched for a bit, and then Jeff held up a piece and said, "You left this out." The salesman, quickly recovering, said, "See. Even a kid can assemble one of these," corrected his error and finished assembling the gun. The customer, a middle-aged woman eyed them and asked, "Can you take this apart and put it back together?" Danielle pulled over a crate and climbed on it. Taking the gun she checked that it was empty and then took it apart, laying the pieces on the mat on the counter. She examined to make sure it was cleaned and oiled properly and then reassembled it. The entire process took less than two minutes. Impressed the woman asked, "Have you ever fired one?" Jeff answered for both of them, "No ma'am. Today will be the first day." The woman looked at the sales clerk and said, "I'll see how they do. Then I'll get back to you." He smiled and said, "It will be waiting for you." Then to Jeff and Danielle, "I hope you do well today." Mike, having finished his discussion with Tommy and having paid for the three of them, drove the truck to the pistol range, and unloaded the pistols and ammunition.

He was as slow and meticulous with this training as he had been with the breakdown, cleaning, and reassembly. He carefully explained range etiquette to them and then walked down to tack bullseye targets on their lane board. When the range was "hot", he handed Danielle a .22 semi-auto pistol and a full magazine and told her to use the upper left hand target. Barely containing her excitement she confirmed the pistol was unloaded, slid in the magazine, racked in a round, released the safety, and sighted down the barrel as she had been taught. As she lined up the rear and front sights with the X on the target things seemed to click into place, and she knew where the round was going to hit the target. She fired all ten rounds, and all were in the X. Mike handed her another magazine. Ejecting the empty magazine, she slid in the new one, released the slide and the safety, and fired ten more rounds. The X had pretty much disappeared now. Mike said, "Okay, Jeff. Your turn." Danielle ejected the empty magazine, laid the pistol on the bench, and stepped back. Jeff took her place. Mike handed him his other .22 semi-auto pistol and a magazine which Jeff slid into place after confirming the pistol was empty. Releasing the slide and the safety, he aimed at the top right target. Something clicked in his head as it had with Danielle, and he knew where the bullets would go. He fired ten rounds and all ten were in the X. Mike handed him another magazine, and Jeff repeated the process. Again, the X was pretty much obliterated. By now, the other shooters on the pistol range had stopped shooting and were watching. Jeff and Danielle were both beaming. Danielle exclaimed, "This is fun!" and Jeff agreed. They spent a half hour there, taking turns firing the pistol, using left hand, right hand, and both hands. When they had finished, all of the targets on their boards were missing the X. There were no stray holes outside the X. They cleaned the pistols and put them back in their cases and in the truck.

Next, they moved to the 100-yard range and put up targets. Beginning with the .22 semi-auto rifles, they had the same results. Danielle shot first, and placed all ten rounds in the X. The next ten were also all in the X. Jeff took a turn, and all ten rounds were in the X. They spent the next half hour plinking with the rifle, then cleaned and stored it in the pickup. By now, they had a crowd of cheering spectators, many with binoculars who were telling those without how well the children were doing. When the targets were brought in everyone gathered around to see.

Finally, they and the crowd moved to the 500-yard range, and after putting up targets Mike brought out the AR15. This time Mike had Jeff go first. Jeff made sure the gun was empty, took the magazine from Mike, chambered a round, and aimed downrange. The feeling was still there. As he sighted along the rear sight, front sight, and to the target he could feel where the bullet would hit. He could feel where he needed to aim, how he should breathe, how he should squeeze the trigger. Again all twenty rounds were in the X. Now the crowd was silent as Jeff removed the magazine and laid the rifle on the bench. Danielle took her place, and when Mike handed her a magazine she inserted it, chambered a round, aimed, and began firing. All 20 rounds were in the X; Mike stood there giving words of encouragement but without a clue what to think. The kids were good. Scary good. It was shooting from a resting position on a bench, but still. Something was going on here.

When they brought the targets in the crowd gathered around to confirm what they had been told. Some thought it was some kind of trick. Some thought the kids should be in competition shooting. Mike thought he shouldn't bring them to a public gun range again. This was just too high profile. The lady from the store was part of the crowd, and she walked up to ask, "So you think I could handle this rifle as well as you did?" Danielle answered for both of them, "I think you would be able to handle it just fine," and the lady left to finish her purchase, much to the salesman's delight. They cleaned the gun, put it back in its case, then Mike loaded it into the truck with the others, and they all headed back to the city. This was their last trip to a public gun range.

Among the crowd were two men from 2nd Street Bible Church. That evening at their monthly small group meeting, they told about seeing Jeff and Danielle and the man they were with, the way they looked, and the shooting. When he told about the haircuts there was some shock, and more than one wondered if they had joined a cult or a militia. There was more discussion regarding what it meant that they were no longer part of the church and questioning whether they would ever come back. There were questions about Mike, who he was, and what he was doing with the kids. Again they were lifted up in prayer.

Chapter 9

Today was Jeff and Danielle's eighth birthday, and they had celebrated it over and over again, beginning with breakfast at the Brown's. Susan had made birthday waffles with a birthday candle for each of them. There were even presents for them of jeans and shirts. Cindy had bought them each small boxes of nice candy from the bookstore and had even refrained from eating any of it before she handed it over. At 11, they rode their bicycles to the apartment complex where Lacey had arranged a potluck luncheon with all their friends, and the clubhouse was full.

Everyone was now accustomed to their new look: very short hair, bigger, more muscles. And healthy. They were the picture of health. All of their injuries had completely healed, and they moved like two young leopards. Elena and Tisha hugged them, and Elena said, "You guys so have to do songs for the poetry coming up that we have to memorize." Tisha chimed in with, "You could just learn it the usual way," and Elena laughed and nudged her with a "No way!" Jeff and Danielle said they would try, but no promises. They bowed hello to the Fujiokas and hugged the children, who barraged them with Japanese, most of which they understood. Their Japanese was coming along nicely, thanks to regular visits with the Fujioka family as well as their once a week Japanese day. Grand-mere was there with her son and daughter-in-law, a rare occurrence due to their work hours, and they spent time with them speaking French.

Angela walked up during this conversation and said, "I heard you speaking Japanese a minute ago, and now it's French. How many languages do you know?" Jeff replied, "Five, counting English. Plus sign language. Plus military sign language." Angela asked, "What besides English, French, and Japanese?" Danielle replied, "Spanish and elvish." Angela raised her eyebrows and said, "Elvish?" Terry, who Lacey had invited, walked up just as she said this and exclaimed, "Oh, yeah. They speak more elvish than anyone else I know." Then he added a few words in elvish. Jeff laughed and said, "You did what to your dog?" Everyone around them laughed at this, and Danielle said, "Don't be mean to Terry. He asked how we were doing." Terry said, "Well that's a relief. I thought I had really messed up," and everyone laughed more, Terry included. Jeff added in elvish, "I have music for you in my backpack," and Terry did a fist bump with both of them. "That is awesome!"

In the middle of the afternoon, they left everyone, their backpacks full of additional birthday presents, and walked through the back gate to Alice's house. Terry left with them, and Jeff gave him the sheets of music, as well as the flash drive on which he and Danielle had recorded the songs. After promising to get together in a couple of weeks after the band had had time to review the songs, they left him and spent a couple of hours with Alice, eating homemade cookies, drinking milk, discussing her spring plans for the garden, and the progress her sister was making towards buying the house next door. It seemed to be moving slowly. Her sister wanted the house, the bank wanted to sell it to her, but the estate was winding its way through probate, as Danielle's court appointed guardian worked to protect her interests in the estate. Danielle suggested burning the house to the ground to speed things along, and a shocked Alice said, "Hush your mouth, girl.

My sister likes that house, and she can turn it into a place that you won't mind visiting." Danielle was skeptical, but made no more comments.

Just before 5 they received a text from Susan, "Home for dinner?" to which they replied, "No. Eating with friends."

After receiving a "K", they said goodbye to Alice and rode their bicycles to the Jacobs' house. Steve opened the door as they pushed their bicycles up the walk and greeted them with a happy "Hi, you two!" After hugging him hello, they followed him into the kitchen to say hello to Amy. She had just finished placing a roast on the table and stopped to hug them. "I still can't get used to your hair," she sighed. Things just keep changing with you two. Relations between the four were still a bit strained, but, thanks to Michelle's advice, they were better than those first awkward weeks after "the day". As long as the conversation stayed away from church or God, things went fairly smoothly, although this was hard for Steve and Amy because God was a big part of their lives.

Over dinner, Jeff and Danielle told them about life with the Browns and Cindy, their progress in home schooling, the get together at the apartment complex, and their visit with Alice. All during the meal Amy's heart ached for the kids, and she prayed for wisdom to know what to say or do. And the answer still came back, "Wait." At the end of the meal, Amy presented them with a birthday cake, and Steve gave them each a birthday card which contained a gift card for their online eBook account. They very efficiently helped clean up the dishes so Steve and Amy could get to church. Steve tried to insist that he drive them home, since the sun would set soon and it would be getting dark, but Jeff and Danielle assured them both that they would be home before dark, and they would be fine. Reluctantly Steve and Amy said goodbye and watched them ride away. Amy sighed and said, "I hope God is watching out for them. I can't imagine how this is all going to end." Steve hugged her and said, "I think it will be something greater than we can imagine."

Jeff and Danielle were still practicing SCUBA every week in Mike's friend's pool. They were wearing heavy-duty wet suits, but Mike said they needed to get used to swimming in cold water, and so they swam every week throughout the winter. The air tanks had to be refilled, and their new friends at the dive shop located near the postal store did this. The owners were a husband and wife team named Marvin and Minnie Wales, and their college age daughter Samantha (Sam to her friends), who attended university, assisted them. Mike had introduced Jeff and Danielle to them, and the children had added the family to their collection of friends. All of the adults were on a team of rescue divers who aided when needed in rescue work in the nearby lakes, ponds, and waterways. They also took several diving trips a year to the Caribbean, lakes within an easy day's drive, and around the world, including the Mediterranean and the South Pacific. The shop didn't make enough to finance all the trips, but they were also living off a trust fund on Minnie's side, using the money to do what they loved.

The family refilled the air tanks for free, but it wasn't entirely charity. Jeff and Danielle were a boost to sales. As in the guns, Mike had made them learn all of their dive gear, various types and brands, and what was best for what type of work underwater. Obviously, they hadn't used all of the gear, but what could be learned by lecture and on the internet they had learned. On a typical Saturday, while Mike and the twins waited for their air tanks to be refilled, Jeff and Danielle walked around the store, examining gear and chatting with customers.

More than one customer was helped along in their purchase decision by one or the other of the children. A typical conversation might consist of a customer asking Danielle, "What do you think of this mask?" while holding one up, and Danielle might respond,

"It's a good mask, but if you'll be using it for diving you might like one of these low volume ones better. And this color would match your eyes. Whichever one you get, be sure to change out the strap for one of these neoprene ones. The silicon ones that come with the mask will pull your hair." Jeff might comment to a customer who was looking at a leg sheath knife as seen in the movies, "Most resorts now won't let you wear a knife, so what you really need is one in case you get tangled in fishing line. Look at the ones that mount on your pressure gauge or your BC where it's closer to you than your leg." More often than not, the customer would buy what the children recommended, as they were friendly, not pushy, and they did give good advice. When asked how many dives they had made they would cheerfully say, "None outside the swimming pool. Can't wait for open water!"

Two more new friends were Bart and Jolene Sanders, a middle aged couple who worked as house parents at a women's shelter on the other side of the high school. The four bedroom, three bath house could hold three families of abused women and their children. It was a little tight, but the kitchen was large enough to cook for everyone, there was space for everyone to eat at the large dining room and kitchen tables, and a laundry room had been added to the back of the house, with two large washers and dryers. Perhaps it wasn't the best of solutions, but it was better than where the women and children had come from and was a starting point for where they were going. Jeff and Danielle had ridden by one day on their bicycles while exploring the neighborhood and saw Jolene in the front yard picking up trash from an earlier storm. They stopped and asked if she needed any help, and the woman gratefully accepted. Before the yard was cleaned to Jolene's satisfaction, they knew each other's names, who was living in the shelter, where Jeff and Danielle lived, and that they were the twins who had been injured the previous year. After this initial visit, Jeff and Danielle stopped by when they could to help paint, entertain the children, and run errands.

Over the winter, Jeff and Danielle had added another tool to their arsenal of knives: slingshots. This came about because of two incidents. They had never told Steve and Amy, but on the ride home from their house on the evening of their 8th birthday, they had been attacked as they followed the bike trail along the creek near Jeff's apartment. As they were riding along where the creek passed closest to the trail, a man came charging out of the bushes along the creek and grabbed for Danielle. Faster than thought, she and Jeff drew knives, and the man circled them as they kept him at bay. Jeff also called the police, and before the man realized what was going on, a policeman had appeared on the bike trail and arrested him. Although he swore up and down that the children had assaulted him for no reason as he was out walking, two things hurt his case. First, a quick run of his ID through the system showed he was a child molester out on parole. The second was the video Jeff's bike-mounted camera had made as he rode behind Danielle. As a second policeman arrived, the first one hauled the man away to jail, and the second officer, a friend of Officer Freedman, proceeded to admonish them for being out by themselves after dark, to which Jeff responded, "If it wasn't for that creep we would have been home before dark." The officer loaded their bikes in the back of his vehicle and drove them the rest of the way to the Brown house. As they were walking up to the front porch Danielle said, "We need something for longer range," and they started researching.

The second incident occurred one late afternoon at the high school. The easiest way to the women's shelter was to go from Jeff's and cut through the school grounds. On one of their trips as they were passing the outdoor basketball court, four boys ran over and confronted them. "What are you doing walking through our property?" Danielle raised an eyebrow. "You own the high

133

school?" The tallest of the boys said in a serious voice, "It's our turf. No one walks through here without our permission." Jeff smiled and said, "Good to know," and he and Danielle started to continue on their way. The tall boy shoved Jeff to the ground. At least that is what he thought he was going to do. As in the bathroom incident that had gotten them expelled from school, this group of young people found they had tackled bobcats instead of kittens. At the end, when the group was backing away, Danielle said in a cold voice, "Leave us alone." Then they continued on their way. When they arrived back at the Browns' house that evening they immediately ordered the slingshots online.

When the slingshots arrived, they practiced with them in the field between their houses, using the leaves of branches stuck in the ground as targets. They tried smooth rocks and ball bearings. The ball bearings were more accurate, but the rocks were less noticeable when lying on the ground. With practice, they were able to strip the target leaf off the branch every time at 50 feet. Farther than that, their accuracy suffered, although they could consistently hit a man-size target at 150 feet. From then on, along with their knives, they carried the slingshots in one of their cargo pants pockets along with a supply of rocks and ball bearings.

Shortly after the slingshots arrived, they were walking through the high school grounds on their way to the women's shelter to help paint the back deck. As they reached the basketball court, eight teenagers stepped from behind a storage shed and moved toward them. Four of them were the ones from before, two with bandages on their hands. Some of them held knives. Some held baseball bats. One girl had her camera phone out taking pictures. Jeff and Danielle didn't even slow down. Steadily walking forward, they pulled the slingshots out of their pockets, loaded them with ball bearings, and shot. Danielle took the camera phone out of the girl's hand, smashing it in the process. From there things went from bad to worse for the gang, and in the end, they again took off running. They ended up with badly bruised rear ends before they were out of range; a few rocks whizzing past their ears hurried them along. Jeff and Danielle continued through the school grounds to the women's shelter, ignoring the group that had stopped running and were watching them from several houses away.

In addition to homeschooling, SCUBA lessons, self-defense and knife fighting classes, weight training, swimming, and the rest of the things in their lives, Mike had added home building. Every Saturday he took them with him to a job site and put them to work, teaching them as he went along. They learned about surveying and staking, forms and foundations, electrical and plumbing, pouring concrete, framing a house, walls, running wires and pipes, air conditioning and heat, and all the rest. They weren't big enough to do much, but Mike treated them as though they were 22 year old professionals, putting them to work where he could. Danielle was excellent at painting small areas such as window frames and baseboards, and her work very quickly looked professional. Jeff caught up to her eventually, but mainly helped her with the taping before painting. He turned out to have a knack for taping and bedding, and when he finished with a seam, it was impossible to tell it from the rest of the wall by feel. All of this was supporting Mike's overall goal, which was to make them feel less helpless. He also didn't want them to feel like they had to attack everything that threatened them. Along with pride in their accomplishments, there lingered a tiny bit of guilt that he was teaching them so many dangerous skills, but he was able to justify in his mind what he was doing by the results he could see. Watching them laugh as they worked on a window was good enough for now.

One spring night Jeff was having trouble sleeping. Someone was staying the night with his mom, and the apartment was full of the smell of burning leaves. At 2AM he texted Danielle to see if she was awake. "You awake?" "Yes. What's up?" "Can't sleep. Want to visit King?" "Sure. Meet U in middle of field." Jeff dressed, took the blanket off the couch, and quietly left the apartment. Slipping like a ghost over the fence he trotted under the night sky down the path he and Danielle had worn between their houses over the past months. In the middle of the field, he stopped, and Danielle shortly appeared carrying a blanket of her own. They headed east until they reached the back of Michelle and Elizabeth's house and called softly to King, who came to the end of his chain and sat waiting. Both of them quietly vaulted the fence and came to kneel beside King who licked them both in greeting. At Danielle's command, he lay down and put his head on his paws. Jeff and Danielle spread their blankets on either side of him and lay perpendicular to him, using his back as a pillow. Once comfortable, they began to talk softly about things that were going on with the various people they knew. This was not the first time they had done this, but it was the first time they were seen.

Elizabeth woke up at 3AM wanting a drink of water. She slid out of bed and walked to the bathroom. On the way, she peeked out her window. Looking around, she spotted King in the middle of the yard, except he looked strange. She stared, trying to understand what she was seeing. It appeared as though there were two people beside King? Lying on King? She ran to get her mom calling, "Mama! Mama! Someone has King!" She heard her mom jump out of bed and saw her bedroom light turn on. Michelle ran to the back door with Elizabeth behind her and flipped the switch for the back light. There was King sitting up in the back yard facing them, tongue out panting softly. No one was in sight, and nothing seemed out of the ordinary. Michelle called to him, and King trotted over to her. Michelle told Elizabeth, "You must have been dreaming, sweetie. King is fine." Elizabeth protested, "No mom. Someone was there. King must like them.

Do you think it was whoever gave King his bath?" Michelle told her, "I don't know, baby, but everything looks okay now, so let's go back to bed." Elizabeth went reluctantly, but she didn't go back to sleep easily.

At the first sound from inside the house, Jeff and Danielle had snatched up their blankets and flowed back over the fence. By the time Michelle turned on the porch light they were back in the middle of the field, crouching. Danielle commented, "That's a first. I hope we didn't scare them." Jeff replied, "Me, too. Maybe no more night visits for a while." They bumped fists and returned to their homes.

Although they didn't visit the Strong house late at night for a while, Michelle and Lizzie were on their minds a lot. The thing Michelle had said, about being one major expense away from big trouble, was brought to mind when they saw her one day having trouble starting her car, as they were walking to the women's shelter with supplies. Two days later on their way to Randy's auto repair center, they saw the same thing. Danielle remarked to Jeff, "I bet she doesn't have enough money to get her car fixed. Maybe we can get Mr. Brown to do something." Jeff replied, "We have to be careful. I think she would get really mad if it looked like charity. We need a way to give her money without her knowing where it came from. Maybe we could slip a gift card through her door." Danielle agreed. "Good idea. To some place she shops like the grocery store. Then she could use the grocery money for something else, like getting the car fixed." Jeff added, "Maybe we could pay her water bill or electric bill or something, too. They take those payments at the grocery store." Danielle pondered the idea. "It needs to be paid somewhere she doesn't go so she doesn't find out who did it. Maybe somewhere in the old neighborhood."

With this idea in mind, they rode their bicycles to the Shepherd house for school. Afterwards, they stopped by the first store they came to that would take utility payments. Saying their mom had lost the water bill, but needed them to stop by and pay it, they gave the young lady behind the counter the name and address of the Strong house. She gave them the amount, and Jeff gave her his debit card. One bill down. They rode down the street to the next place that allowed payment of utilities and repeated the process with the phone bill. This time Danielle used her debit card. Two down, one to go. Another stop, and the gas bill was paid. They made one more stop at the grocery store nearest Michelle and Lizzie and bought a $100 gift card and a thank you card. In her best calligraphy Danielle wrote, "Thank you for all that you do!" They placed the gift card in the note, sealed the envelope, and wrote Michelle and Elizabeth's name on it. Danielle waited while Jeff calmly walked up the sidewalk and slid the envelope through the mail slot. Then they rode their bicycles home to discuss car repair expenses with Randy.

Danielle raised the subject first as Randy was sitting in his easy chair, reading the paper and watching the news. He was surprised, as he wasn't usually involved in what went on around the house, including discussions, but he did enjoy talking about his work. When Danielle asked if he ever ran specials or sales he said, "Sure. All the time. We're running one now for 15% off any repair over $200." Jeff asked where the specials were run, and Randy said, "In the newspaper." Danielle asked if he would show them, and Randy sorted through the discarded newspapers on the floor around his chair until he found the auto section and then flipped through pages until he found the ad. Jeff and Danielle read the ad, thanked Randy for his help, and took the sheet of newsprint to the kitchen to cut it out while Randy went back to his paper and the news, the excitement of the moment over. Then he looked up and asked, "Would you two like to learn about engines?" Jeff and Danielle responded together, "Yes, we would." Randy nodded to himself and went back to reading while Danielle cut the ad from the newspaper.

The next day they taped the ad to Michelle's front door as though it were a flyer. Meanwhile Michelle's life was getting stranger and stranger. First of all, Lizzie had picked up the mail from in front of the mail slot and found the envelope. When Michelle opened the card, she could not imagine who had left it for them. Then, later in the week when the bills arrived, she opened them with trepidation knowing she couldn't both pay them and fix the car. One after another, she opened the electric bill, the phone bill, and the gas bill to find that the balance on each account was zero. The next day she called each utility to ask about the bill and was told that each one had been paid in full. No one could tell her who had paid the bills, only where and when. And finally, she had taken the car to Randy's auto repair center with her coupon and found that with the discount, the money saved from the paid utilities, and the gift card, she could just cover the bill. That evening she sat at the table, put her face in her hands and cried in relief while Lizzie hugged her and asked what was wrong.

Warm weather was in the air, and on a sunny Saturday in May Mike took Jeff and Danielle to the lake for more SCUBA training. Using a friend's boat, he took them to a little used spot, anchored, and set out a dive buoy. While everyone put on dive skins and wet suits, Mike went over the plan. He had a moment of rage when Jeff and Danielle put the dive skins on over their swimsuits and he saw the crisscrossed scars on their backs and the four nail holes in Jeff's back, but he shoved it down and continued with his instructions. They would be diving to thirty feet and going through their exercises: clearing masks, sitting stationary on the bottom, floating in place, etc. Then, using what they had learned, they would search for something he had hidden. They would tie the floats he gave them to the item, inflate them, and float the item to the surface. When they were ready to surface with the item, he would monitor them to make sure their breathing was controlled and normal.

Jeff and Danielle were excited at the thought of swimming somewhere besides a swimming pool for a change. It wasn't the ocean, and visibility wasn't great, but it was still open water. They listened carefully as Mike explained what they would be doing, especially the part where he mentioned involuntarily sucking water up the nose when removing their mask in cold water and what to do about it. Finally, all of the gear was on and checked, and they were in the water. Swimming to the rocks thirty feet below, they sat, just like they did in the Shepherd homeschool, waiting for Mike's instructions. Hovering in front of them, he signaled Danielle to remove her mask and replace it, which she did. Just as Mike had explained, when the cold water hit her face, which had been kept warm by the mask, she involuntarily sucked water up her nose. She snorted it clear and patiently finished removing her mask, waving it in front of her before putting it back on and clearing it, signaling okay. Mike watched her for a moment to make sure she was breathing properly and then signaled Jeff to do the same, which he did with the same result and the same solution. Next, he had them hover two feet above the rocks to test their buoyancy control, which they also passed with flying colors.

Assured that they were comfortable in the water at thirty feet, he signaled for them to follow and led them another twenty feet out from the shore. There he signaled for a depth and air pressure check. Checking, they reported a 45 foot depth and 60 percent air. He swam over and confirmed they were reading their gauges correctly and gave them the okay sign. Then he signed "find object" and pointed generally where he wanted them to look. Danielle took the lead, with Jeff holding her swim fins and kicking for both of them; Mike followed overhead keeping an eye on them. She kept them pointed due north while searching

to the west as Jeff counted 50 kicks and searched to the east. At
the end of the 50 kicks she aimed them two kicks east, turned
due south, and they searched 50 kicks in that direction. On
their fourth pass, Jeff spotted an object on the bottom that didn't
appear to belong there. He tapped Danielle on the leg, and when
she looked at him, he pointed. Instead of swimming directly to
the object they continued on until they were perpendicular to it
and carefully marked their position in case this wasn't what they
were searching for, and they had to resume their search. After
they were certain they could resume the search where they had
left off, they swam down to the object, which appeared to be
a metal weight with a loop welded to it. Danielle unwrapped
the line wrapped around her waist and tied it to the weight. Jeff
untied the float from his BC and handed it to her. She tied the
other end of her line to the float and filled it with air from her
backup mouthpiece until the weight reached neutral buoyancy.
Then with Jeff on one side of the buoy and her on the other, they
began to slowly guide the weight and buoy upwards. As they rose,
Mike observed their breathing and rate of ascent. Everything was
looking good. As the twins rose, the air in the buoy expanded,
and they released pressure to keep it from moving upward too
quickly. Part of their test would be how much disturbance they
made when the two of them and the buoy surfaced. After floating
motionless at fifteen feet for three minutes, they finished the
ascent. Slowly and quietly, they broke the surface and looked
around. Mike surfaced beside them, gave them the sign for well
done and the sign for release the weight. Danielle pulled the knot
loose, and the weight sank to the bottom, ready for the next
diver's training. When Mike signaled 'return to the boat,' all
three slipped back under the water, swam to the boat, and pulled
themselves on board. As Mike discussed with them what they
had accomplished, what they thought of it, what could have been
done better or differently, the baby seals drank water and listened

to him. He could see their confidence continuing to grow with another success under their belts; the rage inside them tempered what they had learned towards steel.

As they climbed into the truck to return home, they were spotted by divers from 2nd Street Bible Church, who told their Bible study group about it that evening, and once again the baby seals were lifted up in prayer.

Chapter 10

J eff and Danielle had added day trading to all their other activities. It began innocently enough. They had been working with the investment club for their online trading account, following the club's recommendations, and the account was growing nicely. However, one of the studies they were doing at the Shepherd's involved following the stock market daily, and the two had noticed that some stocks swung widely at times, either up or down, and even in the course of a single day as news of one sort or another was released. Kathy had spoken to them about day trading and buying short and what a bad idea it was, but Jeff and Danielle couldn't help looking at those swings, and they decided to try it. Accordingly, they bought $5000 worth of stock in a company. Their choice was not scientific, based on research or P/E ratios or future earnings projections. They bought it because they liked the name of the company and thought it deserved to grow. Amazingly it did. Within a week, the company announced a buyout, and the stock quadrupled overnight. Their $5000 became $20,000. Amazed they looked for another company. This one they sold short because they took a dislike to it and thought it deserved to lose money. Over the next two weeks the company was involved in a scandal, and the price plummeted as people dumped the stock. Jeff and Danielle bought the stock at the end of two weeks, and their $20,000 had become $100,000. It was still just a game to them and not real money. They couldn't spend it, so why not play with it. After putting the initial investment back in the companies suggested by the investment club, they put the rest in their next pick and sat back to see what happened. This strategy became their plan for the remainder of the year, reinvesting the entire amount each time in their latest choice. And they were never wrong. If they picked one to go up it went up. If they picked one to go down it went down. Any normal investor would have had a heart attack at their actions or at the least lost their hair or had it turn white, especially the last trade which took them over two hundred million. Then they stopped. After the last trade, they had a very strong feeling that they should get out of day trading, so they did. They made sure all the taxes were paid, then they reinvested the remainder in the diversified manner described by Kathy in the finance portion of class. It was roughly based on their age, but Kathy's teaching didn't really cover 8 year old investors, so they went with the youngest age she presented. Then they mainly forgot about it except for the portion they tracked with the investment club.

The legal impediments to selling Danielle's house had finally been dealt with, and the house was sold to Alice's sister, Eunice. Jeff and Danielle discovered this on a visit to Alice in June. They probably should have heard about it from the bank or the court, but paperwork moves slowly through the system. Eunice was visiting the day they stopped by, and Alice introduced her. Eunice was older by two years and tall and slender to Alice's, well, largeness. She did have the same light black skin, but her hair was dark even though she was older. She had never been married, and when Jeff asked if she had a garden like Alice's, she laughed and said, "No, child, I am death on plants. I can kill weeds." They sat in Alice's garden and drank lemonade while they spoke about the house. Eunice said, "They should probably be telling you this and not me, but I was told they would have an estate "sale" for everything in the house that you don't want." Danielle asked if she had been in the house, and when Eunice said she had, Danielle asked, "Is there anything in the house you want? Or you Alice?" Eunice said, "I wouldn't mind the TV and there are some mighty fine books in there, but child you should let them sell everything they can to get you some money for your future. You'll be needing it someday." Danielle and Jeff exchanged a glance and Danielle replied, "I don't really want anything from that house. I have everything that was mine." Eunice patted her hand and said, "I have my own things, my own furniture, my own knickknacks, my own pots and pans and plates and such. I hope when I've moved all my things in and made the place mine you'll feel comfortable coming over to visit. We'll drive out all the bad memories from the house." Danielle just said, "We'll see." Alice added, "We're thinking about visiting that church of yours. It's a nice walk, and we thought we'd give it a try." Danielle frowned and said, "It's not my church," and Alice said, "Honey, you've got to get over this mad you have going on with God. At any rate I hear there are some fine folks go there, so we'll see." Danielle didn't say anything to this but looked at Eunice. "I hope you like the house, Miss Eunice. Maybe I'll visit after you've been in it for a while. When do you move in?" "The bank says I can close any time after the end of the month. I already have someone to buy my old one, and the rest is just working out when everyone moves. They'll have to sell the things in the house, and the bank is going to have someone clean up and do repairs, and I'll want to do my own job of cleaning because you know they won't do it right, so maybe sometime in July. I'll have a house warming party when everything is just the way I want it, and you will be first on my invitation list." Danielle stood and hugged her, there were hugs all around, and Jeff and Danielle took their leave. Alice and Eunice watched them go, and Eunice said, "Those poor children. And who shaved the hair off their heads?" The two elderly ladies took a moment to lift Jeff and Danielle up in prayer.

Jeff and Danielle were at the lake diving for statues. There were twenty items placed around the lake, and they had found ten of them so far. Each dive they would sit in the boat with Mike and plan each step: the depth they would be swimming, for how long, the direction they would be swimming, the return to the boat. Mike would review the plan, and if he didn't like it he would just say, "Do it again." If the plan just needed refining, he would point out ways to do it better. This dive they were looking for a statue of a bear at 50 feet. The statue was 6 feet tall, unlike some of the others that were as small as one foot tall, or even just a plaque. Mike would be using a dive computer to check against their numbers using the dive tables. All three jumped into the water and met at the anchor rope. When everyone had given the okay sign, they followed the anchor rope to the bottom, and at 30 feet, Jeff and Danielle started off with Danielle in the lead watching the compass and searching left while Jeff propelled them through the water searching right.

Mike trailed behind them watching his compass. They had estimated reaching the statue in 75 kicks, and when it didn't show up in 100 kicks Danielle guided them to the right, reversed course, and they started back in the opposite direction. Ten kicks later, she spotted the statue fifteen feet to the left and curved towards it. When Jeff spotted it, he released her legs, pulled the camera around in its waterproof case, and gestured for Danielle to pose in front of the statue. That's when he became tangled in a floating ball of fish line and fish hooks that had managed to become anchored near the statue. By the time he realized what had happened, he was well snared with fish hooks caught in his wet suit, his BC, and even the strap of his mask. He pulled out one of his knives to cut himself free and found that the fish line gave too much to cut, and any attempt to pull it tighter just dug the fish hooks in deeper. Mike watched from a distance to see how they would handle this situation, ready to step in if their time on the bottom neared a mandatory decompression stop. As Jeff floated motionlessly in place, Danielle swam slowly around him eyeing the situation while keeping a careful eye out for more floating hazards.

After reviewing how the mess was anchored to the bottom she moved in front of Jeff and signed, "We need to add snips to our dive tools. I think I can cut this mess free from the bottom. Then we can get you back to the boat and carefully cut it free there, so we can remove this hazard from the lake." Mike swam over to hear the plan. Danielle didn't have enough signs in combat hand language to explain, so she wrote the plan on her slate for Mike. He read it and gave her the okay sign. Carefully avoiding being hooked herself, she cut loose the six lines that were holding the mess anchored to the bottom. Danielle let all of the air out of her BC and sat on the bottom. Then she carefully unfastened her weight belt and transferred the weights to the pockets of her BC. Next, she swam to Jeff who was able to extend one arm and grasp the end of the weight belt. Watching her compass, Jeff, and all around her, she slowly towed him back towards the boat with Mike following behind and above.

At fifteen feet, they floated for the three minute safety stop while both of them searched for the boat. It was slightly to the right of where they thought it would be, but not far, and Danielle towed Jeff over to hover under the boat. She signed him to stay under the water, and swam up until she could reach in the back of the boat for the toolbox from which she pulled a pair of wire cutters. She also grabbed the cooler, removed the lid, floated the cooler in the water, and used some line to tie it to the boat so it wouldn't float away. Then, with infinite patience, she removed the fishhooks one by one, cut the line, and tossed line and fishhook into the cooler. Finally, Jeff was completely free, and the cooler was overflowing with fishhooks and line. When the three divers and the cooler were all safely in the boat Mike said, "Well done, both of you. What did you learn?" Danielle answered, "If we're going to dive where there are fish line hazards we need something to cut them." Jeff added, "Some nylon or cotton line would be good, too. Maybe ten feet or so." As Mike started the motor and headed back towards shore he asked, "So how are we going to get to the drinks under all those fishhooks and line?"

Jeff and Danielle were on speaking terms with some of the gang from the high school. It came about because of a chance meeting a few days after they drove the gang off with their new slingshots. Once again, the two were crossing the high school grounds on their way to the women's shelter. As they passed the basketball court, they found the girl who had been taking pictures with her phone camera sitting hunched over on a bench. She looked up as they approached, and the black eye and bruising on her face stood out starkly, as did the bruises on her arms. They stopped in front of her, and Danielle asked, "What happened to you?" The girl looked back down and snapped, "What's it to you?" Patiently they just stood there. Eventually the girl huffed and said, "My dad found out I lost my phone." Jeff asked, "The phone in your hand the day of the fight?" The girl snorted, "Yeah, that one." Danielle asked, "You told him you lost it?" Looking up, the girl replied, "Well I wasn't going to say we got our butts kicked by two little kids." Jeff and Danielle looked at each other. Unintended consequences. Danielle sighed and said, "Meet us here tomorrow at the same time. We'll bring you another phone." The girl asked, "Why?" Jeff answered, "Because it should have been over when the fight was over." The girl laughed bitterly. "Yeah, well Mario and Tomas are in trouble, too. They had to go to the emergency room, and their families can't afford those kind of medical bills. They won't be paying them, but they'll have creditors on them forever." Danielle asked, "What emergency room?" and the girl answered, "East Side Memorial. They had to make up a stupid story about falling on a broken bottle. Both of them. Good thing their parents don't talk to each other." Danielle asked, "What's your name?" and the girl replied, "Maria Sanchez." Now there was a faint glimmer of hope in her eyes. Danielle told her, "Okay. See you tomorrow," and she and Jeff continued on their way to the shelter. Maria called after them, "Hey! What are your names?" Turning around Jeff replied, "I'm Jeff." Pointing to Danielle he said, "She's Danielle." Smiling he added, "We're the baby seals." Maria said, "What?" but they continued on their way.

After finishing at the shelter, they rode their bikes to the store where Jeff had bought the disposable phones and purchased one more phone and a 1000 minute prepaid card. Next, they rode to the hospital, locked the bicycles to a tree, and rode the elevator up to the billing office. As they stood in the elevator Danielle said, "We're idiots." Jeff stared at her. "Okay, why this time?" Danielle stared at him and said, "We need to pay OUR bills." Jeff shook his head, "You're right. But what are we doing? If we try to pay any of these bills people are going to know there is money, and my mom will find out, and it will not end well." Danielle leaned against the wall. "So what do we do?" Jeff thought for a moment, and as the elevator door opened and they stepped out on the floor, he said "Let's see how much the bill is and send it in anonymously. We can send in money to pay for Mario and Tomas the same way." Striding up to an available desk, they sat in the two chairs in front of the desk and Danielle told the lady sitting there, "Hi. I'm Danielle. This is Jeff. We wanted to check on our bill." The lady behind the desk said, "Hi, you two. You're the baby seals, aren't you? I'm Candice. You're looking pretty good. How are you?" Jeff answered, "We're fine now, thank you." Candice continued, "What have you been up to since you left us?" Danielle replied, "Mainly school," and explained that they were being homeschooled. Candice said, "How nice. And how can I help you today?" Jeff explained again that they wanted to know how much their bill was, and Candice laughed. "Your bill was paid shortly after you left us. Someone started a fund for it, and a radio station picked it up. Before long, there was more than enough in the fund to pay your bill. The remainder was donated to the pediatric ICU." Jeff and Danielle looked at each other and said, "Wow!" Candice continued, "So you two don't need to worry about that at all. It's taken care of." Not knowing what else to say the two thanked her and left.

As they rode back down in the elevator Danielle said, "Well that takes care of our bill. What about Mario and Tomas?" Jeff thought a moment. "Let's ask Steve and Amy." They arrived at the first floor, unlocked their bicycles, and rode to the Jacobs' house. Amy answered the door with a bowl and spoon in her hands. "Hi, you two! I was just making cookies. Want to help?" Walking into the kitchen with Amy, the two children removed their gloves, washed their hands at the kitchen sink, and helped Amy drop the cookie dough onto baking sheets and place them in the oven. While the cookies were baking, they explained that they wanted to pay the medical bills of two kids in their neighborhood. When Amy asked why Danielle said, "We may have been the ones who hurt them." Amy looked thoughtfully at the two of them and said, "Okay, what do you want me to do?" Jeff explained that they wanted to do it anonymously and wanted to know if Amy and Steve would talk to Pastor John about giving the money to the hospital if Jeff and Daniel would provide it. Amy asked, "Why don't you ask him yourself?" They just stared at her. After a few moments, she sighed and said, "I'll talk to Steve. I know Pastor John is on the chaplain staff there, so I think he'll be able to find out an amount. I'll let you know." They thanked her, and after taking the cookies out of the oven and bagging a few to take with them they left. As they rode home, they discussed unintended consequences.

That evening after Steve arrived home Amy told him about Jeff and Danielle's request. Steve called Pastor John and put him on speakerphone with Amy. Pastor John added Sarah. Amy described the visit and the request, and Sarah said, "So they still aren't talking to us?" Amy sighed. "No. I'm not sure where they are these days. Things are changing for them. I think they're the same kids we knew, but they're still mad at God and just about everyone in the church except me and Steve. I don't know why we get a pass." Pastor John asked, "Where would they get the money for this? I never got the feeling that either of them had any." Steve answered, "I think they hid it so their parents wouldn't find out. I know they were being paid for doing things for several people in the neighborhood. Maybe they won't be able to afford what they want to do. Can you find out how much it is?" Pastor John said, "I'll be up there tomorrow, and I'll stop by the billing office and tell them I know a couple of people who want to contribute to the bills and see if I can find out how much is owed. Then I guess we'll see where it goes from there." They had to be content with that for the time being.

The next day Pastor John rode the elevator up to the billing office and spoke to the billing manager. He explained how he knew a couple of people who wanted to contribute to the bills of a couple of people who had visited the emergency room and gave him the names he had and the dates. The manager looked up the information for him and gave him the amounts. Pastor John called the Jacobs and gave the number to Amy who called Danielle and gave the number to her. Danielle thanked her and hung up, and the Pattons and the Jacobs waited to see what would happen.

On the evening of that same day the twins met Maria at the high school and handed over her new phone and prepaid card. As she accepted them, tears began rolling down her cheeks. She wiped them away, pretending there was something in her eye and tried to give a nonchalant, tough "Thanks." Danielle said, "So, why don't you come help us at the women's shelter?" Maria asked, "Doing what?" Jeff responded with, "Whatever you're good at. They need help with everything. We'll text you next time we go." With a "Maybe" Maria walked off, and the baby seals returned to the Browns.

Over the next few days, they withdrew cash from the ATM after class until they had enough to cover the amount Amy had given Danielle. When they had enough, they stopped by the Jacob's house on the way home from school and left the money with Amy. When they handed her the envelope Amy said, "Guys, where did you get the money? You aren't robbing banks or selling drugs or anything are you?" They smiled at her, and Jeff said, "We have money. It's just safer for us if no one thinks we have any." Amy left it at that, and after they had ridden away on their bicycles, she strolled over to the Patton house and handed the envelope to Sarah, telling her what the two children had said. Sarah shook her head, and that evening she handed the envelope to Pastor John. The next day he stopped by the hospital and handed the envelope over to the billing manager, and for the time being that was the end of that.

A few days later Jeff and Danielle were again walking to the shelter to help put bunk beds in one of the rooms. Before they left Jeff's apartment Danielle texted Maria to meet them at the high school if she wanted to go with them. When they reached the basketball court, three people were waiting there: Maria, Mario, and Tomas. As they walked up to the three, Jeff and Danielle had knives in each hand ready to open, but Mario and Tomas put their hands out, and Mario said, "Chill. We came to help out. Maria told us about her phone, and Tomas and me got letters from the hospital saying we didn't owe nothing. We figure that was you." Jeff and Danielle slid the knives back in their pockets, and Jeff said, "Come on then." As they walked across the school grounds towards the shelter Maria asked, "So why are we helping these people?" Danielle said, "They need help. We can help, so we do. Besides, there are kids there. We like to help kids." Tomas asked, "What is this place where we're going?" Jeff explained, "It's a place where women can go when they're abused by their husbands and need to get away. Some have children, some don't. A woman with two children is coming there tomorrow, so they need to set up some bunk beds in one of the rooms." Mario wanted to know how long they stayed there, and Danielle told him, "A few weeks. Maybe a couple of months. They have to figure out where they'll be living now, if they'll even be staying here or moving to another city or what. It's a mess when a family breaks up."

Arriving at the shelter, Jeff introduced the three newcomers to Bart and Jolene. Bart took Tomas and Mario to help assemble the bunk beds, Jolene asked Danielle and Maria to finish painting one of the walls in the room, and Jeff set to work patching a hole the doorknob had made in the wall when the doorstop fell off. As they worked, Bart and Jolene asked about Maria, Tomas, and Mario and how they had met the baby seals. Maria immediately asked why Jeff and Danielle were called the baby seals, and Danielle rolled her eyes. Laughing Jolene told her, "When they were in the hospital one of the nurses said they looked like baby seals, and the name stuck." Mario asked when they were in the hospital, and Jeff said, "last year," and left it at that. Jolene asked again how the kids had met, and Danielle just said they had met when they were walking through the school grounds to reach the shelter, and no one added any details. The work continued rapidly amid discussions of what would happen when they started building houses in the horse pasture, and classes at the high school. In no time everyone was finished, the beds were made, and the room was ready for its new occupants. As they left Bart and Jolene thanked everyone for their help, told Jeff and Danielle they would see them soon, and told the other three they hoped to see them again. As they walked back through the school grounds Maria commented, "That was pretty cool. You do stuff like that all the time?" Jeff explained, "When we have time. We're pretty busy." Tomas asked, "Busy with what?" and Danielle answered, "Training," and with a wave goodbye the two left the three at the basketball court. Mario raised an eyebrow and said, "Training? What does that mean?" Tomas snorted, "Training to kick our butts."

Mario, Tomas, and Maria were not the only ones receiving financial help from Jeff and Danielle. A church met near Randy's auto repair center, in space rented from one of the companies located there. It was called the Pueblo Community Church, and its pastor was Marcus Hall, a large, intense man in his mid-50's. His wife had died a few years earlier, and after her death, he had gone back to school to get his degree in theology. After receiving his degree, he had preached various times until a few people in the neighborhood, who remembered him from his college football days, had asked him to preach regularly to them, and the church was born. It wasn't a large congregation, and was mainly his age and older, and mainly lower middle class. Jeff and Danielle had never officially met him, but they had overheard him one day speaking to a member of his congregation at the grocery store and saying how he wished he had $10,000 help the kids in the neighborhood. He outlined a plan to the man to have the church pay the kids to help their elderly neighbors, thereby giving the kids some money and helping people at the same time. Jeff and Danielle liked the plan, and they followed Marcus home to see where he lived. It turned out he lived behind the building where the church met, just down the street from the shelter.

They followed him up his sidewalk, and spoke to him as he reached his front door, "Hello, Pastor Marcus." He turned, and seeing them he said, "Hello, children." Jeff said, "We didn't mean to listen, but we heard you in the grocery store talking about a plan to help the kids and old people in the neighborhood if you had the money." He responded, "Yes. That's right. There are some things I'd like to do to help the people in my congregation and the kids in the neighborhood if the money was available." Danielle asked, "What if we could get you the money?" He chuckled and said, "That would be very nice. It would certainly help some people out." Jeff said, "$10,000?" and Marcus said, "That would be a great start for what I have in mind." Jeff said, "If we could get you the money, the source would need to be anonymous. Otherwise, it would cause all sorts of problems. Can you do that?" Marcus smiled and said, "The only person that would know is me." Jeff and Danielle looked at each other for a while, communicating silently. Then they nodded to each other, and Danielle said, "We'll get you a check." And with that, they turned and left, leaving a bemused Marcus behind, shaking his head. They had only walked a couple of steps before they stopped and turned around. Jeff said, "Please don't tell anyone you've seen us." Then they continued on their way.

That evening they moved $10,000 from their online trading account to their checking account. When the funds showed up in the checking account, Danielle wrote a check to the church, and one evening after dark, they knocked on Marcus' door. He answered it and smiled when he saw them. "Hello, children. What brings you by so late?" Danielle said, "We have something for you," and handed him the check. He examined the check and smiling said, "What would happen if I tried to cash this check?" Jeff responded, "They would cash it." Marcus said, "Perhaps the two of you should come inside and tell me about it." He led them into his living room and waved them to the couch while he sat in the easy chair. "What do your parents think of this?" Danielle said, "I'm in foster care. Jeff's mother is a drug addict." He said, "I see. And where did this money come from?" Jeff answered, "Some from jobs, some from music, mainly from the stock market." Marcus tilted his head to one side. "You invested in the stock market?" Danielle smiled. "More like gambled in the stock market. If anyone found out we had it, we would probably lose it." Marcus frowned. "So you're asking me to keep a very big secret." They nodded. "We want to help people. But we're kids. We can only do so much. But we have money, so we can give it to people who can help people. We think you're one. If you want to be." Marcus considered. "Tell you what. I'll think about it and pray about it and let you know. How can I find you?" They gave him their phone numbers. He walked them to the door, and as they started down the sidewalk he asked, "Are you two Christians?" Jeff replied, "We're mad at God," and they continued into the night.

Cindy was in Danielle's room sitting on the floor leaning against the wall, while Danielle sat cross-legged on the bed. They were discussing Jeff and Danielle's upcoming 9th birthday, and Cindy wanted to know what they had planned besides breakfast with the Browns. Danielle explained, "We'll spend the day with our friends in our old neighborhood. There are some at the apartments where Jeff used to live, and there's my next door neighbor. Her sister bought my old house. We'll eat dinner with a couple from our old church." Cindy asked, "You don't go to church anymore?" and Danielle just said, "No." Cindy didn't let it go at that and asked, "Why not?" Danielle sighed. "It's a long story. I'm mad at God, and I'm mad at the people in the church." Cindy kept going, "Why?" Danielle gave her a hard stare. "If you are playing the "Why" game with me I will hurt you." Cindy looked up in alarm. "No! I just wanted to know. I've never been to church." Danielle looked at her hands in their gloves. "I'm mad at God for letting this happen to me and Jeff after all we did for the church. I'm mad at the people in the church for telling me God would look after us." Cindy thought about this. "Does it work, being mad at God? I mean, if he's God and all. Is that like a bug being mad at you or something?" Danielle snorted. "I don't know. It's just all I've got." Cindy commented, "You have a lot of friends." Danielle laughed, "Yeah, I guess so. How about you?" Cindy shook her head. "Not really. I don't get along with most people." Danielle explained, "Sometimes you have to be around people you can like. I mean, I love my old neighbor Alice's garden, but she also likes me and lets me like her garden. My friend Lacey likes to teach music, and I like to learn to play the guitar. My friend Angela likes to teach swimming, and I like to learn to swim. I met most of my friends through Jeff, though. He's just likeable, you know? I don't think he means to be. He doesn't try to be. He just is. And I get to be part of it." Cindy asked, "Because he's your brother?" Danielle laughed, "Yes. He's stuck with me for good or bad." Cindy sighed, "I need friends." When Cindy eventually got up to leave Danielle said, "Why don't you come with me and Jeff on our birthday, and Cindy shrugged, "Maybe I will," and moved to her own room. As she walked out Danielle's door, she tossed her long hair and said, "I could never have cut my hair as short as yours."

Chapter 11

Thanksgiving, Christmas, and New Years went by and Mike had the baby seals at the lake in heavy wet suits training for long-distance underwater transit dives. He took them to a point just off the south shore and gave them a destination 3.25 miles away where he would be waiting, going over the details of the destination. It was a small island in the middle of the lake, a challenge to hit at the end of a three-mile underwater swim. "Maintain a depth of 30 feet. You have flares and strobes if you get in trouble. This is timed. You have an hour and a half." Jeff and Danielle pulled down their masks, gave the okay sign, and slid into the water. They were using closed circuit rebreathers today, and there were no visible air bubbles. After waiting ten minutes, Mike started the engine and pulled away.

Meanwhile under water Jeff and Danielle had sunk to thirty feet and adjusted their buoyancy until they hovered motionless. Then both took compass readings and headed north with Danielle primarily watching their heading and Jeff, swimming to her right with his head even with her waist, monitoring their depth and number of kicks. When he estimated they had reached the first half mile point, he touched her leg, and they swapped positions and jobs with Jeff monitoring his compass and Danielle their depth and kick strokes. Every half mile they swapped, and with steady kicks made rapid progress across the lake.

No one else appeared to be out on the lake. For a while after Mike left, they heard the sound of the boat, but it had faded into the distance. They glimpsed the occasional fish, but the bottom was out of sight in the limited visibility. With the rebreathers there was no sound, and the journey to their destination was silent. The silence and the lack of visual stimulus made boredom a threat and daydreaming tempting. That could be dangerous as, among other things, it wasn't a good idea to assume their rebreathers were working properly. Too much CO_2 or O_2 could be dangerous, and those gauges needed to be monitored. A failure would be subtle. Still, the miles passed steadily, and as they swam through the estimated three-mile mark and approached 3.2 miles, they began searching for an upslope. There was none straight ahead, and they began an east/west search pattern. Twenty-five yards to the east the bottom rose rapidly, and they swam around it cautiously, searching for an anchor rope. Finding none, they swam to fifteen feet and scanned for a boat, spotting the hull of a boat directly above them. Approaching from the stern, one on either side of the propeller, they edged above the water and glanced in the boat.

Mike was leaning back in the driver's seat with his feet propped on the steering wheel, drinking a beer. Danielle slid a knife from its sheath on her chest, opened it carefully underwater, and slowly raised it out of the water, fully intending to spear the can out of Mike's hand. However, just before she threw Mike said, "Do not put a hole in my beer can. It would annoy me greatly. Climb in." Jeff and Danielle eyed each other, shrugged, and throwing their fins into the boat climbed aboard.

Presently they were sitting in sweats and coats, drinking hot chocolate from a thermos while Mike reviewed the mission. "How much did you miss the island by?" Jeff answered, "Twenty-five feet or so." "Which direction?" Danielle's turn, "To the west." Mike nodded, "We need to work on your navigation skills underwater. Not bad, though. You made it in time. I would have knocked off some serious points for a hole in my beer, though." The two kids grinned around their hot chocolate, and Mike continued with a review of their equipment and the swim. Finally, Danielle untied the boat from the tree stump to which Mike had attached the bowline, Jeff fended them away, and the three cruised back to Mike's truck and home.

In February, they celebrated their 9th birthday. Cindy went with them to their birthday festivities and met their friends at the apartments, Alice, and the Jacobs. Amy and Cindy hit it off at once. They both had the same strange sense of humor, and Jeff, Danielle, and Steve rolled their eyes more than once at the two, when they giggled hysterically over something only the two of them thought funny. Steve stage whispered, "We've created a monster!" setting off Amy and Cindy again. As Cindy wandered around the living room she came across pictures of Steve and Amy snow skiing. She squealed, "Oh, I love to snow ski! I've only been once, but it was so much fun!" Then she and Amy started demonstrating how to snow plow and jump moguls, while Steve and the baby seals laughed.

Steve asked Cindy how she had ended up in foster care, and she told him about the father who left when she was five, and the alcoholic mother who left her for days at a time. Eventually someone had called CPS, and Cindy had ended up in foster care. "My case worker said my mom is most likely going to lose custody, and I'll be in the system as long as I'm a minor." Everyone said they were sorry to hear that things were working out that way. Cindy just shrugged. When they left, Amy said to come back anytime, and Cindy smiled. As they rode their bicycles home she commented, "I like them. Do you mind if I go back to visit?" Danielle laughed. "I think they would like that a lot. You and Amy are weird the same way." Jeff agreed. "We're too intense for them. It's nice for them to be around someone normal," and Cindy laughed. "I will, then."

Jeff and Danielle were still training five nights a week with Mike and working on their own or with him on Saturday. They were also still growing, and were above average height and weight, and definitely above average strength. Each could perform handstand pushups with one hand, and they were obviously bulking up. In February Mike added combat medical training, and they learned CPR (on a CPR dummy Mike borrowed from somewhere), bandaging and stabilizing broken bones, IV procedures, penetration wounds with severe bleeding, emergency medical evacuation procedures, and more. They had custom dog tags made with their names and blood types on them. This training went on for weeks, with class work and fieldwork.

One evening when they knocked on Mike's door for training, Mac was there with wooden practice swords, and he announced that they would be learning to fight with swords, which would also train them to fight with sticks, pipes, and other similar items. Their eyes lit up. Being able to fight with whatever was at hand sounded good, but swords sounded amazing. An hour later, they were not so sure. Even though Mike had been pushing them relentlessly for almost two years, they were sweating hard as they used muscles repeatedly in ways to which they were not accustomed. Their wrists were sore, and their forearms were burning. However, they were learning quickly, soaking up the knowledge like sponges, and by the time Mac called it quits for the evening, even he was smiling.

Mike did not let it end there. Pointing at Jeff he said, "Jeff has just been hit in the arm with shrapnel. It cut a vein and broke his arm. Get the bleeding stopped, the arm stabilized, and call in a med evac. Danielle grabbed her backpack and pulled out supplies. Soon, she had the pretend bleeding slowed if not stopped, the arm splinted and strapped, and using her pretend radio had called in a chopper, popped smoke to identify their location, thrown Jeff over her shoulder and carried him to the helicopter when it landed, being careful not to bang the injured arm. When Mike declared himself satisfied, Jeff and Danielle cleaned up all the used supplies and threw them in the trash, resupplying Danielle's backpack from Mike's first aid stores. Their backpacks now contained an interesting assortment of items not typically found in a 9 year old's backpack: sterile gloves and wipes, all types of cravats and gauze bandages, different sizes of medical tape, trauma shears, medical Cyanoacrylate glue, and more. They were not up to sharps such as catheters yet. That would come later. The backpacks would definitely raise an eyebrow if searched, though.

Jeff and Danielle had resumed their nighttime visits to the Strong house, and Elizabeth had been watching them. She had developed a sense for the times someone was in the back yard at night, and more than once, she had awakened during the night, looked out the window, and seen two figures with King, usually lying on either side of him using his large body as a pillow. She was even beginning to think she might know who it was. To test her theory, one evening in March when she felt they might come that night, Elizabeth carefully printed a homework question on a piece of paper with a request for help and, while her mother was putting away laundry, taped it to King's collar. She slept through the night, and the next morning she jumped out of bed and rushed to see if her question had been answered. The paper was still taped to King's collar, but when she removed and opened it, she found her question had been carefully answered with diagrams and simple explanations. Holding the sheet of paper over her head she danced around the kitchen singing, "I know who it is, I know who it is!" Michelle stared at her in amazement and said, "Child, what has gotten into you this morning?" Elizabeth handed her the sheet of paper, and Michelle examined it asking, "What is this?" Elizabeth explained how she had written the question on the paper and taped it to King's collar the night before, and this morning the question was answered. Michelle responded, "This is a little scary! And why are you singing you know who it is?" Elizabeth laughed, "It's the baby seals! I know it is! I've seen them in the back yard leaning on King, and I know that's who it is!"

Michelle didn't know what to think, whether to be happy or sad or mad or something else. "Why wouldn't they just knock on the door like normal people?" Elizabeth shook her head. "I don't know. Maybe they don't think they know us well enough. We only saw them for a couple of weeks years ago. Maybe they're the ones helping us, and they don't want us to know it's them!" The payment of the utility bills had continued, as had the weekly gift cards. Try as she might, she was unable to find out who was paying her bills, or where the gift cards were coming from. Still, with the additional financial help, she was finally able to put a little money aside for emergencies and no longer felt like she was one disaster away from financial meltdown. However, Michelle was focusing on the idea that her daughter had seen someone in the back yard and not told her, and Elizabeth, realizing her possible error in letting this particular piece of information slip, was beating a hasty retreat to get ready for school. Michelle was having none of it. "Elizabeth! You march yourself right back in here, young lady!" Elizabeth shuffled her way back into the kitchen looking as innocent as possible. "When did you see someone in our back yard?" The young girl gave a shrug and murmured, "Lots of times. I wake up during the night and look out my window and they're there, leaning on King. If King likes them, can't I like them, too? He wouldn't like anyone bad." Michelle was in a quandary. She didn't want to tell Elizabeth she couldn't trust King's judgment, but there were some strange things going on, and she didn't like not knowing. So she said, "Next time you see someone in the yard, you tell me, hear?" and Elizabeth agreed that she would.

One evening in April, Jeff and Danielle were sitting in the Brown's living room rolling weights tied to a cord onto sticks to strengthen their wrists and forearms. Cindy was watching them and asked, "Now what are you doing?" Danielle answered, "Strengthening our wrists and forearms." Cindy rolled her eyes. "Okay, why?" Jeff responded, "It's good for using swords." Cindy rolled her eyes again. "Again, why? Do you think you're going to be attacked by people with swords in this neighborhood?" Danielle laughed. "Not really, although you never know. But we like swords. You might, too. You should try them." Cindy laughed. "No thanks. You two are already starting to look like freaks. I don't want muscles like that. But I mean that in a good way." Jeff pretended to kick at her, and she moved out of the way. "Seriously, why are you learning to fight with swords?" Danielle responded, "It doesn't have to be swords. It could be sticks or pipes or anything. But swords are just cool. They can be beautiful, and it helps us focus and not think about other things." Cindy snorted. "You really need a new way to fight. I know a thousand isn't enough. One thousand and one might cut it. So what are you working on now?" Jeff told her, "We'd like to set up more women's shelters, especially for women with children that need some place safe to stay. We really don't like abused kids." His eyes grew dark for a moment, and then he shook it off. Cindy looked at them as though they were crazy. "How are you going to do that? Are you rich, and I don't know it?" Danielle replied, "We know a lot of grownups. Someone will be able to do what we want." Another Cindy eye roll. "Good luck with that." They continued discussing what it would take to set up women's shelters as Jeff and Danielle rolled the weights up and down.

Early the next month Jeff and Danielle went to visit Marcus. They found him sitting on his front porch reading his Bible, and climbing the steps they sat cross-legged near him until he finished and looked down at them. "Hello, Jeff. Hello, Danielle. How are you today? What brings you to my doorstep this fine morning? I haven't seen you since you gave me that check, but I have already put it to use." Jeff replied, "We know. We've seen the kids doing stuff around the neighborhood. So, do you know the women's shelter up the street?" Marcus replied, "Yes, I do. It's a fine place run by fine people. It's a shame there are so few." Danielle asked, "I don't suppose you know a couple who could run a place like that?" Marcus didn't even have to think about this one. "I know two couples who I think would be excellent at this. They have the heart for the work, and it so happens they have the knowledge for it as well." Jeff asked, "What would it take for them to be doing it?" Now Marcus sighed. "The money. Money to buy the houses, money to pay them to live on, money to support the women and children who would live there. Chances are they would be coming out of a situation that would require support while they put their lives back together. As a matter of fact, it has been on my heart a great deal lately. I've spent some time driving around, looking at houses and neighborhoods, praying over them, asking for direction. So, why are you asking about this?" With a smile he asked, "Did you want to fund this, too?" Danielle answered, "Yes. Can you tell us how much you'd need?" Marcus eyed them speculatively. "There would be startup money to buy the houses and get them ready and then ongoing costs for maintenance, utilities, salaries, supplies, and the like. Say $300,000 to start and $200,000 a year after that." Jeff nodded. "Could your church watch over it and make sure it was done right?" Marcus nodded. "The church is small, but it is mainly older people, and there's a lot of experience there, including people who have run businesses, plus accountants and contractors, you name it." Danielle smiled and said, "Tell us how much you need and when. Give us a couple of days." Marcus frowned at the two of them sitting on his porch. "Who is watching out for you two and keeping you from getting into trouble? What are you, nine? Two nine year olds should not be doing the things you're doing." They just stared at him. "Okay, last time you were here I asked you if you were Christians, and you said you were mad at God. What did you mean? Jeff explained what had happened to them, and Marcus said, "You're those children. You know God loves you and is watching over you." He saw their faces grow stony. "You know we can't always see what God has planned. Shoot, we seldom see what God has planned. When I was playing football, I had no idea I'd be pastoring a church one day, yet here I am, and in a position to help you with your plans as well." Silence. More stony looks. He continued, "I'm not sure I should be helping you with this plan of yours." They stood up to leave, and he added, "But I will. I can see God is working in your lives. We'll see where it leads." He held out his hand, and one by one, they put their smaller hands in his and shook. As he watched them walk down his sidewalk, he sent up a quick prayer, "God, please watch over them, and send them the right person at the right time to lead them back."

Jeff and Danielle were walking side by side in a wooded area east of the city. They had continued their shooting training on this land after the unwanted attention at the gun range. The land was owned by a buddy of Mike's named Stuart. He had been a member of Mike's team in the military and had retired about the same time as Mike to these 1,000 acres of trees, brush, fish ponds, and gullies. Shorter and leaner than Mike, his appearance was bearded and scruffy, and he could switch very quickly from down home friendly to cold as ice. He took great delight in calling Jeff and Danielle the baby seals, and they took it with friendly resignation. Today they and Mike were helping him clear his property of wild hogs that were tearing up his garden and destroying the land for other wild animals. There were two herds that Stuart knew of, and today they hoped to eliminate one of them. As the four walked through the brush and trees to the area Stuart thought most likely to contain them, they fired on any movement or shadow in the area ahead of them, less concerned with scaring the feral hogs away than ending up in the middle of them. And they were still surprised by the herd. Just as Jeff and Danielle passed on either side of a tall oak tree, a huge boar charged, apparently out of nowhere, straight at Danielle. She calmly leveled the AR15 she was carrying and fired. Or she would have had the gun not misfired. In a fraction of a second, the boar was on her. The others had their hands full, as the boar was not alone. The humans had come upon the herd which had remained still and hidden even with the occasional firing of guns drawing closer to them. Ten pigs, a mixture of sows and young hogs, joined the boar in its rush, and everyone was firing. As the boar reached Danielle, she jumped and pivoted in the air so that as the boar passed under her and hooked with its tusks she was three feet over its head and parallel to the ground. It immediately pivoted and charged back, but she had touched down lightly behind him and leaped for a branch three feet over her head. On the other side of the tree, Jeff had also leaped for a branch and was now hanging by his legs, holding his body close to the branch, and firing down into the herd. Quickly, Danielle jacked out the misfired round and started shooting into the herd, beginning with the boar that was charging back and forth beneath her. In seconds, all of the feral hogs were dead, and Jeff and Danielle dropped to the ground to join Mike and Stuart. Stuart just shook his head and smiled, but Mike looked at Danielle and asked, "What happened?" She shook her head and said, "Dunno." Stooping, she picked up the unfired bullet from the ground and looked at it. There was a dent in the primer where the firing pin had struck it. She showed it to Mike. "Primer didn't fire." Mike shook his head. "Those primers practically never misfire, but leave it to Murphy, when they do, it's at the worst possible time." Then he added, "Let's get to it." Working quickly they dragged all of the animals, except the boar, a hundred yards to a clearing that could be reached by pickup. Using a 2X4 ramp, they hoisted all nine hogs into the bed of Stuart's pickup, and Stuart took off for a neighbor's house where the hogs would be processed into bacon, pork chops, sausage, etc. Mike, Jeff, and Danielle walked back into the trees with a pair of shovels, and Mike watched while Jeff and Danielle buried the boar. Finally, they headed back to Mike's truck. As they walked along Mike told the two, "Y'all did good today. Danielle, I only saw what you did out of the corner of my eye since there were hogs charging everywhere, but it looked pretty amazing. And I noticed both of you only used one round per hog. You didn't leave much for me and Stuart." Jeff and Danielle just grinned at him as they climbed in the truck for the drive to the neighbors to help with the butchering. Just another successful milestone in their training.

Jeff and Danielle were sitting in Danielle's room working on more songs for Terry. Cindy was cross-legged on the floor leaning against the wall listening to the back and forth conversation. They had finished songs about the dive crossing the lake, the feral hog hunt, learning to fight with swords, their birthday party, working at the women's shelter, and fighting with the gang. Today they were working on one about learning medic training. Some of the songs were funny, some were sad, some were frankly scary. Cindy commented, "All of your songs tell stories about your life, don't they?" Danielle shrugged, "The newest ones do. It's a good way to remember." Cindy frowned, "The pig one is scary. Are you sure people want to hear that?" Jeff smiled and said, "Maybe. Maybe not. But you know how people like to be scared, as long as they're comfortable while they're listening. Terry mostly sings at clubs, so people will be sitting with their friends, sipping on something, and listening, so they'll be fine." Cindy wasn't convinced. "If you say so. At least you got to eat them. I like bacon. And ham. And sausage." They had brought some of the meat home for the Browns who were quite happy to receive it.

Marcus also received a supply of meat, which pleased him no end, although he wasn't thrilled at the way they had acquired it. "The people you are hanging around with have no more sense than the hogs you were hunting, and they are probably just as mean. However, I do love fresh pork, so thank you, children." They took this opportunity to discuss the women's shelters, and he told them that the houses he was interested in were for sale, the two couples were ready and willing to take on the challenge, and they were ready for the first block of money. "Is there anyone at the bank you trust to tell what you're doing? Two nine year olds writing these kinds of checks is going to raise some eyebrows." Jeff just said, "We'll see."

Marcus' words were prophetic. That evening they transferred funds from their stock account to their bank account, and when the money was deposited and showed available, they wrote a check to Marcus and delivered it to him. The day he deposited the check, Jeff received a phone call from Adeela asking to speak with him and Danielle. The following day they rode their bicycles to the bank and sat in her two visitor's chairs while she examined them. They waited patiently, and finally she said, "I happened to notice an interesting transaction in your account this week. You moved in a large sum of money from a stock account and then wrote a check for that amount to Pueblo Community Church. It was flagged because of the amount, and I happen to know the account belongs to two nine year olds. Would you mind explaining what you're doing? And where the money is coming from? And does anyone know what you're doing besides me?" Danielle calmly answered, "Setting up women's shelters, the stock market, and no." Adeela sat back in her chair. "Setting up women's shelters is nice. Do you have a trust fund? And what do you mean no one knows what you're doing?" Jeff took his turn, "We day traded in the stock market. We gambled." He shrugged, "We won. And no one knows about this account but us. We would like very much to keep it that way." Adeela sighed. "Would you at least let me know when you write big checks like this, $10,000 or larger, so I have a heads up?" Danielle smiled and said, "No problem." As they left the bank after this little meeting Jeff remarked, "I wonder if she could set up a charity or something for us? Then the charity could write the checks, and it wouldn't be us doing it." Danielle added excitedly, "And Marcus could be on the board. And maybe Steve and Amy. And Angela. It would mean more forged signatures, though, which might be bad." Jeff frowned, "Maybe so. We'll see."

Robert Freedman passed them as they were riding back to the Browns and pulled over to chat. They had seen him every week since they resumed homeschooling, and, when he could, he always pulled over to say hi and talk for a few moments before continuing on patrol. Today the first thing he said after hi was, "Michelle tells me someone has been paying her utility bills and putting gift cards through her mail slot. You wouldn't know anything about that, would you?" They stared at him blank faced. "I thought not. You two are really good at not showing anything. You'd be good at poker. She also says someone has been sneaking into her yard at night to visit her dog. Know anything about that?" More blank face. "And why haven't you told her you live in her neighborhood? I thought you were friends." Danielle explained, "She only saw us for a couple of weeks, and we were just more patients. We really like her and Lizzie, but we didn't know if she would want to be our friends." Robert snorted, "She likes you just as much as I do. Go tell her you are her neighbors. And stop sneaking into her yard at night." With that he drove away. Jeff and Danielle looked at each other, and Jeff asked, "What do you think?" Danielle shrugged, "It would be nice to visit her and Lizzie. She may be mad since it's been over a year." Jeff winced. "Let's get it over with this evening."

At 7:30 that evening, they were knocking on Michelle's door.

They heard running, scraping, "It's them!" more scraping, and the door opened. Lizzie stood there beaming. "Hi! Come in. We're just eating dinner. Mom brought Chinese food. Want some?" Michelle walked over and first Danielle and then Jeff hugged her. "Look at the two of you. You have grown! Where are you living now? Come sit down! Want some Chinese food?" Jeff and Danielle thanked her and explained that they had just finished dinner. Then Jeff told her, "I live on Cherokee, Danielle lives on Navaho." Michelle stared at them. "That's a block away. You've lived a block away for a year and a half? Why didn't you come by? Does Robert know where you live? Why didn't he say anything?" Now there were tears running down her face. "I don't know whether to be mad or sad or what." Danielle sighed. "We messed up. We didn't know if you would want to be our friends, or if we were just patients. We're sorry." Elizabeth pointed at them and said, "You're the ones who washed King that day he smelled. And helped me with my homework. And were always in our yard at night visiting King." Jeff smiled. "Guilty. But Officer Freedman is going to have to speak for himself. We never told him not to. It just never came up. We've only seen him a few minutes at a time when he's on patrol." Michelle rubbed her eyes. "Are you the two paying our bills? And putting gift cards through the mail slot? How would you be doing that?" They just looked at her blank faced, and she continued, "Of course that isn't you. Robert says it isn't him. It's driving me crazy!" Danielle asked, "Are you seeing Officer Freedman?" and Elizabeth started singing, "He likes her. He wants to kiss her." Michelle swatted at her and said, "You stop that, or I will post your baby pictures all over the internet for your friends to see." She added for Jeff and Danielle, "He comes by occasionally. He's a very nice man." Elizabeth rolled her eyes, Jeff and Danielle laughed, and the tension was broken. Jeff and Danielle spent the next two hours bringing them up to date with a sanitized account of what they had been doing. Elizabeth was excited about all they were doing, but Michelle was clearly not buying all of it. "You are leaving a lot of things out, and I will be watching you. I know where you live now," she threatened. They smiled at her and left, promising to visit more often.

They were back at Stuart's place training in the woods. Mike's friends had taken a real interest in the baby seals, as they all called them, and were putting real effort into their education. Today was a paintball gun day. They loved paintball gun day! Ever since the first day they had been introduced to it, they looked forward to paintball days. Mike, Mac, Stuart, and a fourth of their friends named Travis were teamed up against Jeff and Danielle. Jeff was hidden behind a log and covered in a ghillie suit. His line of sight was limited to four inches left and right and two inches up and down through an open space in the log. It was not his first choice for a hiding place. It was also not his second, third, fourth, or even fifth. It was frankly a bad hiding place that no one in their right mind would choose. However, he and Danielle had planned an ambush that they thought would work against the four men tracking them. He had set up carefully camouflaged sites at his first two choices, but not the third, with sticks barely visible that might be rifle barrels. Danielle was up in a tree out of sight on the side away from Jeff's hiding place. She was completely out of sight from Jeff's side and fairly well hidden from the other side, although probably not from this team. Their hope was that Jeff would get one shot, and, when the others focused on him, Danielle would pick off one or two more and drop from the tree, and then she and Jeff together would take whoever remained. Probably what would happen was the four men would ambush Jeff and shoot Danielle out of the tree, but only time would tell, and they both settled in to wait. Half an hour later Jeff saw movement as a leg passed ten yards in front of his log. He touched the trigger and focused on staring at the ground, thinking of nothing. People could actually feel someone staring at them, and he definitely did not want any of these men feeling his stare. Patiently he waited for another pair of legs, and as they started to pass by the log, he fired, smearing the leg with blue paint. He immediately heard paint splatter on his log, then Danielle firing from the tree, and the paint hitting his log stopped. He saw and heard Mike firing at the base of the tree Danielle had dropped behind. Mike saw the movement to his side and dropped to the ground, but Jeff was already shooting, and Mike was hit several times with blue paint. Jeff dropped back behind his log as orange paint balls hit around him. Then Danielle was firing again, there was shouting, and the rain of orange paint balls stopped. Jeff stayed where he was until the four men stood up, each one marked by green or blue paint, and then Jeff and Danielle joined them in the clearing. Neither of them had paint on them, and Mike shook his head in disgust. Mac commented, "Not a bad ambush. I thought for sure you were in the third best spot. Nice job on the fake guns in the one and two spots." Mike added, "You two are too tricky for your own good. If Danielle hadn't had your back, you'd be dead. If all of us hadn't focused on your ambush, you'd both be dead." Jeff smiled. "Danielle always has my back. We counted on you facing the ambush. This probably wouldn't have worked against amateurs." Travis commented, "I think it's about time to throw them out of a plane," and Danielle asked excitedly, "Really?" Mike gave them a look and said, "Middle of September." All six headed back towards Stuart's house with the twins happily discussing the upcoming parachute jump.

Chapter 12

Jeff and Danielle stood at the long table and packed their parachutes. For the past four weeks they had been training for a parachute jump, but, just as they had spent weeks breaking down guns for Mike and cleaning them before he ever allowed them to fire one, now they had spent weeks training without actually making a jump of any kind. They had learned to land. They had learned to collapse a parachute. They had learned to control spin and roll. Today they were actually going up in an airplane. Danielle would be in tandem with Mike, and Jeff would be in tandem with Travis. All of Mike's friends had their jump wings, but Mike and Travis loved to parachute and had made hundreds of jumps. It really paid to know someone with a plane, just like it paid to know someone who would let you shoot on their property, especially someone who didn't mind bending a few laws here and there. At any rate, today would be their first jump, and they were excited. It was a perfect day for parachuting. The sky was clear and cloudless, the wind was only two knots from the south, and the temperature was a pleasant 85 degrees. Both Mike and Travis had cameras mounted on their helmets to record the experience, and Stuart would be videoing from the ground. Before climbing on board the plane, Mike and Travis checked their jump suits and straps, then had Jeff and Danielle check them. Both men had left a couple of things wrong to see if

Jeff and Danielle would find them, and they did. Danielle would have done an eye roll, but thought it best not to. They climbed in the plane, and Mark, the pilot, took off. He climbed to 12,000 feet, and when he waved that they were almost to the drop zone, Mike had Jeff and Danielle stand up, and he and Travis connected the straps that would hold the two children to the men's bodies during the jump. As they reached the drop zone Mike stood in the door, tapped Danielle on the shoulder to make sure she was ready, and when he received her okay sign, he jumped. Travis did the same with Jeff, and the baby seals were in freefall. For this first jump Mike and Travis just fell. No spins or rolls, just the feeling of flying with the wind roaring past and the ground below rushing up to meet them.

Danielle thought she was in heaven. She felt as though she could go anywhere and do anything, that if she aimed her body right she could land in the Brown's back yard. Or Michelle's. Wouldn't King love that! Jeff was also enjoying the fall, but differently. He was enjoying the view and the sight of the ground rushing up at him and knowing that the solution was riding on Mike's back. For both of them the fall was over much too soon. At 2200 feet, Mike and Travis released the main chutes, and their descent slowed to a crawl as they drifted downwards. Danielle thought this was wonderful, too. The view was magnificent, and it was so peaceful floating slowly to earth under the colorful canopy. Her fingers itched for paper and charcoal to draw it. Jeff was also enjoying the view, although his mind was busy composing music. And planning strategies: if it was him, where would he set up checkpoints? Ambushes? Where would he dig in troops?

Mike and Travis guided the parachutes back and forth over the drop zone, but eventually landed near Stuart's truck. Jeff and Danielle helped collapse the parachutes, and both kids raised their arms in the air and screamed. Danielle yelled, "That was incredible!" Jeff smiled happily as they helped carry the parachutes over to the truck where Stuart had set up tables. The parachutes were placed on the tables, and under the watchful supervision of the three men, Jeff and Danielle repacked the parachutes, which were stored in the back of the truck with the tables. Everyone climbed in, and Stuart drove back to the airfield and a waiting Mark. Mike and Travis strapped on their parachutes again, everyone performed inspections, they climbed back in the plane, and Mark took off.

This time Mike and Travis opened the parachutes as soon as they cleared the plane, and they spent the descent maneuvering across the sky, back and forth, across and around the drop zone. Again they landed near the truck, and again there were yells of delight from the two youngest in the group. Jeff and Danielle repacked the parachutes, carefully inspecting for any damaged or worn risers or panels, and they were soon driving again to the airfield and a waiting Mark.

They made five jumps that day, with one used to demonstrate roll recovery, one for spin recovery, and one from a distance away from the drop zone to demonstrate the distance the parachutes could cover. At the end of the day, after the parachutes were packed for the last time, they drove to the plane, and Mike handed Mark the envelope of cash Jeff had given him that morning when they climbed in Mike's truck at his house. The envelope contained the amount Mike had recommended to cover Mark's expenses, plus some for the favor. Mike had never asked where Jeff and Danielle found the money to pay for the various expenses, such as the ammo they used or the parachute lessons. He had some ideas, but he thought this was something he did not need to know. As long as they weren't robbing banks or selling drugs he was okay with it, and he was pretty sure that wasn't where the money came from.

Sitting in Mike's living room reviewing all the video from

the day on Danielle's laptop, she asked, "When can we make solo jumps?" to which Mike answered, "After we've made twenty-five tandem jumps, and after you're 10." "10!" Danielle exclaimed. "That's months away!" Mike said dryly, "It's not as though you'll be sitting around waiting for the time to go by. You have eight more statues to find in the lake, and we might squeeze in a dive trip to Florida in the next week or so." That perked them up. Jeff asked, "Really? Like real open water? In the ocean?" Mike answered, "Yes. You'll need to get written permission for the trip and for medical care if it's needed. Can you get those?" Jeff and Danielle nodded yes. Mike continued, "Okay. Plan on leaving next Saturday and returning the following Saturday. We'll go by the dive shop one evening this week to get the gear we'll need. Probably Samantha will go with us, and Stuart. We'll stay with a friend of mine. Mark will fly us down and bring us back. I'll let you know after I talk to everyone." At a questioning look from Jeff he added, "I'll let you know how much cash to bring."

Danielle used Mike's computer to print out the forms they would need signed, and she and Jeff left. As expected, Danielle had no trouble getting signatures from Susan. Jeff had less trouble than he expected with his mom. When Jeff told her he needed her signature on consent forms to take a road trip with Mike she only raised an eyebrow and commented, "Nice friends you've made. Are you getting any sort of education at all?" before signing the forms. Since Jeff always gave her the reports Kathy Shepherd sent home, he just shrugged. On Wednesday evening, Mike told them, "Everyone is in. Let's go get the gear," and they piled into the truck for the drive to the dive shop. Walking through the dive shop, Jeff and Danielle stopped at every customer they passed to comment on whatever they were looking at, make suggestions and recommendations, and encourage them to buy the item. When they reached the counter where Samantha was waiting, she laughed and said, "I love it when you guys come up here.

Our sales go up twenty percent!" Jeff and Danielle smiled at her, and she lifted three large backpacks onto the counter. They were unzipped and the contents examined, but everything they needed was there, including the O_2 and bailout bottles. Samantha asked if they were excited, and two pairs of bright eyes looked up at her as Jeff and Danielle exclaimed at the same time, "Oh, yes!" Danielle handed Samantha her debit card; Samantha, warned by Mike, didn't say anything about the card. She just ran it and handed the slip to Danielle to sign. As she took the signed slip back from Danielle she laughed and said, "I love to see your signature. You write so well! Okay, we'll see you Saturday morning at the airfield." Mike, Jeff, and Danielle shouldered the packs, and, leaving behind the line of customers ready to buy, they loaded everything in the truck and drove back to Mike's.

The next two days went by in a blur of homeschool, exercise, shooting, and parachuting. They spent Thursday afternoon at Stuarts, running through the combat range with its popup targets. Friday they made two tandem parachute jumps with Mike and Travis. Early Saturday morning the five travelers met Mark at the airfield and loaded their gear on the plane. By 7:30, they were in the air. The entire week had been beautiful, and today was no exception. The sun rose in a clear, blue sky as they left the city behind. Jeff and Danielle were perched at the windows since this was their first flight in an airplane, except for the parachute jumps. Danielle was busy drawing the ground below, while Jeff took snapshots of the passing landscape, some with the wing of the plane showing, some without. After watching the scenery for about an hour, the two pulled schoolwork out of their backpacks and occupied themselves. Mrs. Shepherd had given them plenty to do and was not going to allow them to fall behind during this trip. They put everything away while they landed in New Orleans to refuel, watching through the windows as the city, the lake, and the Gulf of Mexico came into view. Danielle had never seen the city from this view, and she was fascinated, telling Jeff what she could remember from her time here. They were soon in the air again, and as they flew over the Gulf for this leg of their journey, Mike went over the safety precautions, should they be needed, pointing out the two inflatable life rafts stowed in their containers near the door and the parachutes hanging at the rear of the plane. For a moment, the thought flashed through the two young minds that if the plane was in trouble they would get to use the parachutes and the life rafts, but then they came to their senses.

As they reached their cruising altitude over the Gulf, Mark asked Jeff, Danielle, and Samantha if they wanted to come up and see the controls. Jeff and Danielle scrambled to the front with Samantha following at a more normal pace. Mark gestured Danielle into the copilot seat and began explaining the controls as Jeff and Samantha watched. The three took turns sitting in the copilot seat, studying the controls and watching out the windshield. As young people can do so well, Jeff and Danielle asked a million questions which Mark answered patiently. Eventually they returned to their seats, Jeff and Danielle to continue their schoolwork, Samantha to take a nap. In the late afternoon, they landed at Key West where Mike's friend David met them in a large SUV. After greetings all around, they loaded their gear in the vehicle, and David drove them to his home not far from the airport. Although there was enough time to get in one dive that day the adults decided to wait until morning so Jeff and Danielle could see the clear water of the keys first thing on a new day. For Jeff and Danielle it was like waiting for Christmas morning. They tried to act cool and adult, but everyone could see they were jumping out of their skins with excitement.

The next morning arrived eventually, warm and clear, a perfect day for diving. After breakfast, David ferried the group and their gear to his dive boat, where everyone checked their gear and prepared it for diving. The boat was cast off, and David took them to the first dive spot of the day, which would be a 100' dive off the wall. As he anchored in 25 feet of water, secured the boat, and put out a dive flag, everyone changed into their dive gear. Danielle's one-piece swimsuit covered most of her scars, but as Jeff pulled off his t-shirt to pull on his wet suit there was a gasp and a sudden silence behind him where Mike, Stuart, and Samantha were suiting up. Jeff and Danielle looked over their shoulders and saw Samantha with her hand on her mouth and Stuart with a murderous expression on his face. Mike had seen it before on earlier dives and was somewhat accustomed to it, but Stuart and Samantha were unprepared for the crisscross of scars on Jeff's back and the four round scars from the nails. Also, since the two had taken off their gloves and shoes to put on their wetsuits, the scars on their hands and feet were visible. Jeff and Danielle raised their eyebrows questioningly and then continued putting on their wetsuits, his in the blue he favored and Danielle's in her trademark green. Wiping a tear from her eye, Samantha finished positioning her gear. With a glance at Mike, who had not paused, Stuart also situated his unit.

When everyone was ready, they jumped overboard. As soon as the three adults were in the water they all turned to watch Jeff and Danielle as they saw the underwater beauty for the first time. Both were just hovering in the water looking around, pointing out different things to each other, their hands flashing in sign language. Samantha swam over and handed them each a plastic chart showing much of the sea life in the area. They looked at the charts and gave her big okay signs with both hands. Then Dave led them slowly to the side where the bottom sloped off steeply and took them on a tour at 100 feet. With all six using rebreathers, there was very little noise. The adults were constantly pointing out new sights for Jeff and Danielle, and the two were going into sensory overload. At one point Mike gave them the sign for stay alert, and they snapped out of their dream state and started paying attention to the water around them, just in time to see the large shark swimming out of the depths of the wall towards them. The four adults moved in front of Jeff and Danielle, as the shark swam at Mike, who fended it aside with his shark billy. The shark circled and charged again, this time towards Stuart, who also fended it aside with a shark billy. After one last run at David who also turned it aside the shark swam lazily back into the depths along the edge of the wall. Samantha swam up to Jeff and Danielle to make sure they weren't frightened, watching them sign to each other as she approached. At her okay query, they both enthusiastically gave her the okay sign, and she just shook her head in amazement.

At this point, it was time to return, and David led them back up the wall and into the shallower water. Mike swam in front of Jeff and Danielle and signaled, "Where's the boat?" Jeff checked his compass and pointed. Mike signaled, "Lead the way," and Jeff and Danielle swam slowly towards where Jeff estimated the boat was anchored. Right where he thought it should be, they came upon the anchor buried in the sand, and Jeff gave Mike the okay sign, which he returned. They all rose to 15 feet for a safety stop and then surfaced to climb aboard the boat, Jeff and Danielle talking non-stop as soon as they had their mouthpieces out. Danielle exclaimed, "That shark thought you were a blue tang!" Jeff laughed and said, "Ha! It thought you were a parrot fish!"

Mike, Stuart, and Samantha were sitting in the shade in the bow of the boat while Jeff and Danielle sat with David in the stern going over the fish charts Samantha had given them. Samantha quietly asked Mike, "Does Danielle's back look the same as Jeff's?" Mike answered, "I've never seen it, but I imagine it's worse." He shook his head and added, "I've never seen them act like kids before. Usually they act like feral cats. They are really enjoying this. I think if the shark had gotten past us they would have attacked and made sushi out of it."

After resting on the boat and checking their gear, they made shallow dives for the rest of the day, ending up by snorkeling around the shallower reefs. The adults took turns with Jeff and Danielle, who only came out of the water to rest and eat when ordered to. The adults were caught up in the children's enthusiasm, and showed them everything new they could think of. Finally, as it neared sunset, a happy and exhausted Jeff and Danielle climbed onboard for the last time that day, and David steered the boat back to port.

This set the pattern for the rest of the week. They spent the days diving, one deep dive and the rest of the time in shallower water. They went diving on two nights, which delighted Jeff and Danielle even more, if possible. Thursday afternoon they stayed at fifteen to twenty feet, and Friday they snorkeled around the reefs. During the evenings, Danielle made quick charcoal sketches of their day, while Jeff downloaded pictures to his laptop. Saturday they loaded all of their gear back in the plane, Mark having flown in earlier in the day from Miami where he had spent most of the week. They said goodbye to David who had made out quite well for his week's work, everyone having chipped in for his charter fees, the food they'd eaten all week, and some extra for staying with him. In Jeff and Danielle's case, it was a fair amount extra, which they had given him through Mike. The flight back went as well as the flight in with the brief stop in New Orleans to refuel. Jeff and Danielle spent the time on their schoolwork, which might possibly have been slightly neglected amidst all the diving.

Their progress in school could only realistically be compared to their previous work, though, since they were well ahead of their age level. Their companions had commented among themselves more than once over their education level, especially when Samantha found them working on algebra schoolwork and even more so when she, Stuart, and David had discovered the language a day program (which Mike was already familiar with). It hadn't seemed that strange when they were overheard speaking French. Danielle was, after all, originally from New Orleans. However, the next day was elvish day, which raised some eyebrows. Jeff and Danielle had finished reading *The Lord of the Rings* trilogy and had made a solid start on their elvish/English dictionary. Additions were made regularly as their vocabulary grew, but they could converse quite easily in the language. Spanish day didn't come as that much of a surprise except it made four languages being spoken. Japanese day was a real eye opener, though, and sign language day just made everything, like, Wow! Samantha looked at Mike and shook her head, and he smiled and nodded. Special kids.

Life settled back to normal after their return from Key West. They trained every day: weights, hand to hand combat, medic training, weapons training, SCUBA training, parachuting, navigation, and more. This was on top of their regular home schooling. Thanksgiving came and went. Jeff and Danielle had lunch with Michelle, Elizabeth, and their family along with Robert, who had graduated in his relationship with Michelle to meeting the family. Cindy ate Thanksgiving dinner with Steve and Amy, with Jeff and Danielle's total approval. Christmas also came and went. On a visit with Steve and Amy over the holidays, Amy tried again to tell them how much God loved them. Danielle looked at her and said, "Amy, does God know everything?" to which Amy had to answer yes. She knew where this was headed. "So He knew what was going to happen to us. Can God do anything?" Again Amy had to answer yes, although she added a qualifier with, "If it is in His nature." Danielle nodded. "So, He knew what was going to happen to me and Jeff and didn't stop it. He could have kept us from going home, He could have made my mom and stepdad too sick to do it, He could have had someone show up before it even started. But He didn't. He didn't do anything." Amy tried to tell them that all things work together for good for those that love God, but she could see they weren't buying it, and she sighed to herself. Sometimes you just can't explain things to someone until they are at a place where they can understand. Jeff added, "If you and Steve had known what was going to happen would you have stopped it if you could?" and Amy had to say yes. No matter what the results might have been, they would have tried to stop it. "Isn't God at least as good as you and Steve?" It was an argument she could not win, at least not now, and she let it drop.

Chapter 13

Finally, they were 10. For their birthday, they gave themselves baby seal charms. During a chance stop in a jewelry store on their way home from the Shepherd's one day, something caught their eyes. Custom ceramic on metal charms were a specialty in the store, and one charm shaped like a baby seal quickly led to a discussion with the jeweler, Ann, about making two custom charms to match the pictures on their webpage. When she told them that it would be no problem to make the two custom charms, Danielle sketched the two baby seals for her, both white, hers with a gold rim, Jeff's with a silver rim, hers with green emerald chips for eyes, and Jeff's with blue sapphire chips for eyes. Ann loved the pictures and asked where they came from. Danielle explained that they had been nicknamed the baby seals while they were in the hospital, and that she was green seal, and Jeff was blue seal. Ann was enchanted with the story and stored it away to tell her friends. They discussed the size the charms should be, and when she gave them a price, Jeff paid. Ann promised to let them know as soon as the charms were ready, hugged them both, and they left, knowledge of the baby seals having spread a little farther. More pieces of a plan years in the future were falling into place. The charms were ready in time for their birthday, and they were completely thrilled, adding them to their dog tag chains.

February was also the month they made their first solo skydive. Having made more than 50 tandem jumps, Mike felt they were ready for a solo static line jump as a birthday present. The day was clear with temperatures in the 60's and a light wind. They were covered from head to toe in high altitude jump gear with no skin showing in anticipation of the colder temperatures when they left the plane. Mike had added military grade communications packages as well. As Mark climbed to 12,500 feet, Mike briefed them again on emergency procedures. Jeff and Danielle listened intently with at least half their attention, as they anticipated the thrill of their first solo jumps. THEIR FIRST SOLO JUMPS! After what seemed like hours, Mark signaled that they were over the jump zone. Danielle would jump first, followed by Mike, with Jeff and then Travis behind him. Danielle stood in the door and connected her static line. Mike tapped her on the shoulder, and she shoved herself out the door, Mike close behind her. Jeff stepped to the door, connected his static line, and at Travis' tap threw himself out the door. He had bare moments of freefall before his parachute opened. After checking for anything wrong, he looked around and saw three parachutes around him drifting slowly downwards. Both he and Danielle had managed not to scream for joy as they left the plane, but it was a close thing. Mike said into his throat mike, "Make a counter clockwise circle around the drop zone." Danielle immediately made a slow, sweeping turn to her left, keeping Stuart and his truck in the center of her circle. Mike, Jeff, and Travis followed suit. All four settled gently to the ground, and as soon as Jeff and Danielle had collapsed their parachutes, they began a happy dance, fists in the air while the three men looked on proudly. After letting them celebrate for a bit, Mike said, "So is that it for the day, or do you want to make another one?" Immediately the dance ended, and they carried the parachutes to the truck. With the light wind blowing, they would have to pack them inside, which they did in Stuart's barn. In less than an hour, all four parachutes were packed, and they were back at the airfield loading everything on Mark's plane.

They made two more skydives that day, and while the last two did not have the excitement level of the first one, they were still incredible. Sailing on your own through the sky with your friends around you was even better than SCUBA diving. Okay, maybe not better than SCUBA diving in the Florida Keys, but at least as good in a different way. As they packed the parachutes for the last time before heading home, Jeff and Danielle bumped fists. Another first. And they still had solo free falling to look forward to. Life was good.

Their tenth year was also the year they saved Officer Freedman's life. It was a Thursday in late April. There had been light rain most of the day, and the streets were slick. Jeff and Danielle were riding their bicycles home in the dark after a long day of homeschool, music lessons, visiting with friends, and various errands. As they entered the bike trail from the parking lot, the sound of racing cars and a rapidly approaching siren caught their attention. Since this was not an out of the ordinary situation in the city, they would have ignored it and gone on their way, but suddenly headlights swept into the parking lot behind them and accelerated into the grass of the park a mere forty feet away.

The park was bordered on three sides by trees with the parking lot the only open side, and the car's driver soon found himself blocked, as he slid to a stop in the wet grass, and sat parallel to the parking lot spinning the wheels, as he tried to get tire traction to return the way he had come. A police car screamed into the parking lot and slid to a stop parallel to the other car about fifty feet away, and to their amazement, Officer Freedman jumped out and crouched behind the engine of the car, gun drawn.

Minutes earlier in the evening, Officer Freedman was on the last leg of his beat for the evening, and on the way to the station to sign out, when he pulled alongside Officer Doug Renart who seemed to be heading back to the station instead of starting his beat. Robert pulled alongside and called out, "Hey, Doug, are you heading in the wrong direction?" Doug shouted back, "Man, it was such a sideshow leaving the station today, I forgot my vest. I have to go back for it." Robert gestured towards a parking lot, "Pull over there, and I'll give you mine. I'm heading in." Doug nodded and pulled into the lot. Robert climbed out of his car, pulled off his shirt, removed the vest, and handed it to Doug who asked, "Are you sure?" As he pulled his shirt back on and buckled on his service belt, Robert said, "Yeah. I'm finished for the night. What could happen in a couple of minutes?"

What happened was an armed robbery at a liquor store when Robert was almost to the station. Three men ran out of the store right in front of him, shooting back inside. Jumping into a car, they screeched away. Robert turned on his lights and siren and roared in pursuit, calling in the situation and requesting backup. The chase was short, as the car he was pursuing turned almost immediately into a parking lot and then into the park, which was a dead end, indicating someone unfamiliar with the area. There was little light except from the headlights of the cars and then from the muzzle flashes as the three men piled out of the car on the side away from Robert and began shooting at the police car. With his heart in his throat and cursing the complacency that had led him to give away his bulletproof vest, Robert alternately returned fire over the hood of his car and ducked behind the front wheel as bullets smacked into the side of the car, whined off the hood, or whizzed by overhead. In short order he had fired all of the rounds in his weapon and the spare magazines in his belt pouches and was down to his backup weapon. There was spare ammunition in his briefcase in the trunk, but he didn't think they would wait while he opened the trunk to retrieve it.

It was while he was crouched behind the wheel of his car that one of the three men ran outside the immediate glow of the headlights and approached Robert's position from the side. Jeff and Danielle saw the movement, and laying their bicycles silently in the grass, crept back down the bike path to approach Robert's car from the side. When they reached a spot where they could see Robert, they also saw the man approaching from the side. As he stepped into the full glow of the police car headlights Robert also saw him and raised his pistol to fire, but it was too late. The man fired first, and Robert went down. Danielle threw a knife and the man fell. Jeff and Danielle crouched down and raced to Robert's side, where he lay, trying to get to his feet. Jeff knelt by his side and applied pressure to Robert's chest, while he reached in his backpack for medical supplies. Danielle picked up the gun from the ground, where Robert had dropped it when he fell, and took a quick glance over the hood of the car to where the remaining two men crouched over the hood of their car peering at the police car.

Then, having oriented herself, she popped up, fired two quick shots, and dropped back down. Together they pulled Robert's shirt up and applied field dressings as he yelled at them to get away. Over and over, they assured him that everything was fine, they were all safe, and help was on the way. They could hear sirens approaching from all directions, and just before the first police car pulled into view, Danielle laid Robert's backup weapon near his hand, and the two children faded into the night.

Sgt. McKowsky was the first one to arrive, followed shortly by five others. Spreading out they quickly found the three men lying in the grass, and Officer Freedman lying on his back by his patrol car. At first glance, it appeared that Robert had been able to take on all of the gunmen and get a dressing on his chest wound before passing out. The paramedics arrived while Sgt. McKowsky was directing the setup of the crime scene, and as they placed Robert on the stretcher one commented, "Nice work on the field dressing on his chest and back. It probably saved his life." Then they were gone, leaving behind a puzzled sergeant. Freedman might have been able to put the dressing on his chest (although where had he gotten the dressing?), but there was no way he put the one on his back. Then, he put it in the back of his mind as the crime scene team arrived along with reporters and television crews, and things got crazy.

The story developed, and Robert was declared a hero. Ballistics proved the two men by the car were killed with Robert's backup pistol, and it was assumed he had thrown the knife that killed the third man. Before an Internal Affairs man could question him, Sgt. McKowsky stopped by his room in the hospital to see how he was and take a stab at clearing things up. Robert was lying in the bed, tubes attached and machines beeping, when McKowsky walked in. Michelle was standing by his bed talking to him with two children standing beside her. He thought at first it was two boys because of the short haircuts, but then he recognized them as the two young friends Robert spoke about occasionally, and a question formed in his mind. Michelle and the two children said goodbye to Robert, nodded to McKowsky, and left, and the sergeant walked over to stand next to the bed. Looking down at Robert he said, "It was the two kids wasn't it?" Robert stared up at the sergeant and said, "It would probably be best all-around if it wasn't, don't you think?" McKowsky said, "What are you going to tell IA?" Robert shrugged and winced, "I exchanged fire with the perps until I was shot. I don't remember much after that. Maybe eventually it will come back to me." McKowsky smiled. "Everyone thinks it was all you. Maybe most of it was. The two by the car were killed with your pistol. In the confusion, the police think the paramedics put the dressing on your back, and the paramedics think one of us did it. There are no witnesses that saw anything else as far as we know. It looks pretty cut and dried." He paused and added, "Do you think they'll be okay?" Robert gave a sad smile. "Yes. They're incredibly tough." It wasn't brought up again, and the story stood. Robert didn't like taking credit for it all, especially since he was pretty sure he hadn't done any of it, but he was willing to stand by the story to keep Jeff and Danielle out of harm's way. If any of the other officers had an idea of the truth they didn't say, but there were a lot of officers watching over the two children now, and a call of baby seal down was likely to get as quick and massive a response as officer down.

Jeff and Danielle had watched from the trees as the police swarmed the area and Officer Freedman was loaded into an ambulance. Then they continued down the bike trail to the Brown house. As they rode Danielle asked, "Do you think he'll be okay?" Jeff answered with assurance, "Yes. It was a clean wound, it's patched properly, and they'll have him at the hospital in a few minutes. Plus he's tough. He'll be fine." She asked, "Do you think he knows what we did?" Jeff thought for a few seconds. "If he doesn't know now he'll figure it out. He knows he didn't throw the knife. He may not know if he's the one who took down the other two. For all he knows he may have hit them. He may wonder why you shot his gun, though."

Then Danielle asked the question important to her. She didn't mind that she had killed the three men. They deserved it for hurting her friend. Maybe she had always been this way. Maybe what her mom and stepdad had done had broken her. Whatever the reason, she was okay with their deaths at her hands. The important question was, "Do you think he'll still like us?" Jeff snorted. "We saved his life! Besides, we owed him our lives. He'll still like us. He may even be proud of us." After a pause he added, "Do you think we should tell Mike?" Danielle shook her head. "I don't think we should tell anyone. Let them all come to the right conclusion: Officer Freedman did it all." Jeff said, "They're going to wonder about the dressing on his back. He might have put the one on his chest, but not the one on his back. That might be a problem."

However, the incident passed and time moved on. Jeff and Danielle were making five parachute jumps per week and numerous SCUBA dives at the lake. Visibility was very poor at the lake compared to Key West, but it was an adequate training ground for the lessons Mike was giving them. They were gaining a lot of hours and experience, and Jeff carefully recorded it all. Once a week they parachuted with weapons onto Stuart's ranch, moving, after landing, to the combat course where Mike and his three friends took great pleasure in assaulting them with various popups: some of men with guns, some of men with babies, some of women with guns, some of women with groceries. Anything they could think of to stump the baby seals. From the combat course, they would leave the rifles behind and take up paint guns. Sometimes they would set up an ambush, sometimes they would work by themselves or with one or more of the men to find and destroy an ambush. They were growing very skilled. They were also growing paranoid and too much on edge. As they walked through trees anywhere, all they saw was places for cover and places from which an ambush might come. It was the same when they walked or rode their bicycles in the city. Every alley entrance, doorway, and dumpster was suspect. Steve and Amy noticed. The Browns noticed. The Shepherds noticed. Mike and his friends noticed.

Things began to change, and some things happened that gave them a chance to calm down. First, Mike eased up on the training. They still exercised and shot and went skydiving and SCUBA diving, but now it was for sport and fun. They had friendly competitions on the gun range with bets made and drinks raised, although for the twins the bets involved pushups (which they seldom had to do themselves) and the drinks raised were water. Skydives were made for the joy of flying and floating and the view, and the SCUBA dives were to find all of the statues in the lake. Finally Mike and Travis took them camping in Colorado. They spent a week backpacking in the mountains, living on self-heating MRE's and water from rivers run through purifying kits. After a week, Jeff and Danielle were starting to feel less on edge, and Mike felt a bit guilty since he had an ulterior motive in the back of his mind. For a few weeks, he had been thinking about a final test consisting of a 25-mile trek through the Colorado mountains. This year's trip would familiarize them with the territory. His plan was to have them do it on their own with him and his friends tracking them the whole way by GPS. Maybe sometime next year. This trip was peaceful and uneventful: no bears, nobody injured, no illness. Jeff and Danielle returned home, if not relaxed, then at least less paranoid.

On the first Saturday of June, they began explosives training. Stuart had a plot of land he wanted to clear, and C4 was his method of choice. With Mike watching, Stuart went over the explosive power of C4 and demonstrated its stability by cutting off a piece, lighting it, and using it to heat a pan of water. Next he pointed out a stump that needed to be removed and placed some C4 in a hole he had already dug, added the detonator, and connected wires to it which he ran back to the electrical switch; there, he connected the wires, then had everyone duck, and triggered the explosion. When the dust and debris had settled, he showed them the hole in the ground where the stump had been.

Jeff and Danielle were excited. This was majorly cool! Blowing things up! Stuart began explaining to them the placement of explosives, what different shapes did, how to estimate the amount needed for a particular job, tamping the explosive so the force didn't dissipate, etc. Then he told them to pick the next stump, choose the location for the C4, and decide how much to use. They put their heads together, walked around and around the stump, studied the roots, chose the spot, and estimated the amount to use. Mike watched all of this and shook his head, thinking again that he had jumped on the tiger's back and had no idea how to get off.

Stuart just went over their choice, corrected them on the amount to use, and told them to dig their hole. It didn't take them long to discover that to use the location they had chosen, they would have to blast a hole through the roots to place explosives there, so they ran through the exercise again. Stuart reviewed it and told them to dig their hole.

It took four tries before they found a location that would work and they dug a suitable hole. Then using one of her knives, Danielle cut a piece of C4 off the block Stuart handed her and placed it carefully in the hole. She added the detonator and connected the wires to it. Then she ran the spool of wire a safe distance away and everyone took cover as she connected the ends of the wires to the electrical device to set off the detonator. She raised her hand, and when the other three gave her the okay sign, she squeezed the handle. There was an explosion, and when the dust cleared and debris quit falling, they went to investigate. Where the stump had been there was a hole, somewhat larger than the one Stuart's charge had made. He said, "You used too much. You have to take the texture and depth of the soil into account. This patch was lower and closer to bedrock than mine was so you got more effect. Nice hole, though."

Jeff looked at Mike and asked, "What would you do if we messed up and blew ourselves up?" Mike shrugged. "Bury you and report you missing. You could be on a milk carton." Danielle looked at Jeff and said, "Good to know," and they all laughed. They spent the rest of the day blowing up stumps, and by sunset there was nothing left in the plot but shattered pieces of wood and holes in the ground. Mike said, "Tomorrow you can gather up all the wood and fill in the holes." He laughed at their expressions and added, "Did you think it would be all fun and no work?" Jeff replied, "We can hope." They spent the next two months blowing things up and filling in the holes. To Mike and Stuart's amusement they seemed to have a natural talent for all things destructive.

To finish out the summer the Browns took Cindy and Danielle (and Jeff after he paid his own way) on a three day cruise with three days in Orlando at the end. The kids had their own cabin on the ship and their own room at the hotel, which kept everyone happy. Life on the ship was just fun. Jeff, Danielle, and Cindy only saw the Browns at dinner. There were activities all day long, and the three totally immersed themselves. Since the 10 year olds and 13 year olds on board had different activities, Jeff and Danielle didn't even see Cindy all that much. On the first evening, Jeff and Danielle were sitting at a table in the kid's only lounge, chatting with two friends they had made, Beth and Jamie, two sisters. Beth had a disease that messed her up physically but left her brain totally intact. Jamie had rolled Beth's wheelchair up to the table where Jeff and Danielle were sitting and asked if they could join them. Beth began speaking to her sister, and Jeff and Danielle cocked their heads. The words were garbled, but they could almost understand. When Jamie grabbed two soft drinks from the counter Danielle said to Beth, "Say something else." Beth said a few words, and the twins looked at Jamie for a translation. Jamie, looking a little defensive, said, "She asked what you want her to say." Jeff asked Beth, "Where are you from?" and when Beth said, "Pensacola," Jeff nodded. Danielle asked, "How many are in your family?" and Beth replied "Four. My mom, dad, and me and my sister," and it clicked in their brains and they could understand the words just as though it was a foreign language. From then on, they didn't need Jamie to translate, and the four of them began conversing like old friends. Beth was 13, and her sister was 15. The laughter at their table brought Cindy and other kids over. It turned out Beth had a great sense of humor, and as kids arrived at the table, Jeff and Danielle taught them how to understand Beth. At one point Danielle glared at Beth and said, "Stop being lazy about the way you say your words," and Beth's enunciation improved as Jamie looked on in amazement. Their table became the center of the room, and Beth became the center of attention at the table.

On the next day of the cruise, there was a snorkeling expedition for the young people on the ship, and Jeff and Danielle were signed up for it. When they found that Beth was not, they went with Beth and Jamie to talk to the parents. They found that there was really no physical reason why Beth couldn't be in the water. It was more a matter of the parents' fears. Jeff and Danielle convinced them that Beth would be fine, and they finally consented to let her go with the rest. Jeff and Danielle promised to help Jamie look after her. As they stood in line, moving Beth's wheelchair along with the rest of the youth waiting for the boat to take them to the snorkeling site, Beth asked if they had ever been snorkeling before. Jeff and Danielle looked at each other and laughed but just said yes. When the boat arrived and the gangway was laid, Jamie rolled the wheelchair across. Jeff and Danielle helped lower it to the deck as the crew looked on with some confusion. Danielle said, "Everything will be fine," and as soon as the wheelchair was in place everyone else boarded. There were over 20 young people of varying ages on the boat, and many, having been at their table the night before, clustered around Jeff, Danielle, Cindy, Beth, and Jamie, chattering about what they would see.

As the boat arrived at the snorkeling site, Danielle prepared Beth's mask and snorkel, while Jeff helped Cindy and Jamie. During this time, most of the others had jumped into the water. Jeff told Danielle, Cindy, and Jamie to go ahead into the water. When they were in place he adjusted Beth's mask and snorkel, set his own in place, picked her up, walked to the side of the boat, and as the crew were beginning to say, "Wait a second, " he jumped in, shielding Beth's body with his own. As soon as he hit the water, Danielle was there to help orient Beth. She was breathing through the snorkel, and her excited eyes were shining through the facemask. Leaving her with Danielle, Jeff grabbed his fins off the boat and put them on. Then, motioning for Cindy and Jamie to follow them, they each took one of Beth's arms and began towing her through the water, pointing out the various fish and sea life around the coral reef. Danielle had brought along one of the fish charts from Key West, and as they spotted various items on the chart, she checked them off and showed Beth, then Cindy and Jamie as well. Soon many of the young people were clustered around them, and Jeff and Danielle would take turns swimming down to point out some item of interest to everyone.

The time in the water passed very quickly, and it seemed like no time at all before the crew was calling everyone back to the boat to return to the ship. Jeff told Danielle and Jamie to go ahead on board, and when they were in place, he slung Beth over his shoulder and climbed the ladder to the deck. Jamie, Danielle, and a large crew member helped put Beth back in her wheelchair, and, as the boat cruised back to the ship, they wrapped Beth in towels to warm her back up after her time in the water. Soon, as had happened the night before, there was a crowd gathered around her as she made wicked and funny remarks about her first snorkeling adventure.

It was on the cruise that Jeff and Danielle thought about giving baby seal charms to their friends. Not just anyone, but really close friends. Special friends. Starting with Beth and Jamie. Cindy. Officer Freedman for sure. Michelle and Lizzie. Steve and Amy. When they found that Beth and Jamie would be doing the same three days in Orlando and even staying in the same hotel, they called Ann from the next port to see if she could make three of each charm and ship them overnight to their hotel in time to give them to the three girls before everyone left for home. Ann assured them that she could, and the first baby seal charm giveaway was in the works.

In Key West, they could have called David and gone SCUBA diving, but made the choice to go snorkeling again instead. The joy on Beth's face made it all worthwhile, and the look on her parents' faces as they watched her smiling and the other young people treating her like anyone else was an added bonus. There was a tense moment when one of the boys, trying to show off as boys will do, made an unpleasant comment about Beth, and the group of young people felt as though they had suddenly found themselves swimming with a pair of great white sharks they had thought were porpoises. Before Jeff or Danielle could move towards the boy, one of the other boys punched him in the arm and said, "Not cool, dude!" The boy had the good grace to look ashamed and apologize, and the moment passed, but the other young people maintained a respectful distance from Jeff and Danielle after that.

On the last night of the cruise, a group of young people were sitting around a table with Beth, Jamie, Jeff, Danielle, and Cindy in the center, when Beth asked why the twins always wore gloves. "Is it a fashion statement?" Jeff smiled and said, "No. We have scars that bother some people. It's just easier to wear gloves." Of course, everyone was curious after that and wanted to know about the scars, so Jeff and Danielle pulled off their gloves. Everyone clustered around to see, and James commented, "Those aren't bad!" which led to everyone showing off their scars from sports injuries, falling on various objects, etc. Finally, Beth asked, "What made your scars?" and Cindy said, "Nails." The table grew silent, and someone said, "What?" thinking they had not heard right. Cindy repeated what she had said, and Jamie asked, "By who?" Danielle said, "My mom and stepdad." A girl at the end of the table asked, "Why?" and Jeff said, "Because they were crazy." Jamie asked, "What happened to them?" and Cindy answered, "The stepdad was killed by the police when they arrived, and her mom died in jail the next week." Then everyone had to know the story, and Jeff gave a shortened, cleaned up, suitable for young people, version of the story beginning with the Fourth of July concert. A girl who had walked up said, "I was at that concert! You were the two kids with 2nd Street Bible Church when they sang! It was awesome! Then no one ever heard from you again after that one CD. You two look really different. I wouldn't have recognized you at all, especially with the short hair! Why hasn't the church released any more albums?" Danielle said, "We don't go there anymore," and the girl asked, "Did you change churches?" Jeff replied, "We don't go to church," and he and Danielle picked up their gloves and left. The girl looked around and said, "Uhoh, what did I do?" Cindy explained what she knew about them, what she had learned from Steve and Amy, and the training they had been going through for the last three years. The boys especially were really impressed to find out that they were being trained by an ex-Navy SEAL, and Beth commented that that explained why things had gotten so tense when the boy had made the unpleasant comment. Cindy added, "Yeah, he's lucky he's still in one piece. They are very protective of their friends."

The group broke up then, some to roam the ship, some to dance and listen to music. Jamie pushed Beth around the deck, and they came across Jeff and Danielle in the young people's music room. Jeff was playing a keyboard, and Danielle had taken over one of the guitars. They were playing songs from a new album Jeff was writing for Terry, songs with a nautical flair based on their time in Key West, songs about sailing, diving, and just sitting around. Jamie parked Beth's wheelchair and sat in one of the chairs near the instruments, and they both listened to the music. When they finished with the song they were playing Jamie, said, "I hope we didn't do anything wrong asking about the gloves. We didn't know it would lead to what it did." Danielle put the guitar on its stand and she and Jeff walked over to the two girls. Danielle put her arms around Jamie and Jeff put his arms around Beth. Jeff said, "It was okay. We just didn't want to keep talking about it. It's in the past, and we're moving forward. Besides we

199

have three days of fun and excitement on land starting tomorrow." They sat in the room, played music, and talked until midnight when everyone headed back to their rooms.

The ship docked the next morning, and the Browns with Cindy, Danielle, and Jeff were joined by Jamie, Beth, and their parents on the shuttle ride to Orlando and their hotel for the next three days. It was three glorious days of nonstop entertainment, eating, walking, and riding rides. Many things required no special accommodations for Beth's wheelchair, and the twins and the two men quickly devised a system for the quick movement of Beth from her wheelchair to a ride and back to the wheelchair. Every day after lunch, they would sit inside one building or another, while Beth took a nap and the others chatted or roamed nearby, continuing on after Beth had a chance to recharge.

At the end of the second day Jeff, Danielle, and Cindy were in their room getting ready for bed. Jeff had a strange look on his face, and Danielle asked him what was wrong. Jeff said, "I don't know. I just feel weird. About Beth. I really like her. She's funny and smart, and I like being around her. It feels strange to be away from her." Cindy started laughing. "You have a crush on her! Dude, she's my age!" Jeff frowned and asked, "What's a crush?" Cindy rolled her eyes at Danielle and said, "Really? What's a crush?" Danielle gazed at her calmly and repeated Jeff's question, "What's a crush?" Cindy eyed the two of them in amazement. "Where have you two been all this time? A crush is when you really like someone, and you feel all goofy, and you want to be around them all the time, and you feel weird when you're not with them." Jeff looked horrified. "Does it go away?" Cindy had to sit down she was laughing so hard now. "Well, yeah. Usually. Eventually." Jeff asked, "How do I get rid of it?" Cindy was shocked. "Why would you want to? People live to get this feeling, and hate when it goes away." Jeff was getting angry. "I can't feel like this. It gets in the way of everything. I can't even think!" Cindy frowned. "I don't think you can just get rid of it. It has to wear off." Danielle patted his arm sympathetically and said, "We'll ask Michelle when we get home. You only have to get through one more day. Try to act normal." Cindy added, "I've heard a cold shower helps, but I don't know. I've never had a crush." Then she collapsed laughing into the chair again.

Jeff spent the third day trying to act normal and must have succeeded to some extent because no one commented on his strange behavior. That evening when Jeff and Danielle checked at the front desk their package from Ann had arrived, and they guided Cindy, Beth, and Jamie into the restaurant for late night snacks before everyone went to pack. When everyone was seated, Danielle put the package on the table and said, "We have something for y'all." Slicing the package open with a knife that miraculously appeared and disappeared, she took out the six clear plastic envelopes and handed three to Jeff. "We have something for you to remember us by. We've never done this before, and it only occurred to us on the ship. We weren't sure they would get here in time for us to give them to you." With that, she handed a green seal charm to each of the three girls. Jeff added, "And one from me as well," handing each of the three girls a blue seal charm. Danielle took the three chains Ann had sent out of the package and gave one to each girl, and, as Cindy and Jamie strung their charms on a chain and fastened it around their necks, Jeff took Beth's charms, strung them on her chain, and fastened it around her neck. There were tears of happiness running down the three girls' faces while Jeff maintained a calm exterior over roiling internal feelings. Jeff kept telling himself, "Crush. Ignore the crush." He still found the feelings disturbing to say the least.

Beth asked, "Do you have these, too?" and Jeff and Danielle pulled out their dog tag chains to show the charms hanging there. Jeff said, "They're numbered, too. Ours are number one. Yours are two, three, and four. We couldn't decide what to do with ours.

At first, I just wore mine, and Danielle just wore hers. Then I wore hers and she wore mine. Finally, we decided to both wear both. Anyway we know who has what number, and if one turns up somewhere we'll know whose it is." Beth and Jamie's mother showed up then to fetch the girls to pack their luggage, and having already exchanged email addresses and phone numbers, everyone went back to their rooms. It had been a marvelous end to a wonderful trip.

Soon after arriving home, Jeff and Danielle stopped by to see Michelle and Elizabeth. Jeff explained to Michelle what Cindy had said about him having a crush on Beth, told her what he was feeling, and asked for advice. "How do I get rid of this feeling?" he asked anxiously. Michelle smiled at him indulgently and said, "You don't like it?" "No," he exclaimed. "It doesn't feel real. It's like I feel good just thinking about her, and I don't feel good when I'm not around her. It reminds me of being on painkillers in the hospital. What is it, and why is it happening to me?" Michelle tried to explain. "When you find someone you're interested in your body produces chemicals that make you feel like you're feeling now." A horrified expression appeared on Jeff's face. "What?! Why?" Michelle continued her explanation. "It gives you incentive to get to know them better. Many people don't take advantage of the opportunity they've been given and just spend their time enjoying the feeling. Then, when the chemicals stop, they're no further along in knowing about the other person than they were at the beginning. But, if you take that time to find out about them, what they like, what you have in common, and so on, then when the chemicals stop you may not even notice." Jeff laid his head on the table and mumbled, "So what do I do?" Michelle rubbed his back and asked, "Were you planning to stay in touch?" There was a mumbled, "Yes. I do like her. She is fun to talk to." Michelle said, "Then I think there's nothing for you to worry about. You'll exchange emails and maybe phone calls, the feeling will fade, and you'll be friends or you won't. Either way you'll be fine." Jeff looked up into Michelle's eyes. "Is that why my mom does drugs? So she can feel like this whenever she wants?" Michelle sighed and said, "Maybe. At least some of the time." For the first time Jeff had a little insight into his mom that he had never had before. All in all the conversation with Michelle was a mixed bag of results, and Jeff had to be satisfied with that for the time being.

Chapter 14

For their eleventh birthday, Jeff and Danielle got tattoos. They weren't tattoos of baby seals as one might expect, but Japanese symbols. After much discussion with the Fujioka family, Danielle chose the Japanese symbols for faith while Jeff chose those for hope. They deliberately chose the first two spiritual gifts from 1 Corinthians 13 instead of the greatest. Danielle, with Ayame's supervision, painted them on paper, and the two presented them to Bear at his tattoo parlor in their old neighborhood, along with the permission forms from Susan and Marilyn. They had surprisingly little difficulty getting the forms signed. Susan didn't really care one way or the other, and Marilyn's only question had been "How are you paying for this?" to which Jeff responded, "It's a birthday present," not specifying from whom. Bear looked at the two drawings and said, "Sure. No problem. Who wants to go first?"

Danielle took off her jacket and sat on the stool in her halter-top. Bear put the permission forms in a binder and sat down behind her, making no comment about the wrist sheaths on each arm. Jeff pointed out on her left upper back where they had marked out the spot for the tattoo the night before. There had been much discussion regarding size and location. He had the same spot marked on his right upper back, although he had pretty much left it up to Danielle to pick the location and size.

Bear stared at the scars crisscrossing her back, confirmed that she wanted the tattoo in green, and began. After four years of learning to block pain from exercise and combat training, the pain from getting a tattoo was no big deal, and Danielle waited patiently without moving for Bear to finish. It took a couple of hours. The characters weren't particularly complex, but there was more than one. Eventually Bear placed his tools on the tray and with Jeff's help arranged two mirrors so Danielle could see the work. When she grinned and gave a big thumbs up he bandaged it. Then it was Jeff's turn, and he removed his shirt and sat on the stool. Again, Bear stared at the scars on his back and made no comment about the two wrist sheaths. Danielle showed him where to place the tattoo on Jeff's right upper back, showed him the color of blue to use, and Bear set to work. He finished by lunch, they went through the mirror, approval, bandaging routine, and he went over the care instructions as Jeff and Danielle paid him. He shook his head as they left the store, watching as they unlocked their bicycles and rode away, remembering a day about four years earlier when two ambulances had screamed past as he worked on a special job, carrying two kids to the hospital after her parents had tried to kill them.

In March, Jeff and Danielle went to visit Alice who took them next door to see Eunice. They had not been to the house since Eunice moved in, and the change was startling. It was as though this was a house built to the same floorplan as the one Danielle had grown up in, but one she had never lived in. Everything from her past was gone, down to the carpet and wallpaper. With Eunice leading the way, Jeff beside her, and Alice following, she was given a tour of the house. Her old bedroom was now a workroom for making quilts. As Eunice showed them the room she asked, "Would you like me to make the two of you quilts?" Danielle smiled and replied, "Maybe someday. Right now they wouldn't fit in our backpacks." A puzzled Eunice asked, "What do you mean?" Jeff said, "We only keep what will fit in our backpacks." Alice exclaimed, "Why would you do that?" to which Danielle replied, "It's just where we are right now. Things are always moving, and we travel light." Eunice shook her head, saying, "Well I'll make them anyway and hang on to them for you. Green for you, right," looking at Danielle. When she nodded Eunice added, "And blue for you," to Jeff, and he nodded as well. Room by room Eunice led them through the house, and with each difference a little more of the old memories faded away to be replaced by new ones.

When she led them into the kitchen Danielle ran her hands along the counter tops, the front of the refrigerator, and the top of the breakfast table. Then she turned and hugged Eunice, who hugged her back and said, "Now, now, child. Now, now." Alice looked on with tears in her eyes. Danielle eventually released Eunice and looked at Jeff who smiled and bumped fists with her. Eunice led them into the back yard and explained where Alice would be planting her a garden: the Perineal Winecups here, the Sundrops there, Cutleaf Daises next to the fence, and so on. Eunice asked, "Maybe you two could help if you have time," and Danielle murmured, "We'd love to." After the garden had been laid out in their minds, they all ambled back to the kitchen, where Jeff and Danielle helped prepare a meal. There was much oohing and aahing over the speed with which the twins cut vegetables and prepared a sauce for the meat. They explained about the cooking lessons Susan had given them, and both women complimented them on all they had learned. Eunice chuckled, "I might need a lesson or two myself from the two of you," and Jeff and Danielle grinned.

Eunice prayed over the meal, and the conversation turned towards what was going on at 2nd Street Bible Church. Eunice asked, "Do you two still have your mad on at God?" Danielle sat stony faced, and Jeff simply said, "Yes." Alice sighed. "You two are going to lose this fight." After more stubborn silence, Alice changed the subject. Jeff and Danielle helped clean up the kitchen after the meal, and rode off on their bicycles. As they pedaled down the street Eunice said, "I hope it doesn't come too hard when God sets them straight. They've been mad a long time." Alice shook her head. "Me, too. Those are two stubborn kids. Probably how they survived the way they did." The two ladies went inside and lifted Jeff and Danielle up in prayer.

Jeff woke early one morning in June feeling a strong need to buy a house. He didn't know why, but the feeling said soon. Grabbing his phone, he sent a text to Danielle. "Need to buy house." She immediately texted back as though she were awake and thinking the same thing. "Roger that. Do you know why?" Jeff, "No. Do you know by when?" Danielle, "Soon. Do you know where?" Jeff, "No. We can start looking after class." When school at the Shepherd's was over for the day they rode their bicycles to Michelle and Lizzie's house, and as they were riding down Sioux in front of the High School they saw Pastor Marcus standing in front of a house with a new For Sale sign in the front yard. They looked at each other and said together, "This is the house." As they stopped beside Pastor Marcus, he smiled and said, "Hello, children. Looking for another house to buy?" He was not completely surprised when Jeff answered yes and asked if he knew the owners. Marcus answered, "Yes I do. Jack and Margaret Parker. They belong to my church. Just retired and want to move to Florida. Fine folks." Danielle asked, "When do they want to move?" to which Pastor Marcus replied, "As soon as they can get what they want for their house. They're in no great rush, and they'll eventually get what they're asking. Probably not right away, though." Jeff asked, "What do they want for it," and Pastor Marcus told him. Danielle asked, "Do you think we can see it? And can your church buy it for us?" Pastor Marcus laughed. "Child, what do you two want with another house? Setting up another women's shelter? And you two need to set up your own charitable organization to do your buying. But yes, I imagine we can see the house right now if you want." Jeff jumped in, "If we set up a charitable organization, would you be on the board of directors?" Pastor Marcus looked a little startled as he led them up the walk to the front door. "I suppose I'd consider it. We can talk about that later," and he rang the doorbell. Margaret Parker answered the door with a smile and a "Hello, Pastor. Welcome. Who are your young friends?" She was a large woman with mostly gray hair and a smiling face. Jeff and Danielle liked her immediately. Pastor Marcus introduced Jeff and Danielle and asked if they could see the house, as they knew someone who might be interested in buying it. Margaret assured them she would be happy to show them the house and led them on a tour. She was obviously proud of her home, and Jeff and Danielle noted it had been well maintained. She said, "The roof is new this year, the heat pump was new last year along with the water heater, and the appliances are three years old. We're leaving all of them with the house, including the washer and dryer. Won't need them where we're going." She even showed them the attic, and Jeff and Danielle inspected everything thoroughly, just as Mike had taught them. Margaret commented to Pastor Marcus, "For a couple of kids they certainly know a lot about houses." Pastor Marcus just smiled and nodded. When Jeff and Danielle reappeared Margaret continued, "The carpet and linoleum need to be updated, but we painted everything inside and out last year." Jeff said, "The house is obviously in excellent condition. We think our friend would be interested in it. How soon could you move?" Margaret laughed and said, "Hon, if they bought the house today we would be out by the weekend. We are that ready to move. We've loved this house, but we're ready for the next part of our lives." Danielle thanked her, and she, Jeff, and Pastor Marcus left. As they walked back down the front walk, Jeff and Danielle looked at each other and nodded, and then Jeff said to Pastor Marcus, "We want the house. Will you buy it for us the same as the ones for the women's shelters?" Pastor Marcus replied, "I imagine so. Can you tell me why you want this one?" Danielle said, "We don't know yet. We just know we need to have a house soon." Pastor Marcus looked at them severely and said, "And you two don't think God moves in your lives?" Jeff just shrugged, and Pastor Marcus sighed. Get your money together. As soon as I have it, I'll make the pitch to the Parkers. With that, they separated, and Jeff and Danielle went on to visit Michelle and Lizzie.

The next day after school, they went from the Shepherds to the bank to talk to Adeela. They explained that they would be donating a large sum of money to Pueblo Community Church and would be transferring the money to their bank account from their online account. She looked at them speculatively. "Have you two considered setting up your own charity for this sort of thing?" Jeff nodded yes and said, "We don't want to lose control of the money. Can you help set it up?" Adeela asked, "Who are you trying to protect it from?" and Danielle answered, "Jeff's mother and my foster parents, whoever they might be. And any state appointed guardians." Adeela nodded. "Okay, I'll look into it. Thanks for letting me know about the money transfer. I'll watch for it and the transfer to the church." They thanked her and left. As they rode back towards the Brown house Jeff asked, "Do you think we should set up a charity and put all the money in it?" Danielle shrugged. "If it feels right, sure. Maybe most of the money, not all of it. It would be nice if we could get Officer Freedman and Michelle on the board. And Pastor Marcus and maybe Pastor John. And Steve and Amy." Jeff agreed, and they continued on their way.

They transferred the money that night and gave the check to Pastor Marcus the next day. He made the deal with the Parkers, and within a week of the sale, the house was empty. Some people from Pueblo Community Church helped Jeff and Danielle get the house ready for the new occupant, whoever it might be. One of the helpers was an eighteen-year-old girl named Hope who lived in the neighborhood and went to the university. She was a pretty and energetic blond who Danielle liked even though she thought the young lady was hopelessly naïve, and she often seemed to speak without thinking. She helped them shop at garage sales and thrift stores for furniture for the house, things for the kitchen, linens and bedspreads for the beds, and towels and such for the bathrooms. For no reason they could explain, Jeff and Danielle set it up for a mom and dad and two children. They thought the children would be young girls, but they didn't trust their feelings enough to match the rooms that much and made them generic. As a final touch, they added a TV antenna, TV and DVD player, cable for an internet connection, and a computer. Finally they bought a $200 gift card for gas and a $500 gift card for groceries and such. Then they waited. The house was as ready as it could be, but it wouldn't be a home until someone moved in.

Boyd and Pam Merrill were sitting in their truck in the grocery store parking lot, praying with their two daughters, Madison and Emily. At this point, they didn't know what else to do. They had left their rented home in Kentucky when they ran out of money to pay the rent. There were no jobs available, and they had come to this Texas city in the hope of finding something, but here they sat in this parking lot, the gas gauge on empty and no money to buy gas or even food to feed the hungry children. They didn't know anyone, and they didn't know what to do. As Pam looked up from her prayers, she saw two children pushing their bicycles past the truck. The children were tough looking with hair cut short in military style haircuts, but as they walked past her, something made her say, "Can you help us?" Two pairs of bright eyes looked her way, one pair green, one pair blue, and the girl said, "What's up?" Pam said, "We're broke. Do you have enough money to give us to buy something for our daughters to eat?" She felt like she should be ashamed for asking, but for some reason she wasn't. The boy said, "What do you want for them?" and she answered, "Some bread and some lunch meat would be nice." From the back of the truck one little girl said, "Turkey," and the other little girl said, "Ham." Pam rolled her eyes and said, "Turkey would be fine." The girl said, "Mustard or mayonnaise?" Again from the back one girl said, "Mustard," and the other girl said, "Mayonnaise." Another eye roll. "Mustard would be fine." The boy said, "White bread? Wheat?" Before either girl could comment Pam said, "Wheat."

The boy nodded and walked on towards the store while the girl stood by the truck. "I'm Danielle. That was my brother, Jeff. Who are you? And where are you from?" Pam smiled and said, "I'm Pam Merrill. That's my husband, Boyd. The girls are Madison and Emily. We came here from Kentucky looking for work, but we ran out of money too fast." Danielle nodded and asked, "What do you do?" Boyd answered, "I'm an all-around handy man. Plumbing, carpentering, air conditioning. I could have gotten a job doing maintenance at a school or a company if there had been a job." Danielle nodded and said, "One second," before pulling a mobile phone out of her pocket and dialing a number. "Pastor Marcus? Our family has arrived. Does the company where your church meets still need a maintenance man? He's here. We'll be taking them to the house in a little while. Want to meet us there?"

She hung up as Jeff walked back with two grocery bags and handed them to Pam. In the bags were ham and turkey lunch meat from the deli along with a loaf of white bread and a loaf of wheat, mayonnaise and mustard, lettuce from the salad bar, a bag of assorted chips, two individual containers of milk and two of water, a package of paper plates, plastic ware, napkins, and a box of sanitary wipes for cleaning hands. Pam looked in the two bags and tears started running down her face. She handed a wipe to everyone and made sandwiches, handing paper plates and milk back to the girls first, before making sandwiches for her and Boyd. Boyd said, "This is really nice, and we appreciate it, but why are you doing it?" Danielle said, "We've been waiting for you. We knew you were coming, just not exactly when. When you finish we'll take you over to your house."

The two adults looked up with some incredulity mingled with suspicion and said, "What?" "Jeff and I had a feeling, a couple of weeks ago," said Danielle, "that we needed to get a house ready for someone, so we did. Two grownups and two children. The house is ready. We were just waiting for the people to show up. And here you are." As though that was an explanation that any rational person could accept. Boyd asked, "How do we pay for all this?" Jeff answered, "When you get on your feet, you start paying your own way. When you get ahead you pay it forward. Pastor Marcus can explain. He's meeting us at the house." Then he handed Pam a gift card. "This is for gas." Another gift card. "This is for groceries and stuff." Danielle gave them a slip of paper with an address on it. "This is the house. It's close." She gave them directions. "We'll meet you there." Then she and Jeff rode off.

Pam looked at Boyd, and he said, "This is crazy." Pam said, "We prayed for help. Are we going to reject it now?" He shook his head, finished his sandwich, and drove to the gas station to fill up. The gift card seemed to have plenty to fill the gas tank, so he did. Then, following the directions Danielle had given them, they drove to a pretty house on Sioux Street. The two children were sitting on their bicycles out front. Standing next to them was a large black man. Jeff and Danielle waved them into the driveway. They parked the truck and stepped out. Pastor Marcus held out his hand. "I'm Marcus Hall, pastor at Pueblo Community Church, just around the corner. I gather you have already met Jeff and Danielle. Come on in, and I'll show you around and explain things." He led them into the house, giving them the combination to the electronic keypad and the instruction sheet on changing the combination. While Jeff and Danielle showed the girls their bedrooms, Pastor Marcus tried to explain the house, simply saying that he trusted Jeff and Danielle's instincts, that the church had bought the house, that Boyd had an interview for the maintenance position the next day, and if, when they were settled they liked the house, they could buy it from the church. Boyd and Pam were speechless. Pastor Marcus smiled ruefully. "I know. It kinda takes your breath away. Jeff and Danielle are like that. Oh, and they'll most likely want something from you in the future, like help with the women's shelter up the street."

In August, Jeff and Danielle played in Terry's band when it introduced the new album Jeff had written. It wasn't planned, but Terry, who played lead guitar and his sister, one of the keyboard players, had flown to Atlanta for a family reunion on Wednesday before the band was scheduled to play on Saturday. The early afternoon flight back should have given them plenty of time, but weather threw a wrench in the plans. First, they were hours late getting out of Atlanta, due to storms in the morning that delayed all of the air traffic at the busy hub. They could still have just squeaked in with maybe a slight delay, but a storm over the city as they were coming in to land delayed them just enough that their plane had to divert to refuel. With an hour to go before the band was scheduled to play and no chance of Terry and his sister arriving in time, and with the hotel bar already packed with their fans ready to hear the new album it was decision time. There had been flyers and word of mouth out for weeks, and now there was also a chance to open for a big name group if one important person in the audience liked the music. Finally, the drummer, Andrew, suggested getting Jeff and Danielle to fill in for the night. The discussion went back and forth between the four band members, and with half an hour to go, the decision was made to at least ask them. Marcy, the other keyboard player made the call to Danielle. She and Jeff were in the Brown's backyard fighting (of course) with practice swords when her phone rang. Marcy explained the situation to Danielle, Danielle explained it to Jeff, and they agreed. After a quick cleanup for both of them, they changed into clean cargo pants. For the occasion, Danielle wore a signature green shirt that showed her tattoo, and Jeff wore a blue one that did the same. Andrew pulled up just as they finished dressing, and with a wave to Susan and a "We're going out" they were gone.

On the drive to the bar, Andrew explained that they would be playing the songs in the order listed on the new album, and that Danielle needed to replace Terry while Jeff replaced his sister. Oh, and that Danielle would be singing a couple of solos. Danielle shrugged and said okay. At the bar, they hugged the rest of the band hello and checked out the instruments they would be playing. Right on time, they were announced, and Andrew explained the situation. "Well, two of our band members are in the air over Texas looking for a place to land. Fortunately, we had two replacement singers waiting in the wings who just happen to be the two who've been writing our music. This is probably the only time you will get a chance to hear them play, so I hope you will give them a warm welcome."

The crowd reacted restlessly at this news as the band began the first song. This was a rocking song about getting their first tattoos, choosing the patterns and the colors, and trusting Bear with their skin; and many in the audience could relate to the lyrics. Everyone enjoyed the song. There was appreciative applause when it ended, and they immediately started the next one, a funny one about learning explosives and blasting the stumps out of the ground at Stuart's place. The crowd roared with laughter at the line about sending one stump into orbit to land on Stuart's truck with the classic line, "Do you think you used enough dynamite there,

Butch?" The third one told the story of their first solo skydives, although no one knew it was about parachuting until the last line, "As I go through life on a nylon sail." Then all of the other lines changed meaning. Fourth was a song about saving Office Freedman's life, although there were no details about the incident. Still, when Robert heard the song and found out who had written it, he knew what it was about, as did his sergeant and a few others on the police force. The crowd at the bar just knew they were touched by the words and liked the tune. Next was a song that told the story of their long distance swim at the lake and Mike catching Danielle as she was about to throw a knife through his beer can, and when they sang the line, "Don't throw that knife through my beer can," the crowd erupted with laughter again.

So far, the album was doing really well. The band began the second half of the new album with a hard-hitting song about their first shark in the Florida Keys. Danielle had a guitar solo on this song, and when they finished with the line about the adults getting between the shark and the kids, the crowd was on its feet, for the solo, and for the meaning of the song. They lightened the mood with the next two songs, one about the cruise and one about the amusement park, both of which had the people smiling, especially if they had been themselves and could personally relate to the lyrics. Next to last was a song about the pig hunt, funny and scary, and finally Danielle sang a solo about visiting her house after Eunice moved in that had the crowd in tears but then saying "Ahhh" happily with the closing line, "The bad memories have all been washed away by loving hands."

As the last chord faded away the crowd was on its feet, cheering, clapping, and stomping. Everyone came up as the band left the stage to say hello, meet Jeff and Danielle, and buy CD's. Andrew put his arms around their shoulders and said, "I think we can say this album will be a success." Jeff and Danielle nodded happily, but Jeff said, "If my mom finds out about this she could really cause a lot of trouble." Andrew said, "The album only has your initials, we didn't give your last names, and don't you either. I think we've got you covered." Jeff, Danielle, and Andrew slipped out so he could take them back to the Brown house, and two hours later Terry and his sister arrived in time to hear about the gig and join in the celebration.

In September, after days of intense survival refresher Mike took Jeff and Danielle to Colorado for their big survival test. He dropped them off at the edge of the road, handed them a topographical map with a spot circled and, pointing to a spot on the map, said, "This is here. Meet me at this circled spot in five days." Then he climbed back in his truck and drove off. Jeff and Danielle sat on their packs, studied the map, and planned their line of travel as best they could from the map. There was one river to cross as well as some streams, mountain ridges, and maybe some gorges. Jeff estimated twenty-five miles, and Danielle agreed. They shouldered their packs, took a compass reading, and headed off into the forest. Unknown to them, Stuart and Travis were flanking them on either side about a mile distant, while Mike was trailing them by a couple of miles. Stuart and Travis were in radio contact with each other and Mike, who was monitoring Jeff and Danielle by the GPS devices he had stowed in their backpacks before they left his house. He did not intend to lose these kids.

The path was just a nice hike for the first couple of miles. Then they began climbing higher into the mountains, and the way was more rugged. In addition, a mile of distance walked was not necessarily a mile closer to their destination. As they walked, they watched for edible plants and animals. There would be extra points for each MRE they arrived with intact. When they paused for a lunch break, they had a delicious meal of rattlesnake and edible wild vegetation. The rattlesnake was a chance encounter as Jeff stepped over a log. First, there was a buzz as the disturbed snake coiled at the foot of the nearby tree prepared to strike. Then there was the thunk as Danielle's knife pinned its head to the tree. Since it was nearly one, they stopped to eat and rest, cooking the snake together with the plants over their backpacking cook stove. Together with some of the water they were carrying and a granola bar, it was a fine first meal, and one MRE each saved.

Early in the afternoon, they ran into a fifty-foot wall. According to the map, this ridgeline ran a few miles in either direction, and it appeared this was a low spot, so they climbed it. Putting climbing spikes on their boots and tying rope to their backpacks they went up the wall side by side, moving slowly from handhold to toehold. After an hour of steady progress with rest breaks on convenient narrow ledges, they reached the top and gazed down at the valley ahead before the next upward slope. Mike, watching from the trees below, stowed his binoculars and said into his radio, "They cleared the ridge. No problem." His radio clicked twice as Stuart and Travis responded.

Next came the trek across the valley and three miles of steady uphill climbing. In the middle of the valley Danielle asked, "Did you feel someone watching us as we climbed the wall?" Jeff nodded. "When we were about halfway up I got an itch between my shoulder blades. It was a "we're being watched" sort of itch, though, not an "I'm a target sort of itch." Danielle agreed. "Me, too. Do you think Mike is following us?" Jeff said, "Maybe. Probably. I think someone is on either side of us, too. At least a mile out. If Stuart and Travis show up at the rendezvous point I'd say they're staying with us as we move." Danielle raised an eyebrow. "How do they know where we are?" Jeff said, "I have an idea we should check our packs when we make camp for the night. See if there is anything in there we didn't pack." Danielle snorted. "If he put a tracking device on us we should tie it on a squirrel and let them follow it for a while." Jeff laughed. "It's probably part of the test to see how long it takes us to figure it out. We probably lost points for not finding it before we left his house." Danielle frowned. "You're probably right, the sneak."

They finished the hike across the valley and made their way up the opposite side, climbing around boulders, making their way past trees and brush and over patches of bare rock. As the shadows lengthened, they reached a flat space under some pine trees and picked this as the spot to spend the night. While it was still light, they stripped and checked themselves and each other for ticks. The bug juice seemed to be keeping them at bay. After dousing themselves liberally again, they dressed and set up camp. There were more wild plants and pine nuts for dinner, but they decided to eat freeze dried soup and pork jerky as well. As they munched they discussed setting a watch. Danielle asked, "Do you think they'll try to mess with us?" Jeff said, "I don't think so on the first night. Someone might get killed by accident, and besides, then we'd know they're here. I wouldn't be surprised if Mike checks to see if we set a watch, though. Two and two?" Danielle agreed, two hours on, two hours off. Jeff took the first watch. Halfway through his second watch he felt eyes on the camp and slowly moved his eyes over the surrounding area. He couldn't see anything, but it felt as though the itch came from the west, and he made a note of it. When he went to wake Danielle he told her about it, and she nodded. Halfway into her second watch the itch went away.

The second day went much as the first without the rock climbing or the rattlesnake. They climbed up and down mountains, around more boulders, through trees, and over rocky patches. Jeff took a steady stream of pictures of everything of note, including the mountain goats they saw mid-day when they stopped for lunch. Yesterday they had made seven miles. Today it would probably be five. A tough five. The pace they set was easy enough to avoid altitude sickness, and so far it hadn't been that hard. Of course, after more than four years of physical training they were both in excellent shape. Which was good in case one had to carry the other one out.

The third day made up for the second day. They reached and crossed the river. This cost them a few hours as the river was deep, wide, and full of rapids where they first hit it. After a discussion, they split up, Jeff going upstream for an hour, or until he found a place they could cross, and Danielle going downstream. When Jeff returned to the starting point Danielle was waiting, hidden in the shade of a rock. Jeff reported, "There's nothing easy upstream. Where it would be okay to cross, we would have to climb steep rock two or three hundred feet once we got across. We could do it if we had to, unless you found something better." Danielle nodded. "There a place to cross about half an hour downstream." They spent time running the river water through their filters, refilling all of their water containers, and headed downstream.

Less than an hour after crossing the river, they ran into the mountain lion. Jeff was in the lead as they came over the edge of a ridge and found the lion sunning itself on a rock twenty feet away. It seemed to be, first, hungry, and second, eyeing them as though they were plump sheep. Admittedly, they were about the size of its usual prey, but as it stalked towards them, it found these sheep had teeth. Jeff's first rock from his slingshot hit the lion in the flank causing it to growl and bite at the spot. As it turned back towards them, Danielle's rock hit it on the nose and brought it to a complete stop in confusion. Two more rocks, another on the flank and one on the shoulder caused the lion to start backing up, and two more rocks in the same places sent the lion springing away from them. After this encounter, they stopped to cut staffs for themselves, about six feet long and an inch in diameter. Staffs in hand, they continued.

Mike had watched this encounter from half a mile away with his heart in his throat. He had unslung his rifle and had the lion in the crosshairs, but it was an iffy shot with the baby seals right there. Fortunately, they had driven the lion away. Or, maybe it was a foregone conclusion because they had been training for over four years, and they were the baby seals. What was one lion? Nevertheless, he closed up the distance and was only a quarter of a mile away when they ran into the grizzly bear.

The bear was a young male about six and a half feet tall, weighing around five hundred pounds. He was apparently in the process of staking out his territory by scratching marks on a tree, and he rose up to his full height just as Jeff and Danielle approached through the trees. Mike, who was watching their movement through his binoculars muttered an incredulous, "You have got to be kidding me," as he dropped the binoculars and unslung his rifle for the second time that day. By the time he had the rifle up and the picture in his scope, the battle was in full swing. He cursed to himself as he watched through the scope. There was no way to get a shot with the intermingling of bear, Jeff, and Danielle. He took a second to key his radio and say, "Move up! They're fighting a bear," before bringing his rifle up again. What he saw through the scope was unbelievable. Jeff and Danielle were moving faster than he would have thought possible.

It was like watching a choreographed dance. The bear would wheel and strike with his claws, but the target wouldn't be there. Instead, he would receive a rap on the nose or ear or paw with a staff. Mike watched in disbelief as Jeff actually tripped the bear as it charged Danielle by placing his staff between the bear's two rear feet. As it stumbled, Danielle took the moment to give it another rap on the nose before flipping out of the way. When the bear turned to attack Jeff, the boy actually took the opportunity to thrust the staff in the bear's mouth. The bear bit the staff and struck it with his paw, and Jeff used the momentum to spin and strike the bear on the shoulder, just as Danielle delivered a blow to its ear. Just like that, the fight was over. The bear ambled away from them, not running, but with occasional glances over his shoulder as if to say, "There was so much wrong with this fight, and don't think you won! It isn't over!" Mike followed him with his rifle until the bear was out of sight, then said into his radio, "Resume positions. The fight is over. Bear is headed east. Heads up." Stuart replied, "Anyone hurt?" Mike answered, "Just the bear as far as I can tell." Travis broke in, "I have to hear this story when we meet up," and Mike finished with, "I'm not sure I can tell it so it's believable." He resumed watching the twins as they picked up their packs from where they had dropped them when the bear attacked, strapped them back on, and resumed the trek through the trees.

That was the last excitement for the trip. The fourth day passed without incident, and midway through day five they reached the rendezvous to find an SUV parked beside the road. Shortly afterwards Stuart and Travis arrived, and fifteen minutes after that Mike strolled up, munching on a protein bar. Jeff commented, "All three of you, huh? Did you see the mountain lion? And the bear?" Mike nodded and said, "Well done on both. Good weapon choices both times. And tactics. Were you scared?" Danielle laughed. "After fighting with Mac? They were easy compared to that." The three men laughed, but Mike was glad they hadn't been carrying two bodies out of the forest. These two kids were as much a part of his team as Stuart and Travis, and he would really hate to lose any of them. All five climbed in the SUV which had been left by another of Mike's friends and drove back to Mike's truck, dropping off Stuart and Travis at their car on the way. Both groups then drove to a nearby town and checked into a hotel where Mike had made reservations, to clean up and get some rest before the drive home the next day. Over dinner at a local restaurant, Mike debriefed Jeff and Danielle on their hike. The twins showed the pictures they had taken, including shots from their body cameras of the two fights. The three men just shook their heads at the pictures and the descriptions, knowing that luck or something had played a big part. Sometimes you beat the bear, sometimes the bear beats you.

The year moved on, and Cindy was adopted by Steve and Amy Jacobs. It came as a not unexpected surprise to Jeff and Danielle. Cindy had been going to visit Steve and Amy with and without the twins. When she went with them, they joined Steve in making good natured fun of Amy and Cindy's strange sense of humor, groaning where appropriate. It was obvious that Cindy blended well with the family, especially after she became a Christian and joined 2nd Street Bible Church. For a couple of weeks after she became a Christian, she tried to talk to Jeff and Danielle about her faith until Danielle threatened to break her arms, and after a talk with Amy, she stopped. Steve, Amy, and Cindy announced the news to Jeff and Danielle on a visit one evening after school, and the twins congratulated them warmly. It would be another month before everything was finalized, but as far as the three of them were concerned, it was a done deal. Riding back to the Brown's that afternoon, Jeff asked Cindy if Randy and Susan knew yet. She replied, "I'm not sure. CPS may have said something, but they haven't mentioned it to me." Danielle said, "It will just be me there unless they take in someone else."

Danielle was in pain and wasn't sure why. She knew she wasn't the best match for Steve and Amy, and Cindy was. Taking into account the way she and Jeff had treated them since "the day," she also didn't feel she deserved to be adopted by them. Then there was the freedom she had had with no one really caring what she did. It was just that the option had sort of been out there, and now it wasn't, and it left an empty spot. She wondered what else she had been taking for granted, expecting it to be around forever when there was no guarantee it would be.

As it happened, Randy and Susan were no longer going to be her foster parents either. On a Monday in January, they sat down with Danielle and told her they had decided to get out of the foster care program. The real reason wasn't explained, but basically the two of them were afraid of Jeff and Danielle. Not that they thought the two children would intentionally hurt them, but they had watched over the past four years as they had trained, apparently all in mayhem. They had watched them fighting in the backyard with practice swords and seen them throwing knives. The children's idea of fun appeared to be attacking each other at random or seeing who could throw whom the farthest. Bigger and stronger than when the Browns had first seen them, they might even be stronger than Randy. They were certainly stronger than Susan was. In addition, it was as though the twins expected to be ambushed everywhere: in the grocery store, in the department store, even in the Brown home. There was never a doorway that wasn't suspect or the end of an aisle that didn't need to be cleared, even if they didn't obviously slow down or look. You could just feel it in the way they moved. They were especially dangerous when they were asleep, and the Browns knew better than to wake one of them up if they fell asleep on the living room floor after a particularly tough day. Either the other twin had to do the waking, or both of them had to be left until they woke up on their own, because they woke up dangerous with knives out. Finally, Susan and Randy had had enough.

It was a sad decision, because Susan had enjoyed teaching them to cook, and they seemed to enjoy learning. Randy had enjoyed teaching them about cars, and after four years they could repair just about anything they could physically handle. Jeff hadn't been an added expense. If anything the Browns had come out on the plus side in the deal. Jeff and Danielle bought their own clothes, the few they actually owned. They only wore what would fit in their backpacks. They often brought food home to try for meals. The two were polite and had excellent manners. However, it was like living with two semi-tamed leopards. You never knew if or when they would turn on you, and the Brown's nerves had finally had enough. Rather than take on someone new, they chose to just get out, period.

As one set of foster parents exited the picture, a new set entered in the form of Tom and Audrey McAdams, the two former alcoholics who were baptized the same day as Jeff and Danielle. For the past five years, they had been diligent workers at 2nd Street Bible Church, teaching in the children's Sunday School classes. Their down home wit and understanding made them favorites with the children, and their common sense and no-nonsense attitudes made them favorites with the parents and other adults. They had not touched alcohol since joining the church and had recently applied to be foster parents. Approval came just in time for Danielle to be assigned to them. Someone such as Officer Freedman who had known them in the past might have had misgivings, but five years of good behavior goes a long ways towards smoothing bureaucratic paths.

Since the McAdams lived on 5th Street, Danielle would be moving back to the old neighborhood, a mixed blessing. Many of their old friends were there, but the women's shelter, Pastor Marcus, and especially Michelle and Lizzie weren't there. Jeff and Danielle had been spending a lot of time with the Strong family, and if there was anything they needed to talk about with a mother figure they went to Michelle. Still, it was only a three-mile bicycle ride, so things could have been worse.

As it happened, it would be a three-mile bicycle ride for both of them. Thanks to an interesting chain of events, Jeff was moving back to the old neighborhood as well, and near to Danielle. He and his mom were kicked out of their apartment. Marilyn had been caught trying to sell the appliances from the apartment to buy drugs, and the owner had evicted her on the spot, telling her to move or he would file charges. She called one of her friends who had a van and moved them to a room on 5th street, a little over a block from Danielle's new home. It consisted of two rooms, if you counted the small bathroom with its standup shower, sink, and toilet as a room. The other space was just an empty room with a counter big enough to hold a sink and a hotplate. A small refrigerator stood on the floor under the hotplate. There were no drawers, although there was one cabinet above the sink. The walls had no windows. It was really a storeroom for the pottery shop it was attached to, but the owners, friends of Marilyn, needed a little extra income more than the storage space, so they were willing to rent the 10X10 room for some under the counter money. Marilyn's life was still spiraling downhill, and Jeff was still fighting to stop the decline.

December brought changes to the Freedman and Strong families. Robert and Michelle were married by Pastor Marcus the Saturday after Christmas and joined the Pueblo Community Church. The wedding was well attended by their friends and family. Elizabeth was a flower girl at the wedding, looking adorable in her purple dress. Danielle served cake, and Jeff was an usher. They had pleasant conversations with their former doctors and nurses from their time in the hospital. These friends of Michelle's, who had not seen the twins since their stay in the hospital, were amazed to see how much they had changed. There was the usual growth one would expect between the ages of seven years and almost twelve, but the two had grown even more than average and promised to be large adults. They were also heavily muscled from four and a half years of hard training. To top it off they were well mannered and articulate. Talking to them was like talking to adults who resembled twelve year olds. There was little childlike about them although something would occasionally peek through.

The wedding was a beautiful affair, and the partying continued into the wee hours of the morning at Michelle's house (they were still working out where they would live) before they left early the next morning for a short honeymoon, taking Elizabeth along with them as they drove to the coast for a few days. Jeff and Danielle were extremely happy for them, except for the joining the church thing.

Hope and Danielle were preparing a room for new arrivals to the women's shelter one Saturday in January before Jeff and Danielle's 12th birthday. Hope knew about Jeff and Danielle and their history and was frankly a little disturbed at their attitude and the attitude of everyone around them. It was as though everyone walked on pins and needles, afraid of telling them the truth or upsetting them. Hope was a very loving, caring person, but she was not the most patient person in the world, and on this day, she felt she should say something to Danielle. What she said was, "God loves you, you know." Danielle looked at her and snorted. Hope continued, "I know you're all mad at God, but when you were a Christian did you ever read your Bible?" Danielle wasn't smiling anymore and was starting to look a bit dangerous. "I read my Bible every day. I memorized a lot of it." Hope retorted, "Did you read any of the verses about counting the cost, or taking up your cross every day, or they persecuted Me, they will persecute you, or did you just read the ones about Jesus loves you and Jesus will bless you? Rumor has it that you and Jeff were trained by an ex-Navy SEAL. Is that true?"

At this point Danielle didn't trust herself to speak, so she just nodded. Hope continued, "So when he became a SEAL did he only take the missions he wanted to take and do the things he wanted to do or did he go where he was sent and do what he was told?" Danielle spat out, between grinding teeth, "I imagine he went where he was sent and did what he was told." Hope said, "Danielle, I love the kids coming here as much, maybe more, than you do. But do you think I could really help Tiffany?" referring to one of the kids who had been through recently with her mother. Both had been abused badly by the father. "I grew up in a Christian home with two parents who loved me and loved each other. I've never been through anything like Tiffany went through. I can tell her I love her, and she looks at me like "what do you know". But you can help her, and she can relate to you. Do you know why? Because you have street cred. You've been through bad stuff, too. Danielle, God needed someone who could relate to kids like Tiffany, and to do that He had to give someone street cred. You became a Christian, and you basically told Him to use you as He needed, and He took you at your word. He gave you and Jeff street cred. And it wasn't just that. Do you think Tonya could help Tiffany? She has street cred." Even through her anger Danielle laughed. Tonya was another kid whose mother had been through the shelter. She was one of the most selfish individuals Danielle had ever met. Hope went on, "So it couldn't just be someone with street cred. It also had to be someone who cared about the kids. And He chose you. And you got mad because you volunteered, and He believed you and chose you." Then, perhaps unnecessarily, she went on, "What happened to you was bad, but do you think it was worse than some father in the Sudan who is crucified and watches his wife and children dragged off to be sold into slavery? Or worse?" At that point, Danielle, to avoid killing Hope as she wanted to, stormed out of the room.

It was unfortunate for Paul McKenzie that he chose this morning to violate the restraining order against him, for the third time. When Danielle came storming into the kitchen, Paul was there by his wife, Deborah, while their daughter, Grace, cowered in the corner by the sink, and Jolene yelled at Paul and dialed frantically on her cell phone for the police. Jeff opened the screen door leading to the back yard just as Danielle reached it, dragging an unconscious Paul. When the police arrived two minutes later, they found Paul curled in a ball with his hands tie wrapped to the swing set. Paul was handcuffed, placed in a patrol car, and transported to the hospital. Meanwhile, one officer took statements from Jolene, Jeff, and Danielle who were calming Deborah and Grace.

That evening Jeff and Danielle sat in the Brown's back yard as Danielle told Jeff what Hope had said. Danielle asked, "Do you think Hope was right? Did I get mad because I didn't realize what I had volunteered for, or what?" Jeff sat in thought for a while analyzing the information. Then he sighed. "I guess it might sort of be like Mike being a SEAL and on a mission and then throwing civilians between him and the bad guys. She's right about us not paying attention to the verses in the Bible about counting the cost and being persecuted like Jesus was. Although I'm not sure your parents did what they did because we were Christians. I don't know though. Maybe they did. She is right about us being able to help the kids we did because of our street cred, which we have because of what happened." They sat in thought for a while longer. Then Danielle said, "Crud. I guess that means we owe God an apology. I hate apologizing." Jeff laughed. "Like Steve and Amy say, talk to God like you're talking to a friend. Tell Him what you're thinking and feeling." The two of them sat there for a long time, talking to God, telling Him about their anger and confusion and confessing that they had no idea how to apologize to Him for being mad at Him for almost five years for something that was basically their own misunderstanding. And for the first time in almost five years, they felt like He could hear them, that He understood, and He forgave them for their anger." When Danielle looked up she said, "I'm not angry anymore." Jeff agreed, "Neither am I." Danielle continued, "I don't love my mom and stepdad. Not like I do the Freedmans or the Jacobs or Pastor Marcus or the kids we've helped. If they were alive, I might try to forgive them. But I am not going to let what can't be changed get in the way anymore."

Jeff nodded. Then he sighed. "What about the tattoos? They don't seem right, now. Do we get them removed?" Danielle sat in thought for a while. Then she started drawing in the grass with a stick. Finally, she said, "No. I can fix those. I'll make up new drawings for Bear. They'll be bigger and take longer and hurt more." Jeff said, "Of course they will."

Steve opened his front door the following Sunday morning to retrieve the paper and found Jeff and Danielle sitting cross-legged on the front porch. Eyes open wide in surprise and shock he called to his wife, "Amy, Cindy, we have company!" and opened the storm door to invite them in. Jeff and Danielle rose smoothly upright, walked up to Steve, and hugged him, saying over and over again, "We're so sorry!" Amy and Cindy came to the front door and became part of the hug. Sitting at the breakfast table, Jeff and Danielle told them what had happened the day before, and tears of joy streamed down Steve and Amy's faces. Cindy just beamed at them and said, "You goofs!" Amy asked, "Will you be coming back to the church?" Jeff asked in response, "Will they want us back?" Steve laughed. "Are you kidding? It will be like the prodigal son, and daughter (looking at Danielle), returning. They'll put out the fatted calf, or at least the pot luck. Today?" Danielle said, "No. There's something we want to do first. We'll take care of it starting Monday." Amy gave her a questioning look but said okay. "You should go talk to Pastor John." They agreed that they would later that day if he had time, and Steve said he would talk to him at church that morning. They spent the rest of breakfast talking, until it was time for the Jacobs to leave for church. As they climbed on their bikes Cindy asked, "Does this mean you two are going to be normal now?" and they all had a good laugh over the thought of Jeff and Danielle ever being normal again.

Amy called at lunch and told them Pastor John would like to see them at 2:00 that afternoon if they could come. Jeff and Danielle rode their bikes over with some trepidation, but Pastor John and Sarah welcomed them warmly into their home. After they were seated and munching on homemade cookies he said, "Why don't you tell us about it," and Jeff and Danielle told them about their last four and a half years, editing out some things they thought might get other people in trouble, telling about their anger and how they felt betrayed, and finally about what Hope had said. Pastor John and Sarah listened patiently, asking the occasional question, and when they had finished he said, "I know you have left out some things, and that's okay. It is so apparent to me that God has had his hand on you. It isn't often we get to understand Him at work, but when you think about all the people showing up when you needed them, and the family you have built around yourselves, even the fact that you met each other, His hand in everything is obvious." He continued, "As for coming back to the church, of course everyone will welcome you back! The ones who have never had a chance to do an original Danielle connect-the-dots drawing are totally envious of the ones who have. Adam and the choir can't wait to see new music if you're still writing, Jeff. And you both have a tremendous witness to offer." Danielle asked, "Can we get baptized again?" Pastor John smiled and said, "Of course." Jeff added, "We'd like to do it on our birthday, if it wouldn't be too much trouble." Pastor John nodded and said, "We can do that as well. I'll announce it this coming Sunday. Do you want it to be private or open or a few friends?" Danielle said, "Anyone who wants to can come," not really thinking anyone but the Jacobs would want to come. Pastor John asked, "Would you like to give your testimony this coming Sunday?" and Jeff and Danielle agreed. Jeff said, "It has been four and a half years. A lot has happened. Can we take four and a half hours?" and everyone laughed. As they watched them ride away on their bikes later that afternoon, Sarah leaned on Pastor John's shoulder and said, "Their story is not over yet. It's amazing to see how all the praying that has been done over them the past several years is bearing fruit."

After school on Monday, Jeff and Danielle rode their bikes to

Bear's tattoo studio, and Danielle showed him what they wanted. He looked at the drawings, discussed the colors Danielle wanted to use, and said, "This is going to take a while. Probably the rest of the week, if you can only come after school." Jeff and Danielle agreed, and he had Danielle sit on the stool, pulled everything together, and started. It took until Wednesday evening to finish Danielle and until Saturday morning to finish Jeff. The tattoos Danielle had created incorporated the original Japanese symbols in a cross. Danielle's symbol for faith became part of the left side of her cross. She added the words hope in the right side and love down the center. Her tattoo was mainly in green with the new writing in black. Jeff's tattoo was similar in design with the words faith on the left and love down the center with the Japanese symbol for hope on the right side. His tattoo was mainly in blue. Bear was very impressed with the artwork and asked if he could use it in future tattoos. Danielle kindly told him no, these would be one of a kind, and he nodded in understanding. He liked these kids, and one of these days, he might visit their church. You never knew.

That Sunday, Jeff and Danielle gave their testimony in front of 2nd Street Bible Church. Word had gotten around that they would be speaking, and the church was full. People who might have stayed away for various reasons chose to come instead, even if they had to rearrange their calendars. Pastor John introduced them, and they sat on two stools in front of the congregation. Robert, Michelle, and Elizabeth along with Steve, Amy, and Cindy sat on the front row. Alice and Eunice sat just behind them. Danielle began, "Five years ago we became Christians and began doing things with this church. We prayed and read our Bibles every day, we helped with Sunday School, Jeff wrote music for the praise band, we played with the band for the street fair and at the 4th of July concert, and we thought this was the Christian life."

Jeff picked up here, and they took turns, each telling a bit more of the story. "We read the Bible all the way through although we didn't understand a lot of it. We spent a great deal of time on praise verses and love verses and not much time on verses about the cost of being a Christian." Danielle, "Then the morning after the 4ᵗʰ of July concert my mom and stepdad tried to kill us, and it all just came apart. We felt so betrayed by Pastor John and everyone here and especially by God. We didn't understand how we could be doing what we thought we were supposed to be doing and helping people, and then something so bad could happen to us. It was like everything God had given us He just suddenly took away for no reason, and we were mad at all of you for tricking us, and we were really mad at God. He was just a big unfair bully."

Jeff, "We couldn't not believe in Him. It wasn't that He wasn't real. It was just that for some reason we couldn't understand, He hated us. So we were mad back at Him. And we spent the next four and a half years being mad. "Danielle, "Some of you wondered what we've been doing the past four and a half years. When we got out of the hospital, we moved a few miles to the east and were taken under the wing of an ex-Navy SEAL. He and his friends taught us everything they knew. And along the way we kept running into God. I moved into my foster home and found that Jeff had moved in a block away. When we moved to our new neighborhood, we found ourselves just a couple of blocks from a nurse who had watched over us in the hospital. And she ended up marrying the policeman who rescued us. Officer Freedman is, and will always be, the one who pulled the nails out." At this point, there were few if any dry eyes in the room.

Jeff continued, "Every step along the way the past four and a half years, when we needed someone to teach us something, someone appeared. When we were expelled from school our first week, there was someone to homeschool us. When we needed bicycles, there was a garage sale right around the corner." Danielle, "My hands healed and I could draw and play the guitar again. When we needed a way to strengthen our hands and feet there was someone to teach us how. Over and over again, God put people in our way when we needed them. And we still stayed mad at Him." Jeff, "After four and a half years I guess we were ready to listen. I know you told us over and over how God loved us, but finally, when we were ready, someone told us something different. She told us about the cost of being a Christian. She pointed out all the verses, like in Luke 14 where Jesus talks about the cost of discipleship and carrying your cross, or in John 15, where Jesus talks about the world hating us but hating Him first." Danielle, "And we realized, after four and a half years of learning about duty, and living and breathing it, that we had wanted all the good things about being a Christian but none of the suffering or the pain. And we were ashamed. So we had to come back to God and ask forgiveness. Thankfully God is quick to forgive."

Jeff, "Now we need to ask you for forgiveness, too. Just for the last four and a half years, though, because we will mess up again. Probably tomorrow." The congregation laughed through their tears. "We would ask that you would forgive us for blaming you, for thinking that what happened to us was worse than the trials and sorrows that you live with every day and keep on going and trusting God." Danielle, "We know that many of you prayed for us all this time. And it has been a long time. We were just seven when all this happened to us, and we'd only been Christians for a few months. Now we're much older and wiser." More laughter. Jeff, "So, if you will have us back we would like to come back to 2nd Street Bible Church." As one, the congregation stood and applauded them, and Jeff and Danielle were welcomed back to the church they had left almost five years earlier.

On their 12th birthday, they were baptized.

Sometimes God allows what he hates to accomplish what He loves.
                                                              Joni Eareckson Tada

Characters

Adam Nichols (Music minister at 2nd Street Bible Church)
Adeela (customer service at bank)
Alice Springley (Danielle's next door neighbor)
Andrew (Drummer in Terry's band)
Angela Potts (Taught Jeff to swim; also the investment club)
Ann (jeweler who makes their baby seal charms)
Bart and Jolene Sanders (houseparents at women's shelter)
Bear (tattoo artist)
Beth (special needs girl on cruise; Jeff's first crush)
Bob (runs post office store where they have mail box)
Boyd and Pam Merrill, Madison (8), Emily (6) (Family from Kentucky twins buy a house for)
Paul, Deborah, Grace McKenzie (husband with restraint order; wife and child in women's shelter)
Candice (billing office at the hospital)
Carl (Danielle's stepfather)
Cindy Rogers (Danielle's first foster sister)
Dan and Marla (members of 2nd Street Bible Church. In Jacobs Bible study group.)
Danielle LeBeau (Green Seal)
David (friend of Mike's in Key West. Runs a dive boat.)
Debbie (receptionist at The Web Factory)
Denise (1st grade Sunday School helper)
Eddie (information counter at the bank)
Elaine (night nurse)

Elena and Tisha (Jeff and Danielle write poem song and dance for them)

Elizabeth Strong (Michelle's Daughter)

Eunice (Alice's sister)

Frank (wants hoses moved)

Grand-mere Claudette (Jeff's upstairs neighbor)

Harudo and Ayame Fujioka (live on 2nd floor in Jeff's building)

Hatsu and Cho (Fujioka children)

Hope (the girl who brought Jeff and Danielle back to God)

Jack and Margaret Parker (own house Jeff and Danielle buy for Merrill family)

Jamie (Beth's older sister)

Jeff Mitchell (Blue Seal)

Jim and Sherrie (members of 2nd Street Bible Church. In Jacobs Bible study group.)

John Patton (Minister at 2nd Street Bible Church)

Kathy (sold them bicycles)

Kay (receptionist at the hair salon)

Kendra Taylor (2nd patrol officer at their rescue)

Lacey Reynolds (Music Teacher)

Mac (unarmed combat instructor)

Marcus Hall (pastor at Pueblo Community Church)

Marcy (One of the keyboard players in Terry's band)

Marge (wants cleaning behind hedge)

Maria Sanchez (gang member. Phone shot out of her hand)

Marilyn (Jeff's mother)

Mario (gang member. Knife in hand the first fight.)

Mark (friend of Mike's. Pilot.)

Marty and Scott (members of 2nd Street Bible Church. In Jacobs Bible study group.)

Marvin and Minnie Wales and daughter Samantha (run dive shop)

Mary Johnson (Elementary grades Sunday School teacher at 2nd Street Bible Church)

Melanie (Danielle's mother)

Michael (hair stylist at salon)

Michelle Strong (Emergency Room Nurse)

Mike Smith (Ex-Navy SEAL)

Mr. Amir (clerk at Food Mart)

Mr. Ford (Elena and Tisha's principle)

Mr. Lucas (Elena and Tisha's English teacher)

Mrs. O'Malley (Jeff and Danielle's first grade teacher until they were expelled)

Officer Doug Renart (officer Robert gave his bullet proof vest to)

Randy and Susan Brown (Danielle's first foster parents)

Robert Freedman (Police officer)

Roger and Carolyn Brandt and Allison (Danielle drew a picture for Allison in church)

Ronnie and Marie (members of 2nd Street Bible Church. In Jacobs Bible study group.)

Sam and Kathy Shepherd, Sam Jr., Bailey (homeschool Jeff and Danielle)

Sarah Patton (John's wife)

Sgt. McKowsky (Robert's sergeant.)

Steve and Amy Jacobs (Pecan man, church member)

Stuart (friend of Mike's. Owns land east of city with trees and underbrush and long fire lanes.)

Terry (Musician, lead guitar in his band)

Tina (Jeff's IT contact who stores his pictures at The Web Factory)

Tod Jenkins (owner of The Cabinet Shop)

Tom (wants his front yard watered)

Tom and Audrey McAdams (Former alcoholics)

Tomas (gang member. Knife in hand the first fight.)

Tommy (runs the outdoor gun range)

Toni Patterson (they watch her children for an hour twice a week)

Tony (works in a head shop; friend of Marilyn's)

Travis (friend of Mike's. Also on his SEAL team.)

Here is a sneak peek at Baby SEALs Part 2.

Chapter 1

Twelve year old Jeff Mitchell stood waist deep in the cool waters of the Gulf of Mexico off Padre Island on a Friday before Easter, spring break for many school districts. Under clear, blue skies the water sparkled as the waves made their way to shore where seagulls coasted on the breeze and occasionally swarmed anyone foolish enough to offer them food, with their cries of "Mine! Mine! Mine!" On the shore among the various beach goers, mixed with other church members from 2nd Street Bible Church, Amy Jacobs sat in a lounge chair beside Audrey McAdams, Danielle LeBeau's new foster mother. Danielle, Jeff's twin sister by another mother, stood waist deep in the water near Jeff. Jeff and Danielle were both big for their age at 5 feet, over 100 pounds, solidly built, with military short brown hair and bright, intelligent eyes, blue for Jeff, green for Danielle. To Jeff's left stood Tom McAdams, Danielle's new foster father, and Robert Freedman, both keeping an eye on the various children splashing in the surf. Near them Steve Jacobs attempted to ride a wave on a boogie board. Between the three men and Jeff stood Cindy Jacobs, Steve and Amy's newly adopted daughter and the current object of Jeff's attention. He stared at the fifteen-year-old girl in her silver one-piece swimsuit as she stood four feet away and thought, "Tuna." When he had seen her walking down the beach towards the water in the swimsuit she and Amy had picked out for the church trip to Padre Island, with her long legs and her long, black hair held in a ponytail, he thought, "Nice!" but that wasn't what he was thinking now. A shiver of alarm ran up his spine, and he turned towards Danielle to voice his concern. Danielle was staring at the water at his side. Before he could say anything he felt a rasp on his leg like sandpaper, and a dorsal fin broke the water beside him as a shark headed straight for Cindy. Without thinking, Jeff grabbed the fin with his left hand and the shark's belly with his right, and he lifted the seven foot tiger shark. Danielle launched herself at the tail, which had also broken the water. The shark's jaws snapped shut inches from Cindy's hand, and there was an explosion of water as the now angry, 250 pound shark, turned on Jeff.

CPSIA information can be obtained
at www.ICGtesting.com
Printed in the USA
LVOW10s0556221216
518239LV00001B/1/P